SPECIAL MESSAGE TO READERS

This book is published under the auspices of

THE ULVERSCROFT FOUNDATION

(registered charity No. 264873 UK)

Establi[illegible] to provide funds for research, di[illegible] treatment of eye diseases. Ex[illegible] [illegible]utions made are: —

A C[illegible] [illegible]me[illegible] U[illegible] at M[illegible] [illegible], London.

Twin [illegible] theatres at the Western Ophthalmic Hospital, London.

•

[illegible] Chair of Ophthalmology at the Royal [illegible]ustralian College of Ophthalmologists.

•

The [illegible]verscroft Children's Eye Unit at the Great Ormond Street Hospital For Sick Children, London.

You ca[illegible] help further the work of the Foundation by ma[illegible]g a donation or leaving a legacy. Every con[illegible]ution, no matter how small, is received w[illegible] gratitude. Please write for details to:

T[illegible] ULVERSCROFT FOUNDATION,
[illegible] Green, Bradgate Road, Anstey,
[illegible]eicester LE7 7FU, England.
Telephone: (0116) 236 4325

In Australia write to:

THE ULVERSCROFT FOUNDATION,
c/o The Royal Australian and New Zealand College of Ophthalmologists,
94-98 Chalmers Street, Surry Hills,
[illegible]lia

The son of a Yorkshire businessman, Roger Silverwood was educated in Gloucestershire before completing his National Service. He later worked in the toy trade and as a copywriter in an advertising agency. Roger then went into business with his wife as an antiques dealer before retiring in 1997. He now lives on the outskirts of Barnsley where he writes full-time.

You can find out more about the author at www.rogersilverwood.uwclub.net

THE SNUFFBOX MURDERS

Inspector Angel and his team are looking for a murderer — an antiques thief who tears out the tongue of anyone he fears might give him away. The Inspector also believes the murderer is imitating Herman Lamm, an infamous villain of a century earlier. The suspects are a disparate trio: a conman, extremely interested in an antique gold statue; Mr Van Hassain, a diplomat and businessman; and a rich inventor's beautiful wife. All three delight in acquiring antique gold snuffboxes . . . it's not much to go on but Inspector Angel is determined to catch the killer.

Books by Roger Silverwood
Published by The House of Ulverscroft:

DEADLY DAFFODILS
IN THE MIDST OF LIFE
THE MAN IN THE PINK SUIT
MANTRAP
THE UMBRELLA MAN
THE MAN WHO COULDN'T LOSE
THE CURIOUS MIND OF
INSPECTOR ANGEL
FIND THE LADY
THE WIG MAKER
MURDER IN BARE FEET
WILD ABOUT HARRY
THE CUCKOO CLOCK SCAM
SHRINE TO MURDER

ROGER SILVERWOOD

THE SNUFFBOX MURDERS

AN INSPECTOR ANGEL MYSTERY

Complete and Unabridged

ULVERSCROFT
Leicester

First published in Great Britain in 2010 by
Robert Hale Limited
London

First Large Print Edition
published 2011
by arrangement with
Robert Hale Limited
London

British Library CIP Data

Silverwood, Roger.
The snuffbox murders.
1. Angel, Michael (Fictitious character)- -Fiction.
2. Police- -England- -Yorkshire- -Fiction.
3. Antiquities- -Fiction. 4. Detective and mystery
stories. 5. Large type books.
I. Title
823.9'2–dc22

ISBN 978–1–4448–0719–6

Published by
F. A. Thorpe (Publishing)
Anstey, Leicestershire

Set by Words & Graphics Ltd.
Anstey, Leicestershire
Printed and bound in Great Britain by
T. J. International Ltd., Padstow, Cornwall

This book is printed on acid-free paper

1

129, Bradford Road, Bromersley,
South Yorkshire, UK.
2100 hours. Sunday, 10 May 2009

'Is everybody here?'

'Yes, boss.'

'Right, well close that door and listen up. I've got another job.'

There were mutters of approval and enthusiasm from the five men.

'Right, now settle down. You will have heard of Jack Prendergast. He's the chairman of Frescati Fashions. He's *Sir* Jack now. Well, Sir Jack and Lady Prendergast will be at the Fashion Award dinner in London next Saturday evening, May 16th. Their country place, Fanbury House, Lower Widdop, Bucks, will therefore be unoccupied. It is quite isolated, about half a mile from their nearest neighbour, which is a farm. The house and grounds are well covered by CCTV, heat-sensor-operated lights and alarms, so it's balaclavas, gloves and overalls, all the way, as usual. All right?'

There were mutters and nods of understanding and agreement.

'Lower Widdop is on a loop road just off the B98406. The west end of that needs blocking up *after* you have entered, to slow down any approach of police traffic from the nearest police station, which is Beaconsfield. I will get Irish John to blow the road up. It pays two grand, and he keeps his mouth shut. It will give us fifteen minutes' start in the unlikely event of anything going wrong. We will, of course, when leaving the house, turn *right* out of the gates and travel eastwards before turning up north, but we'll have a rehearsal of all of that before the night.

'It'll need someone to climb the telegraph pole that leaves the telephone exchange on the south side at Lower Widdop and cut the main telephone wire at nine twenty-five to block the automatic alarm signal reaching the security company. They'll get a signal that the connection has been broken, but they won't know why. They might think it's the weather, or even that it's the telephone company pulling the wrong plug out, but they won't *know* that you are emptying the place. Get that man we used on the Lord Line job, Peter Queegley. Tell him it pays a grand and he keeps his mouth shut, as before.'

'Right, boss,' a man said.

'The time to enter the house is at nine-thirty. Now you may have to saw through a chain securing the main gates to open them, so be there by nine-twenty-five, but don't attempt to enter the house before nine-thirty as the phone line may not be cut. You'll go in by the front door. I have had made a copy of the key to the main lock. There's also a Yale lock to which I haven't a key. The safe is in the drawing room, behind a dummy screen in a false fireplace under a painting of King Charles II. It's a Phillips Mark II. Made about 1960. Can you handle it, Alec?'

'I think so. But I'll have to blow the lock.'

'I believe that it's full of twenty-pound notes. Try not to set them on fire.'

Several members of the gang sniggered.

'You may already have heard that the house contains all kinds of treasures including a valuable collection of antique gold snuff-boxes. I want you to be sure of getting all of them. I've got a punter waiting. They are in a very special thick glass case separately alarmed in the library. Second door on the right as you go in by the front door. The house is full of very valuable paintings both downstairs and up. Fill that van. We will have to work quickly. We have only an hour. To be safe we must be out of the house by ten-thirty. Whatever we haven't loaded by then, we must leave behind. Remember, everything you took to carry out the job, hammers, knives, the gelly wrapping-paper, expired fuses, even toffee papers must be brought back with you. On return, all number plates to be changed before the engines are cold. Old plates to be taken to pieces, spoiled beyond recognition and buried. Vehicles to be re-sprayed white this time. Also there's to be no smoking, eating or drinking throughout the job. I know that I always say that, but it keeps us out of prison, doesn't it?'

There was silence.

'*Doesn't it?*' he bawled.

He waited until all five men had replied in the affirmative, then he said, 'And no talking to anyone. Keep absolute stumm! Especially wives and girlfriends. If there's so much as a whisper and I find out who it is, they'll know about it, I can tell you. You understand? You know that I mean it. Do exactly what I tell you and you don't get caught. All right? Rehearsals, every night this week here at 8 p.m. Next week, Tuesday at 8 a.m. for a dummy run, then at 12 noon, the day of the job, for rehearsals and final briefing. Remember, even for rehearsals, leave all items that can identify you at home, as well as your keys and your mobile phones. You will all be issued with clean mobiles the day of the job. The two outsiders, Peter Queegley and Irish John, will be briefed separately at a place to be arranged, but not here. They are not to be told of the existence of this place, or the target address until you're on your way there. All right? Secrecy is also our security, so all of you, watch your tongues, or I'll personally rip them out. Any questions?'

A caravan in Jubilee Park, Bromersley,
South Yorkshire, UK.
1330 hours. Bank Holiday Monday, 25 May 2009

Shirley Vance giggled. 'There's no need for this charade, Alec really,' she said. 'If you want to see me in the all together, I suppose I . . . well,' she said putting her head on one side and smiling, 'I don't suppose I really mind.' She maintained the smile and then giggled again.

Alec Underwood might have been titillated by the forwardness of the young woman, but he had a serious plan in mind. He was fifteen years older and in all ways he considered that he was superior to her.

He breathed in noisily through his teeth and shook his head. 'It's not like that at all,' he sniffed. He spoke in an indignant way, as if his adenoids needed extracting. 'There's a time and place for everything. You have no artistry in your soul, Miss Vance. I really *do* want to take a mould of your body.'

She liked the thought of that. 'What for? And when?' she said, still smiling and looking in the long mirror at herself in the tiny bra and bikini bottom. She liked what she saw and smiled again at the reflection. Alec Underwood looked heavenward for an answer. 'For posterity,' he said. 'But not *now*, anyway.'

'When?'

'I'll tell you when. It's time you got ready for the parade. They'll be picking you up at a quarter past two. You will be second after the mayor's open-top car, on the brewery dray. Look at the time. I'm going to the church to watch the slaughter of the donkey.'

She pulled a face. 'How horrible. They're not going to do that, are they?'

He blew out to signify his surprise at her ignorance. 'They don't actually slaughter it. They drop it off the top of the church tower.'

She screamed and put her hand across her mouth.

He smiled. He didn't smile often. He smiled when he heard women scream.

'Alec,' she squealed. 'Don't say that.'

'It's symbolic,' he said. 'No. No. No. They don't throw a *real* donkey nowadays.'

'Why? What harm has a donkey ever done to anyone?'

'You must read about it for yourself, Miss Vance, in the carnival programme. It tells you *all* about it.'

She put her beautiful chubby lips together and pouted. 'Don't call me Miss Vance. Call me Shirley,' she said, posing suggestively for him.

He looked at her. He was tempted. His hand almost came out to touch her leg, but he stopped and stood up.

She smiled knowingly. She reached out for a bright pink dressing-gown with a big fluffy white collar.

'I must go,' he said. 'Peter is picking me up in the car. We've a bit of business to see to.'

Shirley Vance's smile went.

'You haven't finished telling me about that poor donkey.'

His eyebrows came down. His mouth turned downwards. 'It's all in the programme. You should read it. Today is Saint Marmaduke day,' he began patiently. 'This is the day Bromersley celebrates the death of Septimus Marmaduke of Lebanon, whose parents it is said originally lived here. And in the twelfth century the date of his death, this day, was celebrated by pushing a donkey off the top of the church tower. That's all.'

'Oooo,' she said, pulling a face of horror.

He smiled.

'Anyway, these days it's a symbolic donkey.'

'What's that?'

'What's what?'

'A symbolic donkey?'

'A sack of carrots tied up in a leather strap. They've used the same strap for two hundred years. Then they say prayers for the protection and forgiveness of all donkeys.'

She put her hand to her chest and sighed. 'Thank goodness. I simply love donkeys. But I'm going to miss all that symbolic stuff,' she said. 'And what's the bit of business you and that Peter Queegley have to see to? You know, I'm not too sure about him. I don't think he's altogether honest.'

Alec Underwood smiled knowingly. 'You're missing nothing, I assure you,' he said. 'Now, as the winner of the pageant, you're going to be looked at and admired by all the young men in the town.'

She blinked, then smiled. 'Ooh yes,' she said with a giggle.

'They're going to look at you and wish they were . . . your lover,' he said with a twist of the lips, the best he could manage for a smile.

'Ooo!' she shrieked. Then she screamed again and suddenly said, 'I have to go to the loo.' She rushed away.

There was the sound of a car horn. Alec Underwood looked out of the caravan window. 'Peter's here now.'

He made for the door.

She turned back quickly. 'Where shall I see you?' she said crossing her legs.

'I'll see you back here when it's all over, say six o'clock.'

Her eyes saddened. Her jaw dropped. 'Won't I see you before?'

'Enjoy yourself,' he said with a big dramatic wave of his arm. 'You're their beauty queen. They'll feed you and fête you. You'll be all right. Enjoy your Marmaduke pie.'

'What's Marmaduke pie?'

'Carrots *à la croûte*.'

'What's that?'

He shook his head impatiently. 'Just eat it,' he said. 'I'm off. Just make sure that crown doesn't fall off and break. See you later.'

She clenched her fists by her side and pulled a sulky face. 'Oh, Alec.'

'You'll be all right. The driver knows you're in this caravan.'

'But, Alec,' she said, her bottom lip protruding.

'Stop whining. All you got to do is sit there and look demure.'

'What's that?'

He sighed. 'Pleasant, wholesome, innocent.'

She nodded then suddenly smiled and said mischievously, 'Sexy?'

'No. Well, yes, if you like.'

He opened the caravan door. A big car was standing there with the engine running. 'I'm off.'

He slammed the door.

Shirley dashed off to the tiny cubicle in the corner of the caravan. But she wasn't happy.

Jubilee Park, Bromersley,
South Yorkshire, UK.
1600 hours. Bank Holiday Monday, 25 May 2009

The auctioneer, Mr Pinsley Smith, rose to his feet on the raised platform and looked round the marquee, which was crammed full of people; all the one hundred chairs were occupied and at least another sixty hopeful and curious would-be antiques buyers were standing at the back. As the proceedings began, another twenty or thirty men and women crowded in from the entrance.

Pinsley Smith tapped lightly on the microphone with a finger, heard the drumming, nodded his approval and then said,

'Good afternoon, ladies and gentlemen. May I have your attention, please?'

The chattering mostly stopped. A few more people came in through the two entrances. All faces turned to stare at the man in the smart checked sports jacket.

'I bid you welcome to this very special Marmaduke Day catalogue antiques auction with some very interesting lots. Now today, the first sixty-six lots are on the instructions of the trustees of the estate of Mrs Robinson, late of Hellensmere House, Tunistone, who are clearing the house before offering it for sale. I will have the honour of conducting the sale of that most imposing Georgian house for the trustees sometime in June. Most of the items today are — I think you will agree — quite remarkable. Lot number one is the life-size gold modelled figure of Dorothea Jordan, actress, 1762 to 1816, mistress of the Duke of Clarence, later King William IV, who incidentally bore him ten children. She was reputed to be the most beautiful woman of the day, and on her death in 1816, the duke had a life-size gold-plated figure of her made and placed on a couch in his bedroom. It remained there for the rest of his life, including the period of his reign from 1830 until his death in 1837. Thereafter it was bequeathed to Elizabeth, one of his daughters by Dorothea Jordan, Lady Elizabeth Acton Fitzclarence, and it was later removed to Hellensmere House, Tunistone where her ladyship lived with her husband Lord Acton, until her death in 1856. The gold-plated figure has been there ever since.'

Two men in brown overall coats carefully tilted the shiny gold life-size nude statue of a female figure towards the crowd.

Smith held out an arm graciously in the direction of the statue.

A few people stood up and leaned forward.

There were several camera flashes.

Smith was surprised. He paused a few seconds while he recovered and said, 'So where do we want to be with an opening bid for this unusual historically interesting figure? Twenty thousand pounds? Ten thousand pounds?'

There were mutterings among the crowd, but nobody seemed much interested.

Smith surveyed the crowd. 'Five thousand?'

Still nothing. 'One thousand?' he called.

There was a girl wearing specs on Smith's staff, listening on a mobile phone seated just below him at the table. She waved a hand.

He looked down at her. She nodded towards him and muttered something.

Smith's face brightened. 'Ah,' he said. 'On the phone, I have a thousand pounds.' He glanced round the marquee. 'Two anywhere?'

Silence.

'I'll take eleven hundred . . . '

Still no response. He sniffed.

'Well, it's here to be sold. Last call. I'm selling.' He gave a long last look around the crowd then banged down the hammer and said, 'Sold to the bidder on the phone. The maiden bid of one thousand pounds.'

2

Empire Studio, Fish Box Passage,
London WC2, UK.
2200 hours. Bank Holiday Monday, 25 May 2009

The night sky was as black as a policeman's boot.

A voice in the dark called out: 'Car for Miss Razzle.'

'It's here, sir,' the man at the studio door called.

The stage exit door suddenly shot open into the dark lane, and a tall leggy blonde in the four-thousand-pound dress and twenty-thousand-pound necklace stepped out into the night.

'Goodnight, Miss Razzle.'

A group of eight or nine young people rushed up to her, waving books and pens.

'Can I have your autograph, please, Miss Razzle?' a young man in a duffle coat said.

She made a squiggle in his book. Then a flurry of other books appeared under her nose. Her eyebrows lifted. The corners of her mouth turned downwards. She sighed. She scribbled into some of them whilst still progressing towards the Bentley, the door being held open by a driver with a peaked cap.

There were a few whoops of delight and happy chattering as the fortunate autograph hunters drifted away.

'Straight home, miss?' the driver said.

She nodded, slumped into the back of the limo and closed her eyes.

The car sped away through the city northwards to Staples Corner, the M1 and on to Bromersley in South Yorkshire.

It was half past midnight when the driver pulled on to the drive of The Manor House on Creesforth Road.

'Here we are, miss,' the driver said, 'in record time I think.'

He rushed out of the driving seat, opened the rear door, then opened the boot and took out a small suitcase.

She climbed out. She shivered in the night air and made a dash for the front door. The driver followed with the suitcase. Heat sensors activated a bright light over the steps.

'I can manage, thank you,' she said.

'Right, miss. Goodnight.'

Rosemary Razzle fished in her clutch bag and took out a small bunch of keys. She unlocked the front door, picked up the case and went in as the Bentley purred quietly away.

She closed the front door. 'Charles,' she called. There was no reply. 'Charles, darling, I'm back. Where are you?'

There was a light in the kitchen. She went down the hall into the room. He wasn't there. She called again. Then she opened the door to the basement steps to the cellars. The light was on. There were two cellars. One was very small and was empty. The other was sealed off with a steel-covered door with a large combination lock screwed on to it. She tried the door handle but it was locked. Next to the wall was a telephone. She quickly snatched up the receiver and tapped the figure 9 on the dial pad. She could hear it ring out in the earpiece. She let it ring and ring. There was no reply. She knew something dreadful had happened. She put a hand to her chest. Her heart was pounding. Despite the cold, she felt hot. Her face was red and she was perspiring. There was no reply. At length, she pressed the cancel button on the phone and tapped in 999.

* * *

She went up the basement steps and into the kitchen. She filled the kettle and switched it on. Then she switched it off and went into the dining room to the drinks cabinet, grabbed a bottle, found a tumbler and poured herself a half-glass of brandy. She turned as if she had heard a noise from the front door. She put the bottle down, dashed into the hall, up to the door, opened it and looked out. There was nobody there. She returned to the dining room, made for the brandy then heard the doorbell ring. She turned back again and answered the door.

As the door opened, the light shone on two uniformed policemen.

Their mouths opened expectantly as they recognized the famous and beautiful Rosemary Razzle. It wasn't everyday they got close up to a real live celebrity actor.

'Mrs Razzle.' They knew who she was from her regular television appearances. 'I'm PC Donohue and this is PC Elder. We came as soon as we could. What's the trouble?'

She nodded. 'Come in, please. It's my husband. He's in his workshop. Locked in. Something's wrong. He doesn't reply. I've banged on the door, and tried to speak to him on the extension phone, but there's no reply.'

The two young men followed Mrs Razzle down the imposing hall, through the huge kitchen to the basement steps.

She wiped an eye with the back of her hand.

'He's in here.'

'Can't you open the door, miss?' Donohue said. 'Haven't you a key?'

'It's a combination lock. I don't know the number.'

'We'll see if we can break it down, miss.'

When the policemen tapped on the door, they knew they wouldn't be able to force their way in. It was a heavy steel door with a combination lock in the centre.

PC Elder tried the handle and pulled it. It didn't shift. He banged loudly on the door with his asp. It made no impression.

'How do you know your husband is in there, miss?'

'The light is on. The switch is on the outside and it's on . . . he often works long hours in there. Where else would he be at this time of night?'

'Is there any other way in? Where are the windows?'

'There are no windows and there is no other way in.'

'There is a phone in there?'

'Yes. I phoned him. He didn't pick up. Please do something. He might have had a heart attack or something.'

Donohue saw a phone on the wall. 'Does

this connect to the phone in there?'

'Yes.' She rubbed her long white manicured hand across her brow and said, 'You just dial 9 and hold on, but I've done all that and he doesn't answer.'

Donohue picked up the phone, tapped in the single digit and listened. After a few moments, he pulled the phone away from his ear and said, 'Can't hear it ring out.' He put his ear to the steel door.

Rosemary Razzle said, 'You can't hear anything through *that*.' Then she breathed in noisily and said, 'Oh. This is useless. You're not doing anything. Time is going on. My husband might be in there dying.'

'What else can we do, miss?' Donohue said, replacing the phone.

She turned away and ran her hand through her hair. She turned back. 'I'll have to get the man out that built the thing. He'll surely know how to get the door open.'

'If we phone him, he might turn out more quickly for us. What's his number?'

Her face dropped. 'Oh dear. I don't remember his name. He works for a security business in Sheffield. It's his business, I think.'

'Try Yellow Pages.'

She rushed off.

The two policemen looked at each other,

looked skywards, then shrugged. Donohue grabbed the door handle and yanked it several times. He fiddled with the combination lock and tapped in a few random numbers and tried the door handle. Nothing happened. He kicked the door. It didn't budge.

Donohue's RT blared into his ear: 'Sixty-two, come in sixty-two. Where are you?'

He told the sergeant where he and Elder were and explained the situation. He was told to stay there with Elder as long as they could be useful, but to keep in touch, then they made their way up the steps into the kitchen.

Mrs Razzle came in from the hall while looking into the phone book. She lowered the book on to the kitchen table, feverishly whipping the pages backwards and forwards until she found the page she wanted, then ran her finger down the small print. She stopped as she found a particular name, and read off a number. She then reached out to the phone fixed to the wall next to the large American refrigerator and tapped in a number. It rang a long time. As she waited, her eyes flitted across the room at the brightly lit, spotless kitchen and the two policemen standing by the basement door looking at her.

They stared at her, noticing the sculptured

silver-blonde hair, the slim figure, the long legs covered by a white dress and the necklace with the big diamonds twinkling in the light.

A man suddenly answered the phone. 'Yeah?'

She caught her breath. 'Is that Farleigh Security?' she said.

'Yes. Brian Farleigh speaking.'

'This is Mrs Charles Razzle, you might remember building a security workshop in the basement of our house for my husband?'

'And security lights outside the house, sure do, Mrs Razzle. But, what's the matter? What you ringing me at this time of the night for?'

'My husband is in the workshop . . . the door is locked . . . and I can't get in.'

'Maybe . . . maybe he wants to be on his own?'

'You don't understand. He doesn't answer the phone. He must have been in there hours. I think something may have happened to him.'

There was a pause.

'You don't know the combination?' he said.

'He keeps changing it. Is there another way in there?'

'No, Mrs Razzle. I think you know that there isn't.'

Her face went scarlet. Her lips tightened.

'There must be *something* you can do?'

Farleigh sighed. 'I'll come straight over. You're the big house at the far end of Creesforth Road in Bromersley, aren't you?'

'Please be quick,' she said and slammed the phone back on to its hook.

The two policemen had made some tea for Mrs Razzle and themselves, and were sitting at the kitchen table drinking it. Mrs Razzle had left hers and was walking up and down holding a glass of brandy and sipping from it from time to time in silence, occasionally darting out of the room to check on the front door.

The police officers had tried talking to her about her life and work, and about her husband, but she mostly answered in monosyllables. They had managed to elicit that he was an inventor in the throes of something important that he needed to keep secret until it had been registered with the patents office. His particular work necessitated a secure room, and she explained why she was so certain that he was in there.

She was leaning against the worktop, breathing noisily, looking up at the kitchen clock, watching the second hand sweep little by little round the dial, while the other hands indicated that it was almost two o'clock in the morning, when the front doorbell rang. She banged down the tumbler, ran to the door and opened it.

A big, suntanned man in a suede coat stood on the step smiling at her.

'Mrs Razzle.'

'You've been a helluva time, Mr Farleigh,' she said.

He looked at her in surprise, jaw dropped. 'Came as quickly as I could,' he said as he dragged two valises into the hall.

'You know where it is. Please make your way there.'

He bustled down the hall, into the kitchen, nodded at the two policemen, went through the door to the basement and down the steps.

Mrs Razzle followed close on his heels, with the two policemen behind her.

At the security room door, Farleigh lowered the valises to the floor, turned to Mrs Razzle and said, 'You're certain he's in there?'

'Positive,' she said. 'And he must be ill or something's wrong, otherwise he would have answered the phone.'

Farleigh rubbed his chin. 'Hmm. There's only one way I can open this door, Mrs Razzle. It will take some time.'

Her eyes flashed. 'What? I expected you to open it straight away. You built it, after all.'

He shook his head. 'It's a security room, Mrs Razzle,' he said as he took off his suede coat and draped it over the newel post. 'Access is not supposed to be easy. That's why it's called . . . a *security room*.'

'There's no quicker way?'

'Only dynamite.'

'Well, use that then.'

He grinned. 'We'd need permission from the local authority . . . that would take a month . . . anyway, down here we might blow a hole in the sewer. And you wouldn't like that.'

She threw her hands up in the air and said, 'Well, *do* something!' She breathed in noisily and turned away. She turned back, looked at her watch. 'It's ten minutes past two already.'

She made for the stairs.

The policemen stood back to allow her to pass.

Then she turned back to Farleigh. 'I will be in the kitchen. Let me know as soon as that door can be opened.'

She marched up the steps into the kitchen.

Farleigh looked at the policemen, grinned, then busied himself securing a small processor to the door lock with magnets then, from that, a lead to a USB port in a hand-held computer powered by mains electric from a socket low down on the wall. That done, he began a search for the combination. Starting from zero, illuminated red numbers ticked progressively on the small LCD screen. The lock had a six-digit combination number, so he said it might take a long time.

The policemen, who were on the basement steps leaning over the handrail, watched fascinated. Over Farleigh's shoulder, they could see the numbers slowly tick away. After ten minutes, they became bored and went upstairs to the kitchen.

Mrs Razzle was nowhere to be seen.

Donohue went into the hall. Through an open door, he saw a light. He wandered towards it. It led into the drawing room. The light source was from a pretty lamp on a small table next to a large luxurious sofa. He saw Mrs Razzle full length on the sofa apparently in a deep sleep. She looked like the fairytale princess from some extravagant Hollywood movie. He enjoyed just looking at her. All that was missing was the music from a hundred-piece orchestra. His eyes travelled to the table where he saw the tumbler half-full of brandy. He didn't want to disturb her. He crept quietly out of the room and returned to the kitchen.

PC Elder was looking at an electric kettle that was about to boil. He turned to Donohue. 'Does she want a coffee? Do her good.'

'She's flaked out.'

'Not surprised with all that brandy she's sunk. Do you think she'd mind if I had another cup of tea?'

'Shouldn't think so.'

'It isn't as if they're hard up,' he said, looking up and around meaningfully.

Steam began to come out of the kettle. It clicked off.

'What does *he* do?' Elder said.

'Invents things,' Donohue said. 'You've heard of Charles Razzle?'

Elder frowned. 'I think I've heard the name.'

'Musical tin-opener. Portable flushing toilet. Robot floor-cleaner. He's well known. Been on the telly. He's reputed to be working on something big.'

'Really?' Donohue said as he poured the water into the two cups. 'That's why he built this security workshop, patents, and all that?'

Donohue nodded.

In spite of the tea, Elder yawned and lowered his head into his arms on the kitchen table.

Donohue looked up at the kitchen clock. It said half past three. He leaned back in the chair trying to get into a comfortable position. It was not possible. He put his elbows on the table, leaned into his hands and closed his eyes. In his imagination he could see his bed. It looked very inviting. He was thinking how much he would enjoy a shower and then a long sleep when he heard heavy feet on the cellar steps. He opened his eyes, nudged Elder, who jumped to his feet.

'I wasn't asleep, Sean,' Elder said. 'Just resting my eyes.'

Donohue looked at the clock. It said ten minutes past five.

Farleigh came through the open basement door. He glanced round the kitchen.

'Where is she?' he said with a grin.

Donohue's eyebrows shot up. 'Is it unlocked?' he said.

'Where is she?' Farleigh said.

The policemen glanced at each other. The door *was* unlocked. They suddenly felt wide awake.

Donohue pointed down the hall. 'First door on your left,' he said.

Farleigh dashed out of the kitchen.

Donohue took a quick swig of cold tea, put the cup down on the worktop and crossed to the basement door. Elder followed him.

Mrs Razzle appeared at the drawing room door, swaying like a rope bridge in a gale. Her hair half-covered her face.

Farleigh came up behind her.

'I heard you. I heard you,' she said. Her speech was slurred. 'You've unlocked the bloody thing. About time too.'

She tried to rush, but she couldn't.

'Go on. Go on,' she said waving him on like an impatient driver waving on a bothersome car behind.

He overtook her and ran down the basement steps.

She followed making the best speed she could, precariously gripping the banister with both hands.

The two policemen came up quickly behind.

The security room door was still closed.

When Farleigh reached it, he pressed down the handle and pulled the heavy door silently towards them.

Mrs Razzle leaned forward.

The two policemen closed up behind her.

As it was opening, they heard a voice from inside the room. It was gentlemanly and courteous, but hollow and echoing. 'What do you want me to do now?' After a pause, the voice said, 'Did I do that correctly?' Then after another pause, it reverted to the original question: 'What do you want me to do now?'

It kept repeating the two questions alternately.

Mrs Razzle turned to the men behind her. She frowned, now seemed completely sober but unnerved, and said, 'That's my husband's voice, but it's not him speaking.'

Donohue pushed forward to be at the side of her and said, 'Be careful, miss.'

The strange hollow echoing voice suddenly stopped. It seemed to have heard their two voices and was considering its response.

'I do not understand your instruction,' the robot promptly chanted. 'Would you repeat it, please?'

The door was now fully open and they stared into the long, brightly lit cellar. Immediately they saw a human-sized robot made of clear blue plastic standing upright against the wall facing them. Three small red lights were flashing inside the top of its translucent plastic head. Ominously, they saw that it was holding a handgun in the shooting position.

Beyond the robot, the walls of the cellar were lined with banks of black electronic equipment, LCD screens and powerful batteries. There seemed to be dials on everything. Electric cables ran all over the place. There was a smell of acid and rubber. There was a long bench in the middle of the room cluttered with engineer's and electrician's tools, and an assortment of entirely unfathomable metal and plastic parts. The corner of a desk projected from behind the door.

Mrs Razzle took a short step into the cellar. 'Charles,' she said, tentatively. She peered round the workshop door, and then she saw it. It was the body of a man slumped on the floor by the desk in a pool of blood.

She screamed and cried out, 'Charles! Charles!'

'Stand back, everybody,' Donohue yelled. 'We're in the line of fire of that gun.'

Donohue, Elder and Farleigh stepped out of the doorway.

Mrs Razzle, ignoring Donohue, suddenly rushed over towards the body by the desk.

Donohue instantly reached forward, put his arm round her waist, lifted her out of the doorway and swung her back into the basement, out of range of the gun.

'Put me down,' she screamed, digging her nails into his hand and kicking his shins with the back of her shoes. 'How *dare* you?'

At the same time, the strange voice reverted to saying, 'What do you want me to do now? What do you want me to do now? What do you want me to do now?'

3

DI Angel's office, Bromersley Police Station,
South Yorkshire, UK.
0828 hours. Tuesday, 26 May 2009

Angel looked across the desk at the uniformed constable and rubbed his chin. 'Aye,' he said. 'Then what happened?'

'Well, sir,' Donohue said, 'Clive Elder and I managed to get Mrs Razzle out of the line of fire of the robot, up the basement steps into the kitchen, where she completely gave way to tears. Clive made her some sweet tea and we talked to her . . . tried to comfort her. The security engineer wanted to leave. He said that he had a lot on. So I took his phone number and address and told him that he would be needed as a witness, and he went. Meanwhile, all the time, now that the security door was wide open, through the closed basement door, we could still hear that robot's voice chanting away, 'What do you want me to do now?' over and over again.' Donohue pulled a creased face. 'Fancy a robot killing the man who made it.'

Angel frowned.

'We were thankful the thing didn't follow us up the stairs,' Donohue added. Angel ran his tongue over his bottom lip.

'You said it looked as if Charles Razzle had directed the robot on to himself using a remote control?' Angel said.

'The gun was pointed in that general direction. Sounds ridiculous, sir, but yes. That's about the size of it. On the floor by the body, with a dozen or more control buttons on it, was what looked like a rather crude remote control. Also, as I said, the security door was locked, and we were told there was no other way into the room. There was nobody else in there.'

Angel blinked. 'So it looks like his death was, presumably, accidental . . . or suicidal?'

Donohue nodded. 'Yes, sir.'

Neither spoke for a moment, then Angel suddenly said, 'Did you say that a light came on when you and Elder first arrived at the Razzle's front door?'

'Yes, sir. It also went on when the engineer left at about five-thirty. It was obviously a heat-sensitive light.'

'Did you see any CCTV cameras anywhere?'

'No, sir.'

Angel reached out for the phone and tapped in a number.

Don Taylor answered. He was the sergeant in charge of SOCO at Bromersley CID. His team was already at work at the house.

'Don,' Angel said, 'I want you to look round for any CCTV. We could be lucky and find one in the workshop. I want any tapes you find, asap.'

'Right, sir.'

'No sign of a suicide note, I suppose?'

'Not up to now.'

'Let me know if one turns up. And let me know as soon as I can get on to the scene.'

He replaced the phone and looked up at Donohue. 'With everything he had going for him, it would be tragic if a man as young and talented as Charles Razzle had taken his own life.'

Donohue shrugged then nodded.

'Thank you, lad,' Angel said. 'Now off you go and get some kip.'

Donohue went out. Angel watched the door close.

He was considering what next he might do to progress the case. Forensics must finish the sweep of the scene before he set foot in the place. He considered the situation for a few moments, then reached out for the phone and summoned PC Ahmed Ahaz, a young man in his twenties.

'I want you to find out if there's anything

on the PNC, Ahmed, on Charles Razzle, and his wife, Rosemary. Also see if you can find out where an old lag called Peter Queegley is these days. I saw him at Pinsley Smith's auction last Saturday. I thought he should still be serving a stretch for handling stolen paintings. I tried to get to him but he slipped away in the crowd. It was either him or his double.'

'Peter Queegley, sir?'

'Local lad. Used to live in Hoyland or Hoyland Common.'

'Right, sir. As a matter of interest, there's a piece in the *National Daily Press and Advertiser* about that auction. Have you seen it? It was on the front page.'

Angel's eyes narrowed briefly. Bromersley almost never hit the front page of any newspaper. His face brightened. 'Really? No, lad. Must see that.'

'I'll fetch it, sir.'

Ahmed dashed off.

The phone rang. Angel reached out for it. It was the civilian woman on the switchboard. 'There's a Mr Hargreaves, funeral director, on the line.'

Angel blinked. He had been the man who had organized his father's funeral, that was the only contact he had ever had with the man. 'Right. Put him through.'

'Sorry to bother you, Inspector,' Hargreaves said. 'I have had a burglary . . . I didn't know who I could speak to about it. I've never had to bother the police before.'

Angel frowned and said, 'That's all right. You can speak to me, Mr Hargreaves. What's happened? What's been taken?'

'My workshop and garage have been broken into. I have had a look round. It looks as if thieves have taken three of my oak coffins, silk lined, varnished and complete with best plated carrying-handles and lids. Broken into a garage and then through an internal-door into the workshop.'

Angel rubbed his chin. 'Sorry about that, Mr Hargreaves. Three coffins? What can you do with coffins except bury people in them?'

'Sell them, I suppose. They are quite expensive. Cost four hundred and eighty pounds apiece plus VAT, and I have no idea what a new garage door will set me back.'

'I'll send a man round straight away. Don't touch anything. There might be some fingerprints.'

He replaced the phone. He wondered whether the coffins had been stolen by young drug-and-booze-soaked villains on a whoopee trip, or by others with a more serious intention.

Ahmed reappeared with a copy of the

National Daily Press and Advertiser. 'Front page, sir. There,' he said pointing to the corner of the folded newspaper, which he passed across the desk.

Angel took it and looked at the piece headed: 'Future king's mistress goes down for £1,000.' Underneath was a two-inch double-column photograph of the gold-plated plaster statue of Dorothea Jordan. The article gave her history and her relationship with the Duke of Clarence in brief. The piece was saying essentially that the price paid for the figure should have been much higher considering Dorothea Jordan's place in history, and suggested that the item should have been sold in a prestigious London auction house by a more responsible and competent auctioneer, and not 'given away' in a marquee sale in an insignificant northern town to a maiden bid. There was a comment from Pinsley Smith, who was quoted as saying, 'I am fully aware of the obligation to my vendors, and considered that while one thousand pounds was a low price, I seriously had not expected the item to have fetched very much more whether sold in London or anywhere else.'

The piece ended with the words . . . 'When asked the name of the purchaser, Pinsley Smith said, 'That is a confidential matter. I never divulge information of that kind about my clients.''

'I'm afraid poor old Pinsley Smith doesn't come out of it too well . . . and it doesn't reflect well on the town, either.'

'It's mentioned in the other national papers, sir.'

Angel sniffed. 'Aye, well, they must be short of something to write about then. I thought the silly season was August. Thanks very much, lad,' he said. He handed the paper back to Ahmed. 'Find Scrivens and send him to me, and didn't I ask you to check on Charles and Rosemary Razzle?'

Ahmed's mouth dropped open.

* * *

Angel parked the BMW on The Feathers' car-park and pushed his way through the revolving doors. The hotel was Bromersley's only three star hotel.

Angel made for the reception desk and caught the eye of the desk clerk, who tilted his head to one side and raised his eyebrows.

'Mrs Razzle,' Angel said. 'What room number is she in, please?'

'Mrs Razzle is in *suite* number 1, sir,' said the clerk. He reached for the phone and tapped in a number. 'Who shall I say is calling?' he said, looking up.

But there was nobody there.

Angel had already passed through the double doors, and was making his way up the stairs to the first floor to suite number 1. When he reached the sitting room door, he knocked on it and waited. It suddenly opened.

He saw the most beautiful woman in a frothy pink house coat. Her long blonde hair fell irregularly over her shoulders. She was exactly as he remembered seeing her many times on television.

She looked Angel up and down, and smiled. 'Were you knocking?' she asked.

'Mrs Razzle?' Angel said. 'Of course. I am so sorry to disturb you. Detective Inspector Angel.' he said.

The smile dissolved. She hesitated, then pulled the door open wider and said, 'Oh yes. Please come in.'

The sitting room was decorated in cream and gold, with two sofas, a sprinkling of easy chairs, a coffee table with a large dish holding a mountain of fruit. There were two full-length windows leading to small balconies overlooking the town and hills beyond.

She pointed to an easy chair. He sat down and watched her climb on to the large sofa opposite.

'I didn't much like being evicted out of my house so abruptly in the middle of the night, I must say,' she said.

'I'm sorry. Your house has become a crime scene. It is necessary.'

'That sergeant wouldn't even let me pick up any clothes or collect a toothbrush or anything.'

Angel knew it would have been so. He didn't say anything.

'I couldn't even take my own car. I had to dash round the shops in a taxi and buy some bits to get me by. When will I be able to return?'

'Very soon. A few days. In the meantime, I have a few questions I must put to you, if you are up to it?'

'Of course. You *must*. Fire away.'

'When did you last see your husband?'

'Very early Sunday morning . . . it would be a few minutes to four . . . I brought him a cup of tea in bed before I left for the studio. A car picked me up at four o'clock on the dot to take me up to London to rehearse and then to record a play I am in. I had to be in make-up for eight o'clock.'

'PC Donohue said you told him you arrived back at half past midnight on Tuesday morning, this morning.'

'That's right.'

'It was a long day. A very long day.'

'Doesn't often happen like that, Inspector. Once a month, maybe. Better than staying in hotels. I can hire a car and driver, there and back. I can nod on the back seat, then arrive home and sleep in my own bed. Why wouldn't I do that?'

Angel nodded. 'Can someone vouch for you being in the studio all that time?'

'There was an audience of three hundred and a crew and cast of about forty.'

'I just need . . . a couple of names . . . '

She reached down to a small leather case on the floor by the sofa, quickly yanked out a plastic ring-binder that was bulging with the script of the play she had recorded. She opened it and snatched out the top page. 'Take that. That's got all the cast, the director and the crew with their phone numbers or their agents' phone numbers. They were all there.'

Angel hardly glanced at it. 'Thank you,' he said. He folded the paper roughly and pushed it into his pocket.

'And you dialled triple nine, five or ten minutes after you arrived home?'

'About that. As soon as I realized that something was . . . seriously very wrong.'

He wrinkled his nose. 'I am sorry that I have to ask you, but is there any reason at all why your late husband would have wanted to take his own life?'

She breathed in quickly and swallowed. 'I can't think of any. Certainly not.'

'You see, there was a gun . . . it was in the robot's hand.'

'Yes. It was his plan to build a robot to do all the usual boring repetitive household chores in the house. He hoped to extend its use to factories and so on.'

'It was in the robot's hand pointing at him. Your husband was believed to be holding the remote control.'

'Yes, I know. Horrible.'

'Have you any idea what must have been in his mind?'

'There's no explanation I can come up with, Inspector, except that from time to time he got depressed. He said that he craved adventure, exploration and new places.'

Angel rubbed his cheek. He felt like that every day.

'Did he have any money troubles?'

She laughed. Too much, perhaps. 'Good lord, no.'

'Did you know that he owned a handgun?'

'I had seen it . . . a long time ago.'

'Where did he get it from?'

'He's had it ever since I can remember. He thought it was a good idea . . . if we were attacked or . . . whatever. You hear some ghastly stories these days.'

'Have you ever seen him fire it?'

'I didn't even know it was loaded.'

'Where was it normally kept?'

'In the drawer of the bedside table on his side.'

'Who will benefit from your husband's death?'

She stared hard at him. There was a pause, then she said, 'I am the main beneficiary, but my husband made an enormous allowance to his daughter, Jessica, my stepdaughter. There's nobody else. He also gave her a capital sum. She may be paid additional subsistence from his estate if she needs it.'

Angel's eyebrows went as high as the scales of justice on the roof of the Old Bailey. He pursed his lips. He was wondering whether it was really necessary to ask the next question. At length, just for the hell of it, wearing the expression of a prize poker player he said, 'And who will decide if she needs it?'

'I will,' she said.

'Really?' he said, unsurprised.

Rosemary Razzle did not react to his reply.

'You've been in touch with Jessica?' he asked.

She hesitated. 'I'm not sure where she is. She's on a sort of working holiday in the

States. She doesn't stay long anywhere. Last I heard she had a job doing something with horses . . . looking after a small stable for a family in Texas, I think it was.'

'I'll need her address.'

'It'll be among my husband's papers. I know they were in touch by email quite recently.'

Angel nodded and made a note on the back of an envelope he carried for that very purpose.

'Was there anybody else regularly in the house?'

'Yes, we have a housekeeper, Mrs Dalgleish, Elaine Dalgleish. She comes in part time.'

'I shall need to speak to her. Ask her to come down to the station and tell her to ask for me, will you?'

'I'll phone her, Inspector. Oh dear. She will have been to the house . . . and wondered what's happened. I must remember.'

'Thank you.'

Angel's eyes narrowed as he licked his bottom lip with the tip of his tongue.

'Is that it, Inspector?' she said.

He stared hard into her eyes. 'Not quite, Mrs Razzle. Not quite. Just one more question. But it's a very important one.'

She lifted her head and looked back at him evenly, her face set.

Angel said, 'Did your husband have any enemies?'

She sighed. 'No,' she replied. 'Everybody liked Charles, Inspector.'

He nodded, then said, 'Think about it, Mrs Razzle. Are you really sure?'

'He was generally easy-going. He would be difficult to fall out with,' she said, then she frowned and added, 'but he took his own life, Inspector, didn't he?'

'Certainly looks like it, Mrs Razzle. Certainly looks like it.'

* * *

There was a knock at Angel's office door.

'Come in,' he called.

It was Ahmed. He came in carrying a large envelope with the word EVIDENCE printed in big letters across it.

'Thought I saw you come in, sir,' he said. 'There's nothing on the NPC about Charles Razzle or Rosemary Razzle.'

Angel nodded. 'Right, lad. What about Peter Queegley?'

'He was released from Lincoln prison last month, sir. Sentenced to twelve months for being in possession of two stolen paintings by Van de Longe. He was charged with another man.'

'Alec Underwood. But he got off. Insufficient evidence.'

Ahmed's eyebrows shot up. He was surprised at his boss's memory. He shouldn't have been. 'That's right, sir.'

'Find out where Queegley is living,' Angel said. 'The probation office will tell you. The new lass in charge there . . . with the stringy red hair . . . smells of bleach. She'll know.'

'Right, sir.'

'What you got there,' Angel said, pointing to the envelope.

'DS Taylor phoned to say that he found two CCTV cameras in The Manor House, Creesforth Road, and that they contained twenty-four-hour tapes and that they were actually still running.' He held up the envelope. 'A patrolman delivered them five minutes ago. They are marked for your urgent attention.'

Angel's eyebrows shot up. '*Two* tapes?' He took the envelope, opened it and slid the video tapes out on to the desk top. 'That's great.'

He picked one up and read out the label. 'Camera inside by front door focused down the main hall. Tape was running and withdrawn at 1109 hours. 26.5.09. No fingerprints.' He read out the other. 'Camera concealed in basement focused on security door. Tape was running and withdrawn at 1105 hours. 26.5.09. No fingerprints.'

He frowned. 'Well, Ahmed,' he said, 'nobody could possibly dodge those cameras and gain access to Razzle's workshop. Pity there wasn't a CCTV camera in the workshop itself. I want you to check them off immediately. They're not run out yet . . . a twenty-four-hour tape, about three-quarters through . . . Anyway, mark the tapes and run them through, and we'll be able to work out exactly the time that they were changed. All right?'

'Yes, sir.'

There was a knock at the door.

'See who it is, then crack on. As soon as you see an intruder, even if you can identify him, let me know.'

Ahmed nodded and opened the door.

It was DC Scrivens.

'What is it, Ted?'

Ahmed rushed out with the videotapes.

'About Hargreaves, the funeral directors, sir,' Scrivens said.

'Aye. Come in,' Angel said. 'They were just referred to as plain undertakers when I was a lad. What about them?'

'Met up with Mr Hargreaves,' Scrivens said. 'A padlock on a garage was forced open, presumably with a crowbar and entry gained into where the hearse is kept. There is a door out of the garage into the workshop where all the coffins and parts like coffin handles, trestles and so on are stored. There were piles of coffins, sir, wrapped in bubble wrap and Sellotape . . . forty or more all different sorts of wood and some painted white. Mr Hargreaves said that three mahogany ones were stolen. He gave me a photograph from the manufacturer's catalogue, and he showed me the place they had occupied in the workshop.'

'Was there any unnecessary damage or any graffiti left behind by the intruders?' Angel was wondering whether it was an act of vandalism fuelled by drugs or alcohol, or a serious robbery for gain of some kind.

'Oh no, sir. I don't think it was kids on a drug trip.'

'Well, what do robbers want with three coffins?' He rubbed his chin. All the reasons he could think of he didn't like. He hoped it didn't augur a spate of grave-digging or worse.

'Don't know, sir,' Scrivens said looking at him wide eyed.

'Any forensic?' Angel said.

'No.'

The phone rang. Angel reached out for it. 'All right, Ted,' he said. 'Leave it with me.'

Scrivens made for the door.
Then Angel called, 'Oh Ted.'
Scrivens looked back.
'Nip into CID and tell Ahmed I want him pronto.'
Scrivens nodded, went out and closed the door.
Angel then pressed the button on the phone. 'Angel.'
It was a young PC on reception. 'There's a woman here asking for you, sir. Says her name is Elaine Dalgleish.'
'Good. Show her down here, lad, smartly, will you?' Angel said and replaced the phone.
He sighed. He needed to collect his thoughts.
There was a knock at the door. It was Ahmed.
'Ahmed, I want you to put a poster on the noticeboard.'
He screwed up his face. 'Yes sir?'
'About three coffins stolen from Hargreaves the undertakers.'
The constable blinked. '*Coffins*?'
'Yes. I want to know if anybody comes across them in their travels. Get a photograph and description from Ted Scrivens.'
'Right, sir.' He went out.
A few moments later a PC showed a woman into the office.

'Please sit down, Mrs Dalgleish, or is it Miss?' Angel said.

'Thank you, and it's *Mrs* Dalgleish,' the middle-aged woman said as she settled into the chair nearest the desk.

'How long have you been housekeeper to Mr and Mrs Razzle?' Angel said.

'Three years, Inspector.'

'Are they good employers?'

'They're all right. But listen here, Inspector, are you going to tell me if what I hear is right?'

'What's that?' he said.

'That Mr Razzle pointed the gun of his robot on to himself and took his own life?'

'It certainly looks like that, Mrs Dalgleish. Who told you he took his own life?'

'Mrs Razzle. But, I must say, I don't believe it. Not Mr Razzle. He's not the type. I reckon you'll find out who did it . . . it'll be somebody else who managed to take over control of his robot. You'll soon find him. You are that Inspector Angel, aren't you, who is said to have the mind of a criminal, who always gets his man, like the Canadian Mounties? I've read all about you in the papers. They say you've never had a murder case that you haven't solved. You're that Inspector Angel, aren't you?'

It wasn't easy for him to avoid her eyes.

Eventually he looked up and said, 'I suppose I am.'

'And I expect you're married, Inspector, aren't you?'

He hesitated. 'Yes,' he said.

'I can do that, you know. I mean on the telly. When I'm watching a murder film on the telly. I can nearly always pick out the one who done it. It's the one least likely. The one who is supposed to be a good sort.'

Angel gave her a polite smile.

She smiled back, followed by a nod.

There was a short pause, then Angel said: 'Do you know of anybody who would have wanted Mr Razzle dead?'

'No. He was a fine, upright, hard-working man, and very clever with it. He had several inventions to his name, you know.'

'So I have heard.'

'He was a lovely man. He does get a bit ratty when he's busy in the workshop and someone wants to see him. When I'm there, I always try to put callers off, or put them on to Mrs Razzle.'

'Did someone . . . anyone difficult call recently, then?'

'Only a salesman trying to get Mr Razzle to change who he gets his gas from. We get them at home every week.'

'Have you been in his workshop?'

'Oh yes. I've seen the robot he was building. I don't like it. It might be very clever, but I don't like it. I think the idea of building an artificial man is . . . is against nature. Nothing good will ever come of it. It will murder again given the opportunity. You'll see.'

Angel noted her indignation. He wasn't inclined to say anything.

'Did Mr and Mrs Razzle get on well together?'

'As well as any other married couple, and better than most, I suppose.'

'Well, did you ever see them have a row or an argument?'

'No. Not them. Mindst you, they seemed to have the ideal arrangement. He worked all day down in his workshop, while she was on the floor above learning lines, exercising, or topping up her tan under a sunlamp. I think they usually spent the evenings together, when she wasn't working. She is a very successful actress, you know. Never off the box. Comes from a well-to-do family. Her uncle is Sir Jack Prendergast, boss of Frescati Fashions. They often go to posh dinners and dos like that.'

Angel wrinkled his nose. He was grateful for the information. Then he remembered that that name, Sir Jack Prendergast, had appeared recently in *Police Review*. Sir Jack had been one of the victims of a spate of country-house robberies. He had been robbed of five million pounds' worth of antiques including paintings, and gold snuff-boxes.

4

Angel drove the BMW to The Manor House on Creesforth Road. He parked it behind SOCO's big unmarked white van next to a Range Rover. A uniformed PC on the front doorstep threw up a salute as he approached the house.

'Good afternoon, sir.'

'Good afternoon, Constable,' Angel said.

The front door opened and another PC dressed in white disposable paper overalls, boots, cap, face mask and gloves came up to him and said, 'I heard your car, sir. This way, please.'

Angel nodded, stepped into the house and said, 'Have you any gloves for me?'

The SOCO opened a patch pocket on his chest and withdrew a thin sealed white paper packet.

'Ta,' Angel said. He tore the packet top and pulled out a pair of white rubber gloves and put them on as he stood there looking down the long hall.

The uniformed PC closed the door behind them.

The constable walked down the middle of

a one-metre-wide plastic roll laid down the centre of the hall. Angel followed at a more leisurely pace, looking round at the many pictures and paintings on the walls above dark oak panelling. He was also taking time to absorb the atmosphere of the house. He stopped after a few yards, looked back, lifted his gaze above the front door lintel and said, 'Hey, lad. Where is the CCTV camera?'

The constable stopped, turned and walked back up to Angel. 'There's no tape in it *now*, sir.'

'No. I daresay. But where is it, exactly?'

The constable pointed in the general direction of the area above the door. '*There*, sir.'

Angel stared and stared. All he could see were pictures and picture frames. He walked back towards the door and eventually made out its characteristic shape among all the framed art. He stared at it a moment, grunted and moved on.

The constable directed him into the kitchen and through the door to the basement.

As Angel stepped down the wooden steps, his eyebrows lifted when he saw the big open door of the cellar workshop.

DS Taylor came out to meet him.

'Sir.'

'A very impressive door, Don.'

'Protecting very expensive technical equipment, sir. There's stuff here they probably wish they had at NASA.'

'Where's the CCTV camera? The one supposed to be covering this access.'

'In the corner, behind that cowling.'

Angel peered up and saw a small sheet of card or tin or aluminium that had been secured to the ceiling and painted white. It partly hid the camera, which he noted was also painted white, the same colour as the walls and the ceiling. As he looked closely at it, he also noted that the camera bracket was fastened to a small-bore vertical pipe that ran from a radiator in the basement upwards, then out through into the floor of the kitchen.

He frowned, shook his head and stood there a few moments before he followed Taylor into the workshop. Standing in the doorway he took several long looks round the place. The sight of the blue plastic robot (now without lights flickering in the head or a gun in its hand) caused him to stop briefly to take it in. He stared at it thoughtfully for a few seconds, then shook his head.

'Where was the body?' he asked.

Taylor pointed to the area on the floor in front of the desk. 'Full length down there, sir. Three bullets. One in the chest, one in the head and one in the stomach.'

Angel wrinkled his nose as he visualized the scene. 'You've plenty of photographs?'

'Stacks, sir.'

'Mmm. The gun. Any prints?'

'A Walther PPK/S, sir,' Taylor told him, opening an evidence bag, taking out a handgun from it and handing it to him. 'No prints on the gun. Razzle's prints were on three of the rounds. The clip had five rounds when I checked it. Three had been fired, so the clip had been full.'

Angel saw the three shell cases on the floor near the robot.

'Those from this gun?'

'Yes, sir. No prints. Everything checked. Absolutely in perfect order.'

Angel nodded and returned the gun. 'Now the remote control. Tell me about it.'

Taylor picked up a crudely made piece of equipment that appeared to be a cross between a TV remote and a string puppet-master's control bar.

Angel looked at it, blinked and said: 'He'd presumably not finished this part of his handiwork?'

'It was found on the floor, a few centimetres from his right hand.'

'With his fingerprints all over it?'

'Yes, sir.'

'Anybody else's?'
'No.'
'Did it work? Can it operate the robot, make it aim the gun and fire at a target on command?'
'Oh yes, sir,' Taylor said, pulling a grim face. 'It works perfectly.'
Angel sniffed. Technology was reaching a new low in his estimation.
'You have to put the gun in the robot's hand and set the finger inside the trigger guard, of course,' Taylor said. 'Then, by pressing buttons on the remote control, you can raise its arm, manoeuvre the wrist in almost every possible direction, aim the gun and fire it on command.'
'Would you have to press the button that controls the finger on the trigger on each occasion you wanted to fire a round?'
'Yes, sir.'
'Where was the gun pointing when you arrived?'
'It was aimed about chest height in the direction of the desk. As the desk is just behind the open door, there was a risk that we might have been in the firing line, so I got the armourer to come — wearing suitable body armour, of course — to make it safe by removing the gun from the robot's hand.'
Angel nodded. He was thinking how

dangerous this world could become if there was a proliferation in the use of armed robots.

He rubbed his chin and looked round. 'The only way in or out of this workshop is through that door?'

'Yes, sir.'

'There are no windows, back doors, trap doors, chimneys, air vents or other possible means of access? I want you to be absolutely sure about that.'

'I am sure, sir. You can rely on it.'

Angel had worked with Taylor for seven years and always found him thorough and reliable. He nodded.

'Anybody else's prints or DNA in this place . . . especially on the robot?'

'No. Every sample we have taken in this place has Charles Razzle's prints on it and nobody else's.'

'And you are still going through his desk, then?'

'We've just about finished, sir. Nothing criminal, or even interesting. He has a big portfolio of shares and cash savings in dated bonds. Even though I suppose he took a beating last year when the recession began, and bank shares dropped. However, his holdings are so diverse and big that huge dividend cheques have resumed rolling in. He was enormously rich. Whoever inherits his estate — I suppose it's his missis, Rosemary Razzle, — will be very rich indeed.'

'He has a daughter, Jessica. Turned anything up about her?'

'No, sir.'

'I need her address. She needs to be informed. Check his computer. See what's on the history . . . and let me know asap. Is there a safe?'

'By the desk, sir. We haven't been into it yet. I assume the key went with the body, in his pocket. We'll have to delay opening until Dr Mac releases the personal effects.'

'Aye, Don. I'll chase him.'

'What I don't understand, is why on earth would Charles Razzle want to take his own life in such a peculiar way?'

Angel sighed. 'Ahmed is going through those tapes now. They'll tell us who entered the house when Razzle's wife was up in London doing her acting.'

'He'd need to know the combination or he wouldn't get access.'

'Maybe Razzle worked with the door open?'

'Or if it was somebody he knew he might let him or them in?'

'Let's see what the tapes tell us,' Angel said, then he sniffed and rubbed his chin.

'Have you found a suicide note . . . perhaps on a computer or anywhere?'

'No, sir. No, we've looked everywhere.'

'Well, keep looking,' Angel said and turned away.

He looked at the door and noticed a keypad above the handle on the inside. He raised his eyebrows. 'When that door is closed, you'd need to know the combination to get *out*?'

Taylor frowned. 'I expect so, sir. I haven't tried it out. I don't know the number.'

Angel rubbed his chin. Then he took a last look at the blue, shiny, translucent robot, bit his lip, shook his head and went out.

* * *

Angel returned to the police station.

He paced smartly up the corridor, head bowed and forehead furrowed. His preliminary examination of the crime scene had disturbed him. He couldn't accept the idea that a man had been killed by a robot while he had apparently been in absolute control of it at the time.

He pushed open the CID office door and looked round for Ahmed. There were a few detectives in there, but no Ahmed. Angel grunted. He needed to see urgently what

Ahmed had found. He dashed down the corridor to the darkened room called 'the theatre', where he snatched open the door and peered inside.

Ahmed was there, alone in the small, dimly lit room. He was seated in front of a console looking at a screen. He stood up when he saw it was Angel.

'Ah,' Angel said, pleased to have found him. 'Sit down, lad. Sit down. Carry on.'

Ahmed was looking at a video picture showing the open workshop door in Razzle's cellar. Through the door and a little out of focus was the blue robot with the gun drawn, pointing at the camera.

Angel slid into a seat next to him. 'What have you found?' he said.

'Nothing untoward, sir.'

'*What*?'

Ahmed blinked. He knew Angel wouldn't be pleased. 'That is, nothing until Mrs Razzle arrives, sir.'

Angel frowned. '*What?*' he said.

'There's no audio, sir, but it is obviously night time. She enters by the front door, seems to call out something, then goes briefly through a door on the right, then returns and runs down to the cellar. Sometime later, PC Donohue and PC Elder arrive, then the engineer arrives, wires a machine of some sort to the keypad of the workshop door. It takes for ages, but he eventually seems to unlock it. Then Mrs Razzle, PC Donohue and PC Elder come into the picture briefly. PC Donohue lifts Mrs Razzle away from the doorway in a hurry. She seems to object . . . and they all go out of shot. I'm running the tape on fast from there.'

Angel's jaw tightened. 'I mean *before* all that. Somebody else. An intruder. The murderer. Isn't there anybody else on either tape?'

'No, sir.'

'Have you checked *both* tapes?'

'I've checked the first. Just finishing the second one, sir.'

Angel's face dropped. His mind was all over the place.

He went out of the room, into the corridor, and slowly closed the door.

It was another blow. A blow he had not expected. There were no intruders or potential murderers showing on the tapes. That was in addition to the fact that there were no fingerprints on the trigger of the gun and the dead man was found alone in the workshop that was locked.

He was left with the inevitable conclusion that the robot had somehow shot Charles Razzle.

* * *

An hour later Angel summoned DS Crisp to his office.

Crisp was a great success with the ladies and, on occasion, had charmed guilty pleas out of some of the most hardened female criminals. He had also been seen occasionally with PC Leisha Baverstock, the station beauty, but nothing ever quite seemed to come of it.

'You wanted me, sir' he said bouncing into the room.

Angel pointed at the chair nearest the desk.

'It's this Razzle case,' he began.

Crisp's eyebrows shot up. 'What, sir?'

'I want you to make a close observation of Rosemary Razzle.'

Crisp frowned. 'You're not going to ask me to make up to her, are you, sir?' he said, looking down and shaking his head. 'She won't look at me. She must be worth a bomb. I can't compete with her diamond-and-pearl world.'

'Do you think you've lost your touch, Sergeant?'

Crisp looked thoughtful then shook his head. 'No. I just know my limitations.'

Angel took his point. 'Start by observing her.'

‘Why do you want her observing, sir? Didn’t the robot kill her husband, then?’

Angel’s eyes narrowed, then he said, ‘I don’t know.’

‘You mean *she* murdered him?’

‘I am led to believe that she was in London when her husband died. She has what seems to be a good alibi. She says she was in a TV film studio. I’m checking it out.’

‘Oh sir,’ Crisp said, ‘she’s famous, she’s rich and she’s a cracker. If she’s in need of a man, sir, there are probably a dozen hanging around in the wings . . . and a queue of others . . . all hovering around with their tongues hanging out.’

‘Probably,’ Angel said. ‘Your tongue will need to hang out a bit further, then. That’s all. Start tomorrow morning first thing. She’s staying at The Feathers until we’ve finished sweeping the house. I want to know who visits her, how long they stay and so on.’

Crisp shook his head. ‘Oh sir,’ he said running his hand through his hair.

‘All I need is a *name*,’ Angel said. ‘That’s all. Right. Now you’ve got her address, you know who she is, get on to it.’

‘What about back-up, sir?’

‘Whatever you need.’

‘And expenses?’

‘Yes. Yes. *Reasonable* expenses. Now hop it.’

Crisp smiled. 'Right, sir,' he said.

He went out of the room and closed the door.

Angel watched him leave. One corner of his mouth turned upwards.

Two minutes later he squared up the letters and envelopes on his desk, shoved them in a drawer, put his pen in his pocket, took an old envelope out of his pocket, referred to something written on it, put it back, looked at his watch and then stood up. He went out of the office and up the corridor to the CID office. He peered in and found Ahmed working at his computer.

'I'm going out, Ahmed. I'm calling on Peter Queegley, then I'm going home.'

'Right, sir.'

Angel then dashed down the green corridor, past the cells, out of the back door into the car park. He drove the BMW down Park Road to Mountjoy Street. It was a short street comprising large Victorian houses that had over the years mostly been divided into flats and bedsits. He parked the car at the side of the road among an assembly of old cars, and walked up to number 20. There was a box of eight pushbuttons on the big doorjamb, with names on cards against them and a speak box above it. He found the name 'P. Queegley' against number 6 and pressed the button.

A girl's voice from a speaker answered. 'Yes? Is it Alec?'

Angel was surprised to hear a girl answer. 'Yeah,' he grunted.

'There you go,' she said.

There was a buzzing sound, a click and the door opened an inch.

Angel pushed at it and he was in. He closed it quickly and looked round. It was a dark, musty hallway, cobwebby and smelling of cabbage water. He walked up the hall on bare floorboards and checked off the numbers on the doors. He had to mount two flights of uncarpeted steps and walk along a short landing to the end before he found number 6.

The small thin door was slightly open. He tapped gently on it. A skinny girl in a tight T-shirt and knickers, with bare feet and bare legs, put her head round the edge of the door. She was wearing more eyeliner than might be found in the transvestite's wing in Strangeways, and she was hanging on to a tumbler half-filled with a light-brown liquid.

When she saw Angel her big eyes grew bigger.

'Here,' she said. 'You're not Alec. Who are you? What do *you* want?'

Angel pushed his way into the small room

and looked round.

There was very little furniture. A television set was blinking in the corner with a loud, excited voice shouting out a commentary on the culmination of a horse race. There was a divan bed, two small tables, two chairs, a tiny oven and a sink unit.

On the bed a man's head popped up from behind a newspaper through a cloud of cigarette smoke.

'Here, here,' he said. He dropped the paper, snatched the cigarette out of his mouth, stood up and said, 'What do *you* want?'

He made a lot of saliva and when he got excited he sprayed everywhere.

He nipped out the well-smoked cigarette-end between finger and thumb, and dropped it into his coat pocket. Then, from his trouser pocket, he pulled out a piece of a bedsheet and wiped his face.

Angel spotted an almost empty bottle of sherry on the sink unit. He picked it up and read the label. It was described as 'Beast quality, genuinne sherry wine.' The label showed that it was bottled in Ankara, Turkey. He shook his head and replaced the bottle.

'How you are getting along, Mr Queegley,' Angel said.

Queegley sneered. 'Oh, it's you.'

The girl said, 'Who is it?'

Queegley looked across at the girl. 'It's the copper what banged me up.'

The girl blinked. Her thin lips tightened. 'A copper?' she said. She banged the glass down on the sink unit, rushed determinedly across the room, stabbed her feet into a pair of high-heeled silver sandals, grabbed a pair of jeans and a shiny silver handbag off the bed, and made for the door.

Queegley's face dropped. 'You don't have to go, Gloria,' he said. 'We'll go out later.'

'I'll give you a ring sometime,' she shouted. 'Maybe,' she added as she slammed the door.

Queegley looked like a man found not guilty by the jury, but still given six months by the judge.

Angel's eyes twitched as the TV now emitted the loud banging of guitars and drums.

Queegley then looked at Angel and said something above the racket. It sounded like: 'Now see what you've done. I've missed the result of the last race, and I was winning, and you've scared *her* off.'

Angel saw the remote control for the TV on the divan. He picked it up, pointed it at the TV and switched it off.

The silence was glorious.

He sighed with relief, then tossed the

remote back on to the divan.

Queegley glared at him, snatched up the remote and stuffed it in his trouser pocket. Then he pointed to the door. 'I was on a promise there, Inspector. She's already cost me a bottle of sherry and a haddock and chips.'

'She doesn't look old enough.'

'She said she was eighteen.'

'You want to be careful.'

'What do you want anyway?' Queegley said, taking out a packet of cigarettes. He put one in his mouth, then lit it with a match. 'You've got nothing on me. I've nothing on my conscience. Are you just here to enjoy watching a man down on his luck?'

'You know me better than that. Just anxious that you keep out of trouble, that's all. I saw you at the festivities in the park yesterday. I tried to talk to you but you . . . you dodged out of the way.'

Queegley's eyes slid to the right and back again. 'Oh? Didn't see you,' he said. 'The place was crowded.'

Angel frowned then smiled. 'Seen anything of your friend lately?'

Queegley blinked. 'Friend? Don't know who you mean,' he said, lowering his eyes.

Angel knew he was lying again.

'Come on, Peter. Alec Underwood, of

course. You've just served twelve months because of him, and he got off, scot free. He must be good for a few quid at least.'

Queegley turned away. 'I don't know what you mean. That's all behind me,' he said as he walked towards the bed. 'That's history. I've paid my debt to society and you've no cause to hound me. Now if there's nothing else you want, push off.'

'Have you got a job?'

'I'm looking round.'

'Get yourself a job, lad. You used to work for the telephone company, didn't you? See if they'll give you your job back. Bring in a wage and keep yourself out of trouble.'

'Two million unemployed and rising. Who's going to employ an out-of-work ex con?'

He had a point, but Angel didn't let it go at that. 'It means you've to try harder, take a lowly job and work your way up.'

'Thank you, vicar. Here endeth the sermon,' Queegley said. He flopped down on the bed and looked round for the newspaper.

'Right, I'll go,' Angel said. 'Just keep out of trouble. If you know what's good for you, you'll keep away from that Alec Underwood.'

'Thank you very much. Goodbye, Inspector. Don't call again.'

Angel shrugged and made for the door.

5

M.V. *Golden Mistress*. Off the coast of Nice, France.
0745 hours. Wednesday, 27 May 27 2009

Van Hassain raised his head from the paper he was reading. His monocle dropped on to his tanned bare chest.

'Boy,' he called.

A young steward in a spotless white uniform with a button-up collar, who was loading a tray with used plates and cutlery at a side table, looked up.

'Boy. Come quickly.'

The steward's eyes looked warily at the wrinkled man, tanned by the many hours spent in the glare of the Mediterranean sun. He crossed the deck and came across to him.

'Was something not to your liking, Mr Van Hassain?'

'Tell the captain I want to see him, urgently. Hurry boy! Hurry!'

'Yes, Mr Van Hassain.'

The boy rushed out from under the canopy into the early morning sun, along the deck past the windows of Van Hassain's day cabin and up the metal steps.

Van Hassain picked up the internet printouts of the news he had been reading, reset the monocle and rubbed his chin.

Through an open hatchway midships, two girls in their twenties, burnt dark brown by the sun, appeared wearing brightly coloured bikinis and carrying towels and bottles of perfumed oil. They were chattering and giggling together. When they saw Van Hassain they shrieked with delight, waved excitedly and ran down the deck towards him.

'Mr Van Hussain! Mr Van Hussain!' they squealed, waving their towels.

He looked up from his papers, breathed in, stared at them with eyes of a dead cod and gestured for them to go away.

The girls stopped in their tracks. The giggling stopped. They looked at each other. This was unusual.

'Oh, Mr Van Hassain. Mr Van Hassain,' they said disappointedly.

'Later, perhaps, girls. Later,' he snapped.

The girls turned away with sober faces, their towels swinging, and made their way up the main stairway to the top deck. From there, they knew how to reach the roof of the wheelhouse, which was the most private part of the ship where they could sunbathe.

A few moments later Captain Rose climbed

breathily down the metal steps, landed noisily and made his way aft along the deck, followed by the young steward. Rose then came under the canopy to where Mr Van Hassain was seated.

The steward returned to clearing the side table.

Rose arrived panting. 'You wanted me, sir?' he said wiping his perspiring face with a large coloured handkerchief.

Van Hassain pointed to the bench seat fitted across the stern of the boat. It was an inelegant gesture as he'd had three fingers blown off by explosives and had only a thumb and a small finger with which to point. The incident had also deprived him of hearing in his right ear and he had a hearing aid in the other.

'Sit down, Captain.'

Van Hassain swivelled his seat round to face the captain, then he swivelled back to the steward.

'Boy,' he called. 'Bring us fresh coffee.'

Rose blinked, smiled and said, 'Brandy, would be better.'

'Coffee,' Van Hassain said.

'Right away, sir,' the steward said and rushed off with a tray loaded with the breakfast pots.

Van Hassain said, 'Now, Captain. I have an order for you.'

Rose took off his captain's hat, put it on the seat next to him, looked up at Van Hassain and said, 'Yes, sir.'

'I have to go up to zee UK again, quickly.'

The fat man frowned, scratched the stubble on his chin and said, 'Of course, sir. But it will be so cold.'

'On the east coast of UK is a place called Bridlington. Do you know of it?'

Rose's face contorted as if he had been squirted with a lemon. 'I have never heard of it, sir. It will be very cold up there, sir. You wouldn't want to go there. And you'll have all those English police crawling all over the ship with dogs, examining ship's safety, scrutinizing the paperwork, asking questions, sniffing around your passport.'

'My passport is the genuine article, Captain. You might consider your own. I wonder if they have a harbour there?'

'Not big enough for the *Golden Mistress* I'll wager. We would have to anchor in the dangerous and busy commercial traffic lanes in the North Sea and bouncing all day and all night, sir. It is not healthy for us, for *you*, sir. The English, their skins are pasty. You see them, sir. They don't have the sun, not like what we do. Also, the price of brandy is . . . ' He made a gesture like a rocket being launched, 'Whu!' he said. 'The diesel! Hoo.

You don't want to go there, sir. No.'

'How soon can we get there?'

'It means a journey through the Bay of Biscay. The bilges will fill up. And we will need to take down the canopy again.'

'Well, see to it. It's what I pay you for.'

'And you couldn't take the girls, sir. No passports.'

'We can drop them off at Tangier.'

'Oh,' Rose said, pulling a sad face. 'It will not be the same for you without them . . . and *they* won't like that.'

Van Hassain shrugged. 'I will reward them.'

'I would need to refuel. The chef would want victuals.'

'Do it. Make one stop in Tangier? The question is *how soon can you get me there?*'

The steward arrived with the tray of coffee. He looked at Van Hassain. The little man didn't acknowledge his presence. The steward began to set up the cups and saucers.

'Three days, sir. Maybe more. Depends.'

'No more. Three days. Start straight away. Any more excuses?'

Captain Rose wiped his face with the handkerchief, forced a smile and said, 'No excuses, sir. No excuses. May I be permitted to ask the reason for going all that way, sir? Is it to collect another load?'

'I tell you later.'

The steward poured the coffee.

Captain Rose pursed his lips. 'The crew will ask where we are going, sir.'

'Don't tell them.'

'They might not want to go.'

Van Hassain's lips tightened. 'I do not care if they do not want to go. I will replace them, like I will replace you if you don't do as I say. *Now pull up zee anchor and start zee engines*.'

Rose shrugged. He looked at the coffee in front of him and gave him a weak smile. 'My coffee. May I drink my coffee, first?' he said, reaching out to the cup.

Van Hassain's eyes opened like two fried eggs. The monocle dropped. 'No!' he said. He reached out, picked up the cup, saucer and coffee and threw them over the side of the boat into the sea. 'Now, Captain, that's where you will finish up, feeding zee fishes, if you don't start pulling up zat anchor.'

* * *

It was 8.28 a.m. Wednesday, 27 May 2009.

Angel picked up the phone and tapped in a number.

A voice answered. 'Mortuary. Mac speaking.'

'Ah, Mac, you're there early this morning?'

'You haven't rung me up to tell me that.'

'No, but I expected to get that annoying 'leave a message after the bleep' nonsense, and I had got myself all prepared to leave a message.'

'Well it's me, live. What can I do for you, as if I didn't know?'

'I am anxious to have the results of the pm on Charles Razzle's body, if you would be so good. Also to ask you where the contents of his pockets had got to.'

'The dead man's personal effects are on the way to you by messenger,' Mac said. 'You should have received them this morning, and I'll be emailing the post mortem to you later this morning, as usual.'

'Thank you. You wouldn't like to help an old friend to speed things up a bit and tell me what essentially the report contains?'

'You are always seeking to push the barriers of time, Michael. It'll cost you a double Famous Grouse next time I see you.'

'You're most welcome.'

'Let me have a look . . . here we are. He died around nine o'clock Monday evening. Interestingly, you will see among his personal effects, when you get them, a wristwatch with a smashed glass and the dial showing five minutes past nine when the watch had stopped. Don Taylor says that at some point during the time he was being shot, he believes that Razzle must have thrown back his left arm violently and caught the front corner of the safe, where there is a corresponding scratch.'

'Thanks, Mac. That tends to confirm it. Tell me about the cause of death.'

'Razzle's old Walther was fixed into the robot's hand.'

'Fingerprints?'

'No. There were three bullets fired. Razzle died of the first gunshot wound to the temple. A police marksman could not have aimed better. It was a perfect shot. The second gunshot was to the left ventricle of the heart. Also a perfect shot. Unnecessary, but a perfectly aimed shot. The third was to the stomach.'

Angel frowned. 'All perfectly aimed. Can you tell me how much time elapsed between each shot being fired?'

'That's a tough one, Michael. No I can't. But not long.'

'Are we talking minutes?'

'Oh no. Between a second and ten seconds. No more.'

Angel rubbed his chin. 'Can you be certain that the first shot was the one to the brain?'

'Oh yes. Because of the blood that was pumped.'

'Well then, wouldn't the victim be on the floor and out of the line of fire before the second bullet was fired?'

'Yes. If not entirely horizontal, the victim would have been very near, yes.'

'And if this death was accidental or suicidal, the victim would not have been sufficiently alive to have been able to operate the remote control to change the robot's very accurate aim before the second bullet was fired, would he?'

There was absolute silence from Dr Mac.

'Are you there?' Angel said.

Eventually he came back. 'I hadn't thought of that,' Mac said.

'And a similar, even stronger case would apply to the third bullet, wouldn't it,' Angel said. 'Razzle simply could not have directed the robot, through the remote, to change the aim of the gun before it was fired into the stomach of the man who would now certainly be laid out dead on the workshop floor.'

'That's right, Michael. That's right. You're absolutely right.'

'Were you able to calculate how far from target the gun was fired?'

'Yes. There was the usual spread of powder. The distance was around two metres.'

'And did you note how far the robot was from the dead body?'

'Yes. Around two metres.'

'That doesn't help any then, Mac. If somebody else was in that workshop he must have been standing just about where we found the robot.'

'Or just in front of it.'

'Would that be within the realms of possibility?'

'Oh yes.'

'You're a great help, Mac. As always. Thank you very much for now. Goodbye.'

* * *

'You wanted me, sir?' It was DS Flora Carter.

Angel looked up.

Flora Carter had been enlisted from Sheffield force to replace DS Ronald Gawber, Angel's sergeant of ten years. Gawber had moved down south so that his wife could look after her elderly father. Flora Carter was senior both in terms of length of service and experience in detective work to DS Crisp.

Angel wasn't happy about female officers, particularly if they were pleasing to the eye. He considered the appreciation of femininity out of place in a police station. Modelling clothes, hair or make-up, presenting programmes on radio or television, or being at home bringing up children was where such fortunate ladies should be. He worried in case he came to work one day and found vases of wallflowers in the cells. What with her and PC Leisha Baverstock, he had been heard to mumble, Bromersley police station was getting more like a hothouse for contestants entering the Miss World competition than an establishment for finding criminals and bringing them to justice.

She smiled at him sweetly.

He didn't smile back. He wrinkled his nose. 'Aye. Sit down. Are you fully in the picture with this Razzle case, lass?'

'I think so, sir. I've kept up with the reports. Charles Razzle locked himself in his workshop where only he knew the combination. A robot he had built shot him dead. CCTV confirms that nobody else entered or left the house during the time of the incident. His wife was away in London with many witnesses. So it's either an accident or suicide.' She looked at him, blinked, and waited for his approval.

With eyebrows raised he said, 'Pretty close. Except for the last bit. It wasn't an accident or a suicide. It was murder.'

Her face changed. A cold chill ran down her spine. 'Oh?' she said. Then she frowned. 'How's that possible, sir.'

'I don't know, yet.'

He told her about the forensic he had received from Mac only a few minutes earlier and the deduction he had made.

Her eyes narrowed.

'But what about the CCTV, sir?'

'There were no strangers shown on it,' he said.

'So nobody could have managed to have entered the workshop dodging both cameras, then hide anywhere until the critical time, then come out, take the gun out of the robot's hand, shoot Razzle, replace the gun, wait there until the workshop door was unlocked and opened and sneak out, because all the time after the door was opened, PC Donohue and PC Elder were there in the kitchen and would have seen anybody coming up the basement steps. Also Donohue and Elder stayed there until SOCO took over at approximately 0840 hours and, anyway, the CCTV tape was running the entire time. It would have recorded it.'

'Exactly,' Angel said. 'So there must be another way into the workshop, or a hiding place in there, where an intruder could have been, or a way past the CCTV cameras . . . a door or window or trapdoor in the basement or something like that. I want you to get a squad together and check that out. Do it thoroughly. Take the building to pieces if necessary. It's a pity there wasn't a CCTV camera in the workshop itself. That would have explained everything.'

'I'll have a good look round, sir.'

She stood up to leave.

There was a knock at the door.

'Come in.'

It was Ahmed with a large brown envelope. The word EVIDENCE was printed in red across it.

'Just came, sir,' he said, offering it across to Angel. 'By messenger.'

'I'll go, sir,' Flora Carter said.

'No,' Angel said. 'Hang on a minute. Have a look at this.'

He turned to Ahmed and said, 'Thank you, lad. I was expecting it.'

'I had to sign for it, sir.'

'I know. I know. I'll take good care of it,' he said, taking the envelope and beginning to look at the list of contents written on the outside of it.

Ahmed hesitated, looked at Flora Carter; they exchanged smiles and he went out.

Angel noticed the glances. He frowned a moment then said, 'I hope you're not making up to that lad, Sergeant. He's only twenty-two, you know. He's far too young for you.'

Her face reddened. She inhaled quickly. In one breath, she said, 'No, sir, I'm not. But if I was, it would be my business . . . and his.'

Angel was unmoved. He pursed his lips. 'He's only young. He hasn't a father. He's not up to the . . . he's not ready to . . . I wouldn't want him getting hurt, that's all.'

Flora Carter's lips tightened then relaxed. 'I'm not the Wicked Witch from the West, you know.'

He didn't reply. He opened the envelope and emptied it on to his desk.

'The contents of Charles Razzle's pockets,' he said.

They both peered down at them. Angel pored through them for a few moments. They were mostly coins. There was a small wallet with forty pounds and a credit card in it, a small bunch of keys, a handkerchief and a wristwatch in a small, see-through plastic bag. He picked up the bag. The watch was a very expensive, gold Orcado. Its dial was smashed and it had stopped at five minutes past nine. He showed it to her. She nodded and that was it.

He picked out the keys, repacked the rest of the stuff, handed her the envelope and said, 'Give that to Ahmed on your way out.'

She took the envelope from him. Then he gave her the keys in her other hand and said, 'And ask him to let DS Taylor have these keys asap. One of them probably opens the safe.'

She nodded and went out. He watched her go. As the door closed he rubbed his chin vigorously.

* * *

The phone rang. He reached out for the handset, pressed the button and said, 'Angel.'

There was a loud wheezy cough and a splutter. Angel pulled the phone away from his ear. He knew the caller was Superintendent Harker. There was another cough and a splutter, and that was again repeated.

Eventually Harker said, 'Are you there?'

'Yes, I'm here, sir,' Angel said.

'Aye, well come up here, smartish,' Harker said, then he banged the receiver hard down into its cradle. It clicked noisily in Angel's ear.

Angel's jaw muscles stiffened. Harker was always guaranteed to annoy him.

Angel threw down his ballpoint and got up from the desk.

He went down the corridor to the last door. There was a sign screwed to it. It read: 'Detective Superintendent Horace Harker'.

He knocked on the door and went in.

Harker was at his desk. There were two piles of papers and files rising up to his eye level, and the rest of the desk was littered with papers, reports, a bottle of lemonade, a coffee cup, jar of Vick, bottle of paracetamol tablets, box of tissues and a transistor radio.

The superintendent was holding a plastic inhaler up a nostril and taking a long hard sniff while blocking off the other nostril with the forefinger of his other hand. His eyes followed Angel into the room. He withdrew the inhaler, put a cap on it, placed it on the desk, then sniffed and pointed to the chair immediately in front of the desk.

Angel sat down.

'Aye,' Harker began. 'Well, now it's fortunate that that Razzle case has come to an early conclusion.'

Angel frowned. 'That's not so, sir. There has been a development.'

Harker's bushy eyebrows shot up. 'A development?' he said slowly. 'Why wasn't I told. It wasn't in your report.'

'It was only known a few minutes ago. It arises from the forensic report.'

Angel explained that Dr Mac indicated that Razzle would have been too badly injured by the first bullet to have been able to have aimed and then fired subsequent rounds effectively.

'That's conjecture, lad?'

Angel frowned. He might have expected some argument.

Harker continued: 'Nobody can possibly be inside somebody else's brain and know in the last split second of life whether the person is capable of pressing a button or not. What does the CPS say?'

'There's more to it than that, sir. Because the first bullet entered the brain, death was virtually instantaneous. The victim would not have had the time, even if he still had the inclination, to change the direction the gun was aiming and press the button that operated the robot's trigger finger a second time, and then again, a third time.'

'Did you say it was Mac who put forward this proposition?'

Angel hesitated. 'Yes, sir,' he said. He knew it wasn't strictly true. But if he had said it had been *his* idea, Harker would immediately have rejected it.

Harker rubbed his chin. 'So the remote control that activated the robot was not in Charles Razzle's possession the moment when he was shot?'

'I don't know that for certain, sir. But probably not. There weren't any fingerprints. Of course, there may have been another remote control.'

'Another remote control? That means that somebody else must have been in that workshop?'

'The murderer. Almost certainly.'

'But the door . . . it could only be opened by Charles Razzle?'

'That's right, sir. The CCTV has shown up nothing.'

Harker's small, black eyes made several small movements up and down and then from side to side several times, his mouth open like a goldfish's.

Angel watched him, wondering what he was thinking.

Then Harker breathed in deeply, let out a big sigh and said, 'Right. You'd better get on with it then.'

6

Angel got into the BMW and pointed the bonnet in the direction of the city of Sheffield. He travelled almost to the far extent of Abbeydale Road before he saw a smart aluminium-and-glass building and big blue letters that read *FARLEIGH SECURITY 24 HOURS*. He pulled to the kerb at the front and stopped the car. There were yellow lines all along the road and everywhere else he looked. He pulled on the handbrake and switched off the engine. He reached into the glove compartment, took out a printed card and put it under the windscreen. It read: 'Police on duty. DI Angel. Bromersley Police'.

Then he got out of the car, reached the door of the building and went inside. It was a converted Victorian house, the internal ground floor walls had been knocked down to provide showroom and open office space. An arrow pointed to the reception area. There was a desk at which a pretty girl was seated, looking at a magazine. She was fully engrossed in her reading and didn't notice him. Angel was good at reading things upside down. He'd had plenty of practice in

Harker's office. She was reading an article headed: 'How to lose two pounds a week'. He sniffed. She could lose much more than that if she had taken any notice of the tips Mac had given him over the years.

She suddenly looked up, smiled and said, 'I'm sorry. Can I help you?'

He whipped out his warrant card and badge and said, 'Detective Inspector Angel. Mr Farleigh is expecting me.'

She flicked her eyelashes up at him. The eyelashes looked attractive but dangerous, like flytraps. He supposed they would be artificial. He thought she didn't need to lose any weight. She was perfect the way she was.

'Oh yes. He'll know you have arrived. I'm sure he'll be right down.'

Her voice was gentle and sweet. Nice enough to make you want to buy six safes.

In the distance Angel heard a door close and feet clattering down uncarpeted wooden steps, then a man appeared in the doorway. He came straight across to Angel. He held out his hand. 'I'm Brian Farleigh. Pleased to meet you.'

He shook Angel's hand enthusiastically.

'You wanted to ask me some questions about Charles Razzle,' he said, then he pointed to a small corner of the showroom where there were four chairs around a small table. Catalogues and leaflets were scattered on safes; also on display were vaults, security grilles, unbreakable glass, containers of non-drying paint and so on. 'Is here OK, or do you want to go to my office?'

'Here's just fine,' Angel said.

They sat down.

'What did you have to do with the building of Charles Razzle's workshop?'

'I supplied and fitted the door. That's all.'

'Have you any idea who blocked up the air vents and made that room the secure room it is?'

'I believe he did it all himself,' Farleigh said. 'There wouldn't have been a lot to do to that cellar, Inspector. The door was, of course, the vulnerable part.'

'Hmm. Is it easy to unlock the door from the inside? Would you need to know the combination?'

'You mean if somebody was locked in there, by accident or by mistake?'

Angel sniffed and said, 'Or on purpose?'

'Yes. He would need to know the combination.'

'Hmm. How difficult is it to change the combination of the lock?'

'Very easy. The door must be open. You can't do it when it's closed, obviously. You hold down the set button and tap a six-digit number in, that's all. But you mustn't forget it or you have to call me out and then opening it would take hours.'

Angel thought for a moment, then said, 'Mrs Razzle didn't know the combination?'

Farleigh gave a slight shrug. 'No. I wouldn't know anything about that.'

'You had a good look round the room when you were building the surround and fitting the door?'

'Yes. He asked me to.'

'And is there another way in and out of there?'

Farleigh grinned, not certain at first that he had heard correctly. 'There wasn't when I looked, I can assure you.'

'Any hiding places? Is there a cubby hole, a secret place where anybody could have concealed themselves for a while?'

'Like a priest's hole?' Farleigh said with a smile. 'The house isn't that old, Inspector. No. Not that I am aware of.'

'Did you fit the CCTV for Mr Razzle?'

He raised his head. 'CCTV? It is one of the things I do. But no. I am not aware there was any CCTV in that house.'

'You met Charles Razzle, of course.'

'Didn't talk much. Always seemed to be somewhere else, if you know what I mean. He just said what he wanted, I gave him a price, he agreed. That's all there was to it.'

Angel wasn't surprised. 'Can you think of anyone who would wish him dead?'

Farleigh's mouth dropped open, he turned to look at Angel. 'It was an accident, surely?'

'We haven't completely ruled out foul play,' Angel said. 'Do you know of anyone?'

'No. No, Inspector. I can't think of anyone, but of course I don't know the Razzles *that* well,' he said. The grin returned. 'I'm not on their Christmas-card list. I'm not in *their* social circle.'

Angel squeezed his earlobe between finger and thumb. He was thinking what else he needed to ask.

Farleigh said: 'I shouldn't think it was deliberate, though. Can't see him taking his own life.'

Angel nodded. 'Thanks very much, Mr Farleigh.'

* * *

Angel returned to his office and slumped down in his chair. He looked at the heap of post, circulars and reports on the desk in front of him. He sighed. He put his hands forward to begin to finger through the bumf, when the phone rang. He reached out for it.

It was DS Taylor. 'We've opened Razzle's safe, sir.'

'Yes, Don?'

'And it's empty. There's nothing in it.'

Angel blinked. '*Nothing*? Right, Don.' He pressed the cancel button.

He was surprised and disappointed. An empty safe that was locked *was* unusual. He didn't return the phone to its cradle. After a few moments, he tapped out Taylor's number.

'Ah, Don,' Angel said. 'About that safe . . . There's always *something* in a safe. If there is no money or gold bars or cash, there's sometimes deeds to a property, love letters, promissory notes, account books, a lady's garter, a will, *some*thing. To find Razzle's safe empty . . . is a great . . . a very great surprise.'

'Yes, sir. I agree.'

'Which suggests that it must have been burgled. Any signs of a recent assault on the lock?'

'No, sir.'

'Were there any prints on the safe handle?'

'Funny thing, sir. It had been wiped clean.'

Angel smiled and shook his head. 'Right, Don.'

He replaced the phone.

After a few seconds he reached into his inside pocket and pulled out a used envelope covered with his own small handwriting, which he began to read. From time to time he broke off reading, and, deep in thought, rubbed his chin, and gazed straight ahead in the direction of the green stationery cupboard. Then he would return to deciphering the tiny writing. This was repeated several times, then, after twenty minutes of this, his nose turned up and the corners of his mouth turned down, he sniffed and shook his head.

There was a knock at the door.

'Yes? Come in,' he said and put the envelope back into his inside pocket.

It was DS Carter.

'I was just thinking about you.' Angel said. 'Sit down. Find anything?'

'Nothing, sir. We moved all equipment from the walls and sprayed them with water. We also sprayed the ceiling and the floor. The same with the rest of the basement area. There are no hidden doors, trapdoors or exits, or hiding-places in the basement, I'll stake my life on it.'

Angel frowned.

She continued: 'Also it is not possible to move around in the basement area outside the workshop door without being caught on the CCTV camera, which is fitted right in the corner of the area.'

Angel ran his hand through his hair. 'Somebody expects us to believe that the robot

Charles Razzle built actually murdered him. Then after all that, he was able to cross over to the robot and wipe his prints off its hand and the finger round the trigger of the gun. His prints were just about everywhere else . . . even on the undischarged bullets in the gun.'

'But it has to have been Charles Razzle because nobody could have entered the workshop, sir. They would have been on the CCTV tapes. And anyway the door was closed, locked, and he was the only person who knew the combination.'

'That's all true, Flora,' Angel said. 'It's a puzzle. It would have been tidier if he had left a suicide note.'

'If it was spontaneous there wouldn't have been one.'

'I know. I want you to find out about his state of mind . . . whether he had any serious health issues . . . whether he was on drugs, prescribed or otherwise, also whether he was on the bottle. You can start with Don Taylor. He will have turned up the name of Razzle's GP by now.'

She stood up. 'Right, sir.'

* * *

Angel climbed the stairs of the Feathers Hotel and knocked on the door of suite number 1.

It was soon answered by Rosemary Razzle, who was wearing a brightly coloured summer dress. Not the sign of a woman in deep mourning, he thought.

'Ah, Inspector Angel,' she said brightly. 'Please come in. You've come to tell me I can return to my house?'

He pursed his lips, then said, 'No, Mrs Razzle, I'm afraid I haven't.'

'Oh.' She pointed to a chair. 'Please sit down. I hope you are not going to keep me from it for much longer.'

'Not much longer,' Angel said. 'I need to ask you a few more questions.'

'Oh yes? I'll do my best.'

'It is becoming obvious that your husband shot himself either deliberately or accidentally . . . '

'Accidentally, definitely,' she said.

'Very well, accidentally. By use of a remote control, he aimed the gun at himself and fired it, three times. That would have been very unusual. I need to ask if he was depressed about anything?'

'Huh! Charles Razzle depressed? Certainly not. He was always quietly spoken. Gentle. Confident and always busy. That robot was his biggest venture yet. He was utterly consumed by it. He talked of nothing else.'

'Did he have any health worries, or money

worries . . . were you happily married? Was there another woman? Indeed, was there another man?'

'There was *not* another man, and I am certain there was not another woman, as you so delicately put it. Charles is — or was — extremely wealthy from his work as an inventor alone, Inspector. He has received six-figure advance payments from each of his two recent inventions. In addition, my earnings as an actress are now not inconsiderable, and would in themselves have maintained us in fine style if we had needed to dip into them. As far as Charles's health was concerned, he worked every day up to his capacity. He was certainly not depressed. He was too busy to be depressed. There is no question about that.'

'There is a safe in the workshop . . . our scenes of crime chaps need to look into it. Have you got a key?' he said slyly.

'I regret that I have not.'

He'd expected her to say that. 'Do you know what's inside?' he asked.

'The safe was for my husband's use primarily. I expect there are only papers in there. He wouldn't keep large quantities of cash in the house, there was no need. He should have had a bunch of keys in his pocket. There should be a key to the safe among them.'

She's smarter than she looks, he thought. She had certainly called his bluff.

'Right,' Angel said quickly. 'We'll see what we can find.'

* * *

Angel went straight home from The Feathers. He drove the BMW into the garage, locked it and let himself in the back door of the bungalow.

Mary was pleased he had arrived. He was so often late those days. It pleased her that she knew he would for certain be there when the finny haddock was ready for serving up. She was rinsing some fresh raspberries in a colander to be served with ice cream for pudding.

He gave her a peck on the cheek on his way to the fridge, where he took out a can of German beer, opened it, poured it into a glass and went into the sitting room. He loosened his tie and collar, switched on the television for the news and slumped down in a chair.

The TV screen lit up, the picture came into focus and immediately caught his attention. It was a news item about the gold-plated life-size reclining plaster model of Dorothea Jordan, former mistress of King William IV. He stared at the screen.

He saw film of the handsome statue on a

podium in an impressive-looking bedroom, then it showed two men carrying it inside Spicers', the specialist antique jewellery and work-of-art dealers, through their imposing Georgian stone-pillared doorway on Royal Crown Road, London. The commentary was about King William IV and Dorothea Jordan, and the recent finding of the figure in an attic in a house in Bromersley. The commentator said that it was considered to be highly romantic, historically significant as well as greatly valuable and that it was going to be auctioned by Spicers' shortly. It was expected to bring a princely sum.

The item ended there and the news moved on to a piece about President Obama's dog.

Mary called out to say that tea was ready.

Angel switched the television off and went into the kitchen.

After tea, on a freeview channel, they watched an old film featuring a very young-looking Fred MacMurray. It was about a flying car and a super bouncing invention called 'flubber.' It was entertaining and mildly amusing but not exactly riveting.

Mary noticed her husband's eyelids occasionally dropping lower and lower for longer and longer.

A caption indicated a break for advertisements and a striking picture of a gold and plaster figure of a woman dominated the screen again.

Mary sat up and said, 'That's the statue we saw at Pinsley Smith's auction in the park last Bank Holiday Monday.'

Angel blinked and raised his head.

It soon became clear that they were watching a trailer for a forthcoming television film.

The picture changed to that of a beautiful woman and a handsome man in period clothes embracing each other passionately. It was accompanied by loud, dramatic music and the word 'Dorothea' appeared and filled the screen.

The commentary, delivered in a man's breathy voice. said, 'Dorothea, the life story of the most beautiful woman in the world, played by award-winning actress, Sincerée La More. Dorothea Jordan, mistress of the Duke of Clarence, later King William IV, who bore him ten illegitimate children and died tragically in 1816. The duke adored her so much that he had a life-size nude gold figure made of her in a relaxed pose, and it was placed on a couch in his bedroom. It had remained there during his reign until his death in 1837. Sincerée La More brings this true love story of Dorothea to life exclusively on this channel, very soon.'

The trailer for the film shook Angel out of any immediate thoughts of sleep. He recalled the statue and the auction in the marquee and considered how important that statue had suddenly become. It stirred up memories of Peter Queegley scurrying away from him there and he wondered if there was any connection. He was still thinking about that when the next segment of the film about 'flubber' and the flying car began.

Angel watched it for a while until he fell asleep.

7

It was 8.28 a.m. when Angel arrived at his office that Thursday morning, and the phone was already ringing. He stared at it irritably, sighed, leaned over the desk from the front and snatched it up.

It was the overnight desk sergeant.

'Good morning, sir,' he began. 'I heard you'd been looking for coffins.'

Angel blinked. 'Yes, sergeant. That's correct. Three stolen from Hargreaves.'

'Thought you'd like to know that at 0200 hours a patrol car saw two men behaving suspiciously outside Jeeves the jewellers. The patrolmen stopped the car and gave chase on foot, but the men gave them the slip. Shortly afterwards a man phoned in to say that he had seen two men carrying a coffin in St Mary's churchyard. That's next door to the jewellers, you know.'

Angel nodded. 'And *next* to the Northern Bank,' he said pointedly.

'Yes, sir. So I went down there myself. Had a good look round. Nothing to see. Jewellers' shutters OK. Bank doors OK. Graves untouched. Church door locked. Windows sound.'

'Were they lead thieves?'

'The roof was intact, sir. I really don't know what to think.'

Angel understood him perfectly. He felt the same. 'Thanks very much, Sergeant. Before you sign out, send down for Jeeves's and Northern Bank's CCTV tapes, and arrange to let PC Ahmed have them.'

'Will do, sir.'

Angel replaced the phone and it rang again immediately. He picked it up.

The caller started with a noisy intake of breath followed by a loud cough.

Angel knew that it was Superintendent Harker.

'Yes, sir.'

Eventually Harker began: 'I was at an ACPO dinner in Northampton last night, with twenty-four other superintendents, the Home Secretary's PPS and Sir Miles Luckman, head of SOCA.'

Angel knew all about SOCA. It was the Serious and Organized Crime Agency, a police unit devoted to fighting gang crime. The members were extremely well-equipped and armed. They had been granted special temporary powers to do anything they considered necessary to catch organized gangs of criminals, and they were good at it. Angel didn't care for their methods, though.

Whenever they appeared on the scene, they climbed over everything and everybody, often creating friction and bad blood among innocent, law-abiding bystanders, which the local force subsequently had to put right.

'Most of what was said was confidential,' Harker continued, 'but after the meeting Sir Miles took me on one side and said that the big robbery at Sir Jack and Lady Prendergast's place, in Bucks, last Saturday evening . . . you've heard about it?'

Angel blew out hot breath. Of course he'd heard about it. The day following, on their front pages, the newspapers had shown photographs of masked thieves breaking into the mansion, taken from CCTV cameras. And television news stations led their programmes with some clips of film from the actual robbery. The gang escaped with millions of pounds worth of antiques leaving no clues as to their identities behind.

'Yes, sir. I've heard about it,' he said.

'Well, he's heard a whisper that the gang responsible for the robbery resides on our patch.'

Angel frowned. That was interesting, but if it were true, could he not volunteer more information . . . at least the source of the info?

'That all, sir?' Angel said.

He heard Harker gasp. 'If Sir Miles had known his identity,' he said, 'he would have had his men round the villain's place and scooped him up, wouldn't he? He wouldn't need the likes of you, sniffing around, making everything seem more difficult than it really was, then suddenly, at the right moment, dramatically producing the solution like a conjuror pulling a toy rabbit out of a hat . . . and assuming that look of humility while the newspapers roll out their usual plaudits about how wonderful you are.'

Angel could never understand why Harker didn't like him. After a long pause, in a controlled voice, he said, 'Right, sir,' and replaced the phone before Harker did.

Angel leaned back in the swivel-chair and gawped up at the ceiling. He really needed a long thinking session, to review the facts and consider whether there was any further information that he might be able to ferret out to progress the case. He was settling into that mode as he pulled out the two envelopes from his inside pocket and began to check down his notes. There were certain small matters that were becoming clear to him. Teeth were enmeshing and cogs were beginning to turn when there was a knocking sound. The thinking machinery came to an abrupt halt. Somebody was at the door. He leaned forward in the chair to return it to its normal angle and called out, 'Come in.'

It was DS Flora Carter. She was carrying a copy of a magazine.

'Sorry I'm late, sir. Good morning.'

She handed the magazine to him. He glanced at the cover. It was the previous week's copy of *Police News*.

He waved the magazine at her, tossed it on to the desk and added, 'What's this, lass? It's all about that gang that robs country houses. I've already read it.'

'So have I, sir,' she said.

Angel's nose turned up. 'We've enough on here, Flora, at the moment. Looking for the murderer of Charles Razzle.'

She frowned. 'You've made your mind up it is murder, sir?'

He pursed his lips. He didn't answer the question. He said, 'What did Razzle's GP say?'

'He said that he hardly ever saw him,' she said. 'His records showed that the last time he was in the surgery was two years ago. Mr Razzle had had an accident with a drill in his workshop causing a small wound in his left hand. The doctor dressed it and gave him some antibiotics. It soon healed up. He didn't go back. The time before that was two years earlier, in 2005, when he examined him for an insurance policy.'

'Oh? Did he check his heart?'

'Sound as a bell, sir. He found everything OK.'

'Any history of depression?'

'No, sir.'

'No tranquillizers, antidepressants, sleeping pills?'

She shook her head.

'Did you ask if he thought it was possible he could have committed suicide?'

'The doctor laughed at the idea, sir.'

Angel nodded. He breathed in and then out noisily. 'Very well,' he said. 'I'll answer your question now, Flora.'

She stared at him with eyes narrowed.

'Yes,' he said, 'I am absolutely certain that Charles Razzle was murdered.'

'Wow,' Flora said. 'I knew you were going to say that, somehow. And yet it still seems to be a surprise. And what do we do about the country-house gang? The super seems to want us to clear that up if we can.'

'My job primarily is solving murder cases, you know. Besides, finding those robbers will be much more time-consuming . . . it's in Buckinghamshire. That's miles away. I've seen the clips on the telly, and I've read the report released by the local police. The gang all wear gloves, have their faces covered, and they work to a precise pattern, as if they've rehearsed every move.'

She nodded.

His mouth suddenly dropped open, he looked at her and said, 'Do you know, Flora? I've just realized, that gang are using 'The Lamm Method'.'

She frowned. ''The Lamm Method'? What's that, sir?'

'Didn't they teach you *any* criminal history or methodology at Hendon?'

'Yes, sir. But I don't remember the name Lamm cropping up.'

He blew out a length of air. 'Hermann K. Lamm, known as the Baron, was born in Bavaria, Germany about 1880. Died in Indiana in the US in a gunfight in 1930.'

'That's a bit before my time, sir.'

'Hermann Lamm was a former German army officer, who put his training to use in robbing banks. Before every job he thoroughly cased the place, built replicas of the scene, trained and rehearsed his men, set a time limit that he considered safe in which to do the job, and personally planned their escape route. Every job he planned in meticulous detail, with permutations of optional escape routes and tactics in case anything went wrong.'

'That was ages ago.'

'Yes, but don't underestimate him, Flora. He was a remarkable innovator.' Angel rubbed his chin while nodding, then he said, 'Have you heard of John Dillinger?'

'Oh yes, sir. Wasn't he, at one time, America's Public Enemy Number One?'

'Well, Dillinger used what became known as 'The Lamm Method' of robbing banks, and took on board some other original ideas conceived by Lamm. Historians do not report that Lamm and Dillinger actually met, but they do say that after Lamm was killed at least two members of his gang joined up with Dillinger. They had seen Lamm's tricks and passed them on to Dillinger. Now, after all those years, the gang carrying out these country house robberies are adapting and using 'The Lamm Method'.'

'But things have moved on, sir. Those were times before the mobile phone, CCTV, computers and DNA, weren't they?'

'True, but fortunately — you could say, thankfully — robbers generally do not plan in the meticulous detail that Lamm did. Nor do they incorporate, nor indeed maintain such discipline.'

The phone rang. He reached out for it. It was Don Taylor. 'I've found Charles Razzle's daughter Jessica's email address, sir. She's in the States. I've read some of their recent emails to each other. They seemed to be in contact every week or so. Loving, caring stuff. Interested in what each other is doing. Looks normal, healthy enough to me. What do you want me to do?'

Angel sighed. 'I need to speak to her, Don, urgently. And she's got to be told. Do it gently.'

'Right, sir.'

He replaced the phone and turned back to Flora.

There was a knock at the door. Angel looked across at it impatiently. It was PC Ahmed.

'Now what?' Angel said.

Ahmed brandished two video tapes. 'These have just come, sir. Delivered to me by a patrol driver. He said that you knew all about them.'

'Ah, yes. They will be the CCTV overnight tapes from Jeeves the jewellers and Northern Bank. I want you to run through them, lad . . . I was told that outside the jeweller's two men were behaving suspiciously. Find the place. I want to see it.'

'Right, sir,' Ahmed said and rushed off.

Flora Carter stood up. 'What do you want me to do, sir?'

Angel sighed. 'It's all very slow. I've got Trevor Crisp watching Rosemary Razzle and the company she keeps,' he said. 'Nothing useful has come of that yet . . . I live in hope. Now, I want to stage a reconstruction of the murder. I want to see what happened in that house at the time Charles Razzle was murdered. And I want the Walther, three live rounds to fire, and sandbags to represent the body. Get that set up, Flora. We'll do it first thing tomorrow morning.'

* * *

'Come in,' Angel called.

Ahmed entered the office and closed the door. 'I've run through both tapes, sir,' he said. 'There's nothing untoward on one, but the other shows two men in night light. One is clearly fingering the padlocks on the shutters of the jeweller's shop. I am almost certain that it is that man you had in here not long since . . . Peter Queegley. But I don't think he is doing anything we can book him for.'

Angel blinked. 'Peter Queegley?'

'I think so. Looks like he was wishful thinking, sir. Hoping to find a padlock left unlocked. Anyway, it's run up ready for you to see in the theatre.'

'I'll come down now.'

Angel put down his pen and made for the

door. Ahmed led the way. The two men walked the length of the corridor to the theatre. Angel closed the door and dropped into a chair and Ahmed switched on the videotape.

The screen showed two men through a blue night-vision lens walking purposefully along the pavement on Market Street, passing various shops as they approached Jeeves the jewellers. The jewellers' windows were all shuttered up, with a particularly large shutter across the largest display window.

One of the two men was tall and wore a large dark hat, the other walked with his head jutting forward. This idiosyncrasy reminded Angel immediately of Peter Queegley. The shorter man glanced round to see if anybody was watching and unknowingly looked straight into the lens of the video camera set on the wall of the jewellers. The man then reached up and tugged at the sturdy padlock. It was obviously locked, so he released his hold. The two men then walked on past the Northern Bank, turned right towards St Mary's church and the churchyard and out of shot.

Ahmed stopped the tape.

Angel rubbed his chin. 'You're right, Ahmed. It is Peter Queegley. Can't think what monkey business he's up to out there in the middle of the night.'

Ahmed nodded and smiled, pleased to have discovered something that his boss might find useful.

'Can't be certain of the identity of the big man in the dark hat,' Angel said.

'Is it Alec Underwood, sir? I can take a still of this and see if 'Facial Recognition' will confirm it.'

'Do that, Ahmed. It probably is. He always wears that hat, as if he's in the Gestapo. Anyway, I'm going to take a look round that churchyard right now.'

He came out of the theatre, up the corridor, past reception and out through the front door into the sunshine. He skipped down the steps, turned right and walked on a little way to the end of the side street to Church Street. It was nice to be out of doors and feel the breeze on his face. He passed Jeeves the jewellers and the Northern Bank and went on to St Mary's church, the parish church of the town. He pushed open the wrought-iron gate. It squeaked like a cat in pain. He stepped into the old churchyard with its headstones and boxed gravestones, some topped with stone, marble, iron and other dramatic representations of angels, saints and other monuments to heaven, typical of the excesses of the eighteenth and nineteenth centuries. Most were now neglected, damaged and in need of attention. The monuments were invariably set much too close together, separated by several centimetres of earth only and framed by overgrown grass, nettles, ivy and brambles.

He walked down the flagstone path and round the side of the church to the porch. He tried the door and was pleased to find it unlocked. He walked in and turned down the aisle towards the chancel, then left again to the vestry door next to the lady chapel. An old priest in black was coming out of the vestry carrying a cassock. He looked up, saw Angel and smiled broadly.

'Michael. Nice to see you. How are you keeping?'

They shook hands.

'Fine,' Angel said. 'I heard you had some unwanted visitors last night, Father. Now what seems to be the trouble? Was it lead thieves again?'

'No, thank God,' the priest rubbed his chin. 'To tell the truth, Michael, I don't know what goes on in this churchyard at night. A good man, a regular parishioner, who was on shift work, was passing here in a car at two o'clock this morning and saw two men carrying a coffin down the outside of the church. A coffin, of all things!'

Angel pursed his lips. 'That's what was

reported. And what else happened?'

'Just walked by the side of the church, the man said.'

'Could he describe them?'

'Just two men. In the dark, he couldn't see. That's all he could say.'

'And was there any disturbance to any grave? Any ground disturbed?'

'None at all. That's what worried me. I had a good look round. I would have been greatly worried if any graves had been disturbed. This graveyard is full, you know. There hasn't been an interment here for more than forty years.'

'And was the church broken into?'

The priest smiled. 'No. We haven't had a break-in or lead robbers for more than two years now. We're doing very well.'

Angel nodded his agreement and pulled a wry face. After all, he had seen the crime figures. He rubbed his chin.

The priest said: 'The church would never pay out for closed circuit television, and I couldn't expect you to put a couple of men out here every night on the off chance. We must trust to providence, and maybe they'll go away.'

'Don't worry, father. There *might* be something I can do.'

The priest's eyebrows shot up. 'Really? Is

there really? You *know* something, Michael? I know you're a shrewd copper. I knew that if this was a murder enquiry you'd be certain to get to the bottom of it. The newspapers say you're like the Canadian Mounties, you always get your man.'

Angel rubbed his chin. 'The papers say all sorts, Father,' he said quietly.

The priest smiled and nodded.

'Well, I must be off,' Angel said. 'But I'll see what I can do. I'll have a look round outside before I go.'

He shook hands with the old priest and came out of the church. The sun was warm, and the trees and bushes rustled in the breeze. He had a walk round the perimeter path on the outside of the church, looking down at it for anything untoward that might have been there. He trod some of the overgrown flagstone paths, glanced round at the crowded graveyard, with its big boxed gravestones, crosses and crucifixes, then up at the church roof. There was nothing at all that might have provided an explanation as to why two men should have been seen bearing a coffin there in the middle of the night. He shook his head and made his way to the gate. In the gateway he saw marks on the stones under his feet. He crouched down. There were marks on the surface of the stones, about nine inches long and six inches apart. The same marks were repeated in parallel on the other side of the path. Also he saw that the edge of the worn step had recently been freshly scuffed in two places. He frowned. Machinery of some kind. Probably a grass-mower. But the grass hadn't been cut. Needed to be something narrow to pass through a gate that, after all, was intended for pedestrians. He couldn't imagine what it might be. He heard footsteps behind him. It was the priest.

'Found something, Michael?'

Angel stood up. 'Have you had a narrow-track vehicle through here recently, Father?'

The priest shook his head. 'Like a gravedigger? No, Michael. There have been no graves dug here for years. This graveyard is full.'

On his amble round the church, Angel had already looked carefully for recent digging and there wasn't any. He couldn't help but wonder.

'Have you had builders or workmen in the church?'

'No, sorry. No workmen of any kind, Michael. Not for months.'

Angel pursed his lips. 'Right, Father. I'll give it some thought. Nice to see you again. Goodbye.'

'Goodbye Michael, and good hunting.'

Angel went through the black wrought-iron gate into Church Street, and back past the Northern Bank and Jeeves the jewellers and up to the police station.

He went round to the police car-park at the rear of the building to collect his car. He drove the BMW into town, then out on Park Road to Mountjoy Street. There were so many cars parked on both sides of this back street, it was difficult to find a parking spot. He eventually managed to find a space between a 1997 Passat and a 1992 Ford. He then walked back to house number 20. He pressed button number 6 with the name 'P. Queegley' scrawled against it and reached down to the speak box above it.

Eventually a man's belligerent voice said: 'Yeah? Who is it?' It was Peter Queegley.

'Detective Inspector Angel. Open up.'

The man wasn't pleased. He sighed noisily and said, 'What do *you* want, copper?'

Angel heard the squeal of a female from the speak box. Angel was certain it was in response to Queegley's reference to 'copper' and not the result of any romantic liaison between the female and Queegley.

'Shut up and put summat on,' he heard him whisper, then down the speaker he said, 'Come back tomorrow?'

Angel's lips tightened back against his teeth. 'Open up at once,' he bawled. 'I'm not the ruddy Avon lady.'

There was a pause, then Angel heard the buzzer and then a click. He pushed the door open and made his way into the hall. He charged up the bare wooden stairs to the second floor.

Queegley was outside the room door on the landing. He was wearing trousers, trainers and buttoning up his shirt when Angel reached the top of the stairs.

'Is this absolutely necessary, Angel?' Queegley said.

'I want to know what you're up to.'

'I'm not up to nothin'.'

Angel walked past him and through the open door.

Queegley glared after him and followed him in.

The same girl who had been there before was standing by the bed with her back to him, tucking a T-shirt into her jeans. She turned round, glowered at him briefly, then turned back.

Angel said: 'You're Gloria, aren't you?'

She stopped and looked up at him wide-eyed in astonishment. 'How the frigging hell do you know that?' Before he could answer she turned to Queegley and said, 'Is this the cop you was saying what knows everything?'

Queegley nodded, lighting up a cigarette. 'Angel. Inspector Michael Angel.'

'Frigging hell,' she said.

Angel shook his head. He wasn't for taking credit when credit wasn't due. 'You told me your name when I was here last time.'

She pulled a face of disappointment. 'Aw,' she said, tightening the belt on the jeans.

'How old are you?' he said.

'Nineteen.'

Angel wrinkled his nose. She looked nearer fifteen.

'Wanna see my burf certificate?'

'Probably,' he said.

Queegley came up to Angel quickly and said, 'She told *me* she was nineteen.'

Angel said, 'Better get off home, smartly. Your mother's screaming blue murder. She wants to know where you are and who you're with.'

She was stunned. Her eyes opened wide. She looked terrified. She believed him.

'Oh my god,' she said. Then she looked back at Angel. Her lip curled anxiously. 'What you been saying to her?'

'Every second counts,' Angel said. 'I should run, if I were you.'

She considered whether to reply.

All she could manage was a frustrated, 'Aw.'

She went back to the bed for her shoulder bag, grabbed it by the strap, dashed for the door and was gone.

As the clickety-click of badly fitting high-heeled shoes noisily stabbed the wooden steps, Peter Queegley said, 'I should sue you for harassment, you know. You're ruining my love life.'

'If she's under age you could finish up inside, don't you know that?'

'She told me she was nineteen. That's good enough for me and it's good enough for any judge.'

'You said eighteen before.'

'So what? She's had a birthday probably. Anyway, eighteen's all right.'

If she didn't deny it, Angel knew he was correct. You could get away with murder in some courts.

'You haven't come to argue about the girl, have you?' Queegley said, taking a drag on the cigarette.

'No. I want to know where you were last night?'

'I was here, as usual, of course.'

'Are you sure?'

'I haven't no spare to go down the pub any more.'

‘Were you on your own?’

‘Of course I was on my own.’

‘Well you weren’t here all the time. You were seen.’

‘Couldn’t have been me.’

‘You were seen with a big man in a big, black hat. Now who would that be?’

‘No. You’ve got it wrong.’

‘Where is your mate Alec Underwood hanging out these days?’

‘No idea,’ he said. ‘And he’s not my mate. Haven’t seen him for . . . ages.’

‘You were seen together, Queegley. No point denying it.’

‘You’re wrong. It wasn’t me.’

‘You were seen on Market Street at 1.48 a.m. passing Jeeves the jewellers. You checked the padlock of the middle window.’

Queegley’s jaw dropped.

‘And at 2 a.m. you were seen with your friend parading a coffin round the perimeter of St Mary’s church.’

Queegley started coughing. Smoke from the cigarette seemed suddenly to have caught in his throat. He continued coughing.

Angel ignored the coughing. ‘I can guess who your *friend* is,’ Angel said. ‘It would be Alec Underwood. The man who, two years ago, got you twelve months inside while he got off scot free. Are you going back for more? If you've some scam going with him, you can depend on him dumping you when it gets umpty. Just like he did last time. Did you break in and steal three mahogany coffins from Hargreaves undertakers last Monday night?'

'No. It wasn't me,' he said wiping his wet mouth with an oversize handkerchief.

'What do you want three coffins for?'

Queegley's eyes shone like traffic lights. 'I don't know nothing about coffins and walking about a churchyard with them. You must be off your trolley. I'm absolutely completely innocent. I'm going straight. I've paid my debt to society. You've no evidence . . . you're just stabbing in the dark. If you'd any evidence, Angel, you wouldn't come here pussyfooting round asking me daft questions, and looking at my woman to see if you could get me for bedding a lass under age. You'd be here with a warrant as thick as a prison visitor, a pair of handcuffs and a fresh-faced flunky to fit them on to me, so sod off and don't come back until you've got some evidence.'

Angel was not unhappy to leave. The visit had served its purpose. He came away satisfied that Queegley knew *all* about the coffins, that he *was* one of the men carrying one round the churchyard, that he *was* up to something nefarious with Alec Underwood, and that he would be off like a scared rabbit to tell him all about it, asap. When Angel reached his car, he slumped down in the driver's seat and adjusted the rear mirror so that he had a direct line of vision to Queegley's front door. Then he switched on the car radio for some light music and waited.

Two minutes later, Queegley appeared. He dashed down the steps, his face the colour of a judge's robe.

Angel licked his lips in satisfying anticipation.

A few moments later a large silver Mercedes estate car raced past him noisily. He carefully observed that Peter Queegley was in the driving seat.

He started up the BMW.

He kept his distance behind the Mercedes estate, allowing a blue van to overtake him so that it would be the van that would appear mostly in Queegley's rear-view mirror and not the BMW. That was just in case Queegley was at all concerned that he might be followed. As the convoy made its way through town, the van veered off and Angel allowed a green car to take its place in between them.

Queegley was making his way out of town in the direction of Barnsley. The convoy was passing a row of bungalows when Queegley suddenly braked hard and turned left through the gates into the drive of one of them. The green car had to brake and swerve out towards the middle of the road, before continuing. Angel noted the number 29 painted in white on the gatepost and sailed straight past. He drove as far as the next roundabout, circled it and came back towards the bungalow. About a hundred yards before he reached the bungalow, he pulled the BMW into the side of the road and stopped. He reached into the glove compartment, took out a pair of binoculars just in time to see the tall, black-clad figure of Alec Underwood open the bungalow door and Queegley step inside.

8

It was 8.28 a.m. on Friday morning, 29 May.

Angel arrived at the station and went straight down to the stores to withdraw three rounds of ammunition and the handgun, the Walther PPK/S, the actual weapon that was used to kill Charles Razzle. The duty stores sergeant gave them to him separately wrapped in two sealed envelopes. Angel tore open the paper, checked them, pushed them into his pocket, and signed the receipt and the list of standard conditions permitting the gun to be in his possession. It was, after all, a lethal weapon and an important piece of evidence.

He then drove the BMW down to The Manor House on Creesforth Road and parked on the drive behind DS Carter's Ford. He went through the unlocked front door, straight down the hall to the kitchen, through the basement door and down the steps. The heavy workshop security door was wide open and the lights were on. A shaft of electric light shone outwards on to the basement floor. He went into the workshop.

DS Carter and PC Ahmed Ahaz were

bending down in front of the robot arranging two sandbags on the floor where the body of Charles Razzle had been.

The blue robot seemed to acknowledge Angel's arrival. Three tiny coloured lights in its blue translucent head kept flickering on and off in an irregular sequence suggesting that it was capable of thought as well as indicating that it was switched on.

Carter heard Angel arrive and looked up. 'Are these sandbags all right here, sir?'

'Aye. They'll do fine,' he said.

'Did you put tapes in the CCTVs?'

'Not yet, sir. I brought two new ones. They are here,' she said, taking them off the top of the safe and handing them to him.

Angel took them, glanced at them and said, 'Ahmed, put these tapes in the cameras and make sure they're running.'

'Right, sir,' Ahmed said and rushed out.

Angel looked at Carter, pointed at the robot and said, 'Where's the remote control for that thing?'

'On the desk, sir.'

Angel looked round, found the large, cumbersome control and said, 'Does it work?'

'Oh yes, sir. Just press the red button and it will walk forward . . . and probably start jabbering.'

Angel clicked the red button and the robot

began making a low buzzing noise. It began a rocking side to side movement which progressed it towards them, at the same time, in a hollow voice, it said, 'What do you want me to do now?'

Angel pressed the green button and it stopped. He pressed the green button again twice quickly and it walked backwards. At the same time, it said, 'I do not understand your instruction. Would you repeat it, please?'

Angel pressed the other buttons in turn and discovered that the robot could turn right and left, turn around, and move its arm, wrist, hand and fingers on demand. The performance was firm and positive but much slower than a human.

He took out the Walther and fitted it in the robot's hand.

Carter looked on.

Using the remote control, Angel raised the robot's arm to the approximate position it would have needed to have been in, to have shot the first bullet at Charles Razzle while the man was standing in front of the desk.

'What do you want me to do now?' the robot said.

Angel noticed that DS Carter's mouth was open and that she had put her hands up to her face. The horror of the murder was in her mind.

'The gun's not loaded, Flora,' he said, to remind her.

She knew it wasn't. *Of course it wasn't.*

She nodded and quickly lowered her hands. 'No, sir.'

The robot said, 'I do not understand your instruction. Would you repeat it, please?'

Angel glared at the robot, pulled an impatient face and said, 'Oh, shut up.'

The robot said, 'The automatic voice recognition control unit is closing down. From now on, I will only respond to signals sent by the remote control. To restart voice control, please say 'Robot speak to me'. Thank you.'

Angel's eyebrows shot up. He looked at the robot's head, blinked and grunted with satisfaction.

Carter smiled and said, 'That's how you do it, sir?'

'Aye. Apparently. It's a pity you can't as easily switch off all people you don't want to hear.'

'Can I do anything to help, sir?'

'What? Yes, you can. In a minute, I want you to measure the length of time it takes for the robot to discharge the three rounds, from the sound of the first click to the sound of the third. We know the robot couldn't have killed him, but we ought to know how long it would have taken, in case we have to answer a question from a particularly reflective member of a jury, or even a judge.'

'Got it, sir.'

Angel pressed the button to operate the robot's forefinger. He could see the blue plastic digit tightening inside the trigger guard. Eventually, there was a click, the first click. Angel then quickly found the button on the remote control to reverse the action. Then he quickly lowered the angle of the robot's arm, to be in the position to shoot the victim through the heart on the floor. When in position, he pressed the button to pull the trigger again. He had again to wait for the click. Then he quickly repeated a similar operation for the third and last time, and aimed again at the floor. After the third click, he looked up at Carter, eyebrows raised.

'That's one minute and ten seconds, sir,' she said.

'Mmm. That precisely confirms the fact that there was simply not enough time for Razzle or anybody else to redirect the robot to aim and fire any rounds after the first one. That bullet entered the brain and he would have been dead instantly or certainly within a second or two. It also therefore proves positively that he was murdered.'

She followed the reasoning through and nodded.

Angel released the Walther from the robot and put it in his pocket.

Ahmed suddenly appeared through the door. He was still holding the CCTV tapes and looked puzzled.

Angel looked up at him and blinked.

'I can't find the cameras, sir,' Ahmed said. 'You said there were two.'

Angel turned to Carter. 'Do *you* know where they are, Flora?'

'Yes, sir,' she said. 'I'll show him. Come on, Ahmed.'

They went out, leaving Angel alone in the workshop.

It was very quiet.

Angel withdrew the Walther from his jacket pocket. He loaded the three bullets into the magazine and dropped it back into his pocket. He turned to the heavy workshop security door and gave it a long look. He rubbed his chin.

After a few moments, Carter returned. 'The cameras were not easy to see,' she said.

Angel nodded, then said, 'Do you think Razzle would have worked down here with this door open or closed?'

'He would know the house was locked up, sir,' she said. 'I would have thought open. I know *I* would.'

'Mmmm. The low roof and the lack of

windows . . . in here all day, he might have felt just a little closed in or claustrophobic. I agree.'

Angel went to the door and took it by the handle. 'However, the murderer would have closed it to muffle the sound of the shots, wouldn't he?' He frowned and said, 'I shall have to reset the combination.'

'Six numbers, isn't it?' she said.

'Yes,' he said thoughtfully. 'I must think of an appropriate figure.'

'You could put your birthday.'

'I could, but it might be too obvious.'

'Your wife's birthday.'

'No. A good thief would think of that. *And* my wedding anniversary. No, I'll think of something.'

'The day you first started work?' she said.

'No,' he said, then his face brightened.

'Got to be something you will easily remember, sir,' she said.

'Indeed. I will remember this. Never forget it,' he said and he went out of the workshop to the control box on the door.

Carter followed him and stood at his elbow.

He recalled the directions of the security man . . . 'The door must be in the open position. You hold down the set button and tap in a six-digit number, that's all.'

He approached the number pad cautiously

and carefully held down the set button as he tapped in the number 130864. At the end, the LCD lit up displaying the new number briefly, then it went out. Angel nodded approvingly. It was done.

Carter saw the number and said, '130864? That's the thirteenth of August 1964? What date was that then, sir? What does it represent, sir?' Carter said.

'It's a date I'll not forget.'

'The date of a war?'

'I am not telling you, Flora.'

'Why, sir. Is it a secret?'

There was noise behind them.

He turned to see Ahmed reaching up to the cunningly concealed CCTV camera, which was painted white and fastened to the waterpipe in the corner of the basement. He saw him slot the tape into the camera and check that the red warning light was on and that the spools were rotating.

'Have you finished?'

'Yes, sir.'

'I hope both cameras are rolling.'

'They are, sir. I checked them particularly.'

'Good lad. Come into the workshop then.'

When they were all three inside Angel said, 'Charles Razzle was probably standing, with his back to the safe, facing the robot. Now, I am going to take the part of the murderer in this reconstruction. For safety's sake I shall discharge all three rounds into the sandbags where they are, on the floor. Apart from that, I believe the rest of the reconstruction will be pretty accurate. You both stay here, until I have tapped the combination in the door and opened it to get out of here, then come out with me, so that you can see what's happening. All right?'

They nodded.

Angel looked at Carter and said, 'Have you Charles Razzle's bunch of keys?'

'Yes, sir,' she said. She felt inside her suit jacket pocket and handed them over to him.

He went over to the sandbags, leaned over, tucked the bunch under the edge of one of the sandbags and said, 'There. They are supposed to be in his pocket.'

He stepped back, then pushed the door into the half-open position.

'Charles Razzle may have had the remote control in his hand when the murderer entered,' he said. 'He may have been checking its response to his vocal commands, who knows?'

He glanced round the workshop.

'Right,' he said. 'The reconstruction will start in a couple of minutes. I just have a couple of things to see to out of here.'

He stared at the robot and said, 'Robot, speak to me.'

The lights in the robot's head did a short dance then the voice said, 'What do you want me to do now?'

Angel looked at Carter.

She smiled.

Carter and Ahmed glanced at each other, then at Angel.

Angel shook his head, went out of the workshop, dashed up the basement steps along the hall to the front door. He went out of the house to his car, parked on the drive behind Carter's. He opened the BMW's boot and took out a slim white packet and tore off the top. Inside was a pair of skin-tight rubber gloves. He pulled them on, snapping them tight. Then he took out a plastic shopping bag. He peered in it to check that the items he wanted were there. Then he went back to the house and stood on the front step for a moment, thinking out what he had to do and the sequence he had to do it in. He let himself into the house, closed the door quietly, dashed through the hall into the kitchen, and down the basement steps. He silently put the plastic shopping bag on the floor of the basement, withdrew the gun from his pocket and entered the workshop.

DS Carter and PC Ahmed watched him with eyes like well-sucked gob-stoppers.

He closed the security door behind him,

crossed to the robot, stood in front of it with his back to it, and carefully pointed, then fired, three rounds into the sandbags.

The noise was deafening in such a confined space and there was a strong smell of cordite.

The robot said, 'What do you want me to do now?'

Everybody ignored it.

Angel carefully took the remote from the desk and used it to set into position the Walther in the robot's right hand, its forefinger touching the trigger. Then he placed the remote on the floor where it had been when Razzle's body was found. He reached down to the sandbags, retrieved the bunch of keys he had placed there earlier. Then he stepped over the sandbags, unlocked the safe, and reached in as if to take something out.

'I am taking the booty,' he said, 'whatever it was.' He then closed the safe, locked it, put the bunch of keys back under the sandbag, crossed to the door, tapped the combination on the pad, opened it, stood back to let Carter and Ahmed out of the workshop ahead of him. He then pulled the heavy door until it was closed, and checked the handle to make sure it was locked.

He picked up the plastic shopping bag he had placed on the basement floor earlier and took out a videotape. He reached up and changed it for the one Ahmed had set in the CCTV opposite the workshop door only a few minutes earlier.

Ahmed watched him open-mouthed.

Then, taking the plastic bag containing another new videotape, Angel went down the hall followed by Flora Carter and Ahmed. He opened the front door, silently ushered them outside, then he changed over the videotape in the CCTV camera there and closed the door.

When all three were standing on the front step, he said, 'And that's how I think it was done.'

There was a pause, then Carter smiled up at him and said, 'It certainly explains why the murderer doesn't appear anywhere on the tape, sir.'

Angel said, 'And we can prove exactly what time they were changed by calculating how long the tapes had been running when SOCO took them out of the cameras. We know from Mac that the approximate time of Charles Razzle's death was 9 p.m. on Monday night. So the murderer would have changed the tapes three or four minutes or five minutes after that. If that checks out, this will be proved.' He turned to Ahmed and said, 'You can do that as soon as you get back to the station, can't you?'

'Oh yes, sir,' Ahmed said with a grin.

Carter said: 'But how did the murderer get into the house, sir? There are no signs of a break-in?'

'That bit I don't yet know. He must have had a key.'

Carter frowned. 'And how did the murderer know the combination to the workshop?'

'He didn't, but it didn't matter. He reset the combination before he shot him. As I did.'

'Could he really do that, sir?'

'As long as he'd got a loaded Walther in his hand, he could pretty well do anything he damn well wanted, couldn't he?'

The logic was sound. Flora Carter had to agree.

Angel said, 'Well, tidy up here. Lock up the house. I'm off to see Rosemary Razzle . . . see if she can throw any more light on the matter.'

'What was that number again, sir, to get back into the workshop?' Carter said. '130864? That's the thirteenth of August 1964. Was that the date you were born, sir?'

'No it wasn't. Don't be so nosy. I'll tell you what it represents later. You should know. It's to do with the history of crime.'

She frowned.

'I'm off,' he said.

She smiled as she watched him dash down the steps.

Angel got into the BMW, started it up and pointed the bonnet through The Manor House gates. He turned left and drove up to the traffic lights then right on to Park Road and up the hill towards the town. It was a straight road and there was little traffic . . . his mind naturally wandered back to recent events. He was pleased that he had been able to demonstrate how Charles Razzle had been murdered, and that it had not been in a locked room by a robot; also, that he had worked out an explanation as to how the safe came to be empty. That morning's work, so far, had been satisfactory. He could see that progress had been made.

Halfway up the hill, he found that he was driving towards slow moving traffic in both lanes. He had to slow down and then stop the BMW in a stationary line of traffic. It didn't move for a couple of minutes. He put his head out of the window and peered out. There was no traffic coming in the opposite direction either. He banged the heel of his hands on the steering wheel and got out of the car. There was now a long line of traffic behind him. He began walking up the hill to find out the cause of the stoppage. Ahead he could see a crowd of people swarming over the road outside a large new retail furniture shop that used to be Woolworth's. Motor traffic was stationary in every direction. He stood on the pavement and looked at the sight in amazement.

A big uniformed policeman in the midst of the throng saw him and battled his way through. It was PC John Weightman.

'What's happening?' Angel said.

'Another furniture shop opening, sir,' Weightman said. 'It's unbelievable. I can't do anything with them on my own. I've phoned through for back-up. They're sending two patrol cars.'

Angel nodded.

'It's being opened by that Sinceree La More, sir. She'll be driving off any second. She's in a white stretch limo.'

Angel frowned. 'Sinceree La More? Who is she?'

'That leggy lass from that new film. An English royal duke from way back made a gold statue of her, his mistress. Supposed to be the most beautiful body in the world.'

Angel remembered. 'Dorothea Jordan. Had ten kids to the Duke of Clarence before he became King William IV,' he said.

'*That*'s the one, sir.'

Angel sniffed. 'Hmm.'

There was the whine of sirens. Police patrol

cars were arriving.

'Get me out of this, John, asap,' Angel said. 'I'm down there and I want to go straight on to The Feathers.'

'Yes, sir. Right away.'

Angel eventually arrived at the Feathers Hotel car-park and made his way up to suite 1 on the first floor. He knocked on the door.

As he stood there waiting, out of the corner of his eye he saw the door of the room adjacent silently open only the thickness of a truncheon. The chandelier on the landing caught the reflection of somebody's eye peering out at him.

Angel sucked in air as the muscles of his hands tightened instinctively, preparing himself for an attack of some sort. The door then suddenly opened much wider and a very familiar face smiled at him. It was DS Crisp.

Angel gave a little sigh, acknowledged him with a nod and, with a small gesture, indicated to him to go back into the room. He didn't want Crisp risking blowing his cover.

The door facing Angel was suddenly whisked open.

Mrs Razzle, who was in a fluffy housecoat, glared at Angel with eyes like needles. He thought that her hair in a dishevelled state in no way detracted from her attractiveness, made her seem even more overpoweringly desirable but also very dangerous. The more he saw of her the more he worried about her.

'Oh it's you,' she said.

'Good morning, Mrs Razzle,' Angel said.

The corners of her mouth turned downwards. She held on to the door with one hand and stared at him without replying.

'I need to ask you a couple of questions,' he said.

'Like what?' she said.

He could see over her head into the sitting room behind her. There were clothes everywhere . . . dresses and coats and underwear draped over the chairs and in boxes, some on the floor.

'What are *you* looking at?' she said.

'We can talk better inside, Mrs Razzle,' he said, applying his weight to the door.

She resisted at first, but he pressed his advantage.

She released her grip on it, turned away, took in a very deep breath, put her hands on her hips and turned back to face him.

Angel pushed the door open and came into the room.

'Are you allowed to force your way in, like that, Inspector?'

'No. Not really,' he said turning back from closing the door. 'But then again, I could prosecute you for obstructing a policeman in the course of his duty. Particularly as these inquiries are into a case of murder.'

Her eyes flashed. 'Murder!' she said.

He looked round at the mass of clothes everywhere. 'What's all this?' he said. 'Going away somewhere?'

'My husband was *not* murdered. He couldn't have been. It's not possible.'

'Yes it is. How many keys are there to the front door of your house?'

'You're not answering my questions.'

'You haven't asked any, and you're certainly not answering mine. Keys, Mrs Razzle. How many keys are there?'

'Three keys, Inspector. *Three keys*.'

'Thank you. And who has them?'

'There's one on my husband's key ring; you have that one, I believe. Another in my handbag and a third we had cut for Elaine.'

Angel wrinkled his nose. 'Ah,' he said. 'Elaine Dalgleish?'

Rosemary Razzle's eyes flashed again. 'That woman is as straight as a die.'

He pursed his lips. 'How long have you known her?'

'Four years. And I don't want you accusing her of anything.'

'Nobody has anything to fear if they've done nothing wrong. To save me time, can you give me her address again?'

'I can't remember.'

He peered down at her. 'That's not the answer, Mrs Razzle.'

'You mustn't bully her and push her around.'

'I never bully or push anybody around. If you don't tell me, I've only to ring my office.'

'Canal Road. Number 22.'

'Thank you.'

'What makes you think my husband's death was murder?'

'I am now certain of it, Mrs Razzle. Chiefly, because it was impossible for the robot to have discharged the second and third bullets after the first bullet, since that shot went directly to his brain.'

She shuddered and looked down.

Angel pursed his lips. 'I'm sorry. That was very . . . I could have put that more . . . delicately.'

'No. No, it's all right. If anybody said anything kind to me just now, I would collapse in a heap.'

He nodded his understanding, then he waved an arm round the room at the clothes and said, 'What's all this?'

There was a pause, then she straightened up, squared up her shoulders and said, 'It's no business of yours, Inspector, but I am trying to find something to wear.'

Angel looked at the piles of clothes and noted that none of them was black or of conventional mourning colours.

She turned away from him, then turned back. 'When am I to be allowed back into my own house?' she said.

'Quite soon, I expect. Sorry that you have been inconvenienced, but it really *is* necessary.'

She glared at him briefly. 'Well, if there's nothing else . . . ' she said.

'There's nothing else, for now,' he said. Then he turned and made for the door.

9

Angel knew exactly where Canal Road was. It was adjacent and parallel to Sebastopol Terrace at the bottom of a hill in the lowest part of Bromersley. The two streets consisted in total around 160 old, small, terraced houses, and in the middle of the houses was located a notorious public house, the Fisherman's Rest. The pub was frequented by prostitutes, pimps, thieves, rogues and vagabonds as well as many a trusting, honest fisherman and passing innocent traveller. Angel had visited the pub many times over the years, quelling fights or to make enquiries. Two years previously he had actually investigated a case of murder in the public bar.

He turned the BMW left off Wakefield Road on to bumpy, uneven Canal Road and stopped outside number 22. A young girl was bouncing a ball against the wall. Two small boys were racing up the street taking turns to kick an empty lager can ahead of them with remarkable accuracy. The house door opened straight on to the pavement and was only twenty doors away from the pub.

Angel got out of the car and knocked on the door. As he waited he noticed that the house had been freshly painted; also, that it had had its front step recently scrubbed and a two-centimetre white border carefully painted on the edge of the tread. The windows were gleaming, and the white net curtains with their embroidered design were well worn but spotless. Number 22 was generally smarter and cleaner than all of the other houses in the street.

He knocked again and shortly heard a rattle of keys, the sliding of a bolt, followed by the opening of the door. Elaine Dalgleish appeared, wearing an overall and a headscarf. Her face was red and moist with perspiration. When she saw who it was, her mouth dropped open in surprise.

'Oh, Inspector Angel,' she said. 'Oh dear. I am in such a mess. My washing machine is broken down. The floor in the kitchen is wet through. Anyway, come in. Come on through. You'll have to excuse the mess.'

'That's all right,' he said.

'I've got an engineer looking at it,' she said as she closed the door.

He followed her through the tiny sitting room, across the bottom of the stairs into the even tinier kitchen.

Angel's eyes narrowed when he saw the

soaked mats and puddles round the furniture. Through the jumble he saw the back and legs of a man in a white coat and wellington boots. He had his head inside the door of a front-opening washing machine.

Above, suspended from the ceiling was a clothes rack overloaded with clothes drying out.

The back door was wide open. There was the row of a radio playing music, a baby crying, the thump of a ball being kicked and children squealing excitedly as they seemed to be engaged in their own rowdy version of football.

'Mind your feet,' she said. 'You'd best stand on the stairs, Inspector.'

He took up a position on the first step up and peered round the corner into the room.

Elaine Dalgleish had snatched up a mop and was feverishly pushing it around the linoleum-covered floor, squeezing the soapy grey water into a yellow plastic bucket. 'I'll just have to do this, Inspector. Save my rugs, if you don't mind.'

Angel waited.

After two or three minutes, when she had soaked up most of the water, she leaned on the mop, turned to him and said, Now then, Inspector, what can I do for you?'

Before Angel could answer, the engineer

came out of the machine waving a fistful of black material. '*That*'s the cause of the problem, missis!'

He placed the wodge of mangled material on the plastic-faced table.

She glared at it. 'It's a glove,' she said. 'That's where it went to. I've been looking for *that*.'

'A glove is it?' the engineer said with a grin. 'Well, I'm afraid his tiny hand will have to stay frozen. Won't be much use to him now.' He stood up, pointed at the washing machine and said, 'It needs a new bearing-seal, missis. I've got one in the shop, I think. I'll be back in about ten minutes.'

He glanced at Angel, blinked with surprise, then rushed out of the back door.

Elaine Dalgleish picked up the soggy remains of the glove, glanced at it and dropped it in the waste bin by the sink. She turned to Angel and said, 'He's gone. Thank goodness. I don't want everybody knowing my business. Now, what did you want, Inspector?'

'Just a few questions, Mrs Dalgleish,' he said. 'It's a matter of the key to the front door of the Razzle's house.'

She pulled her head back. She wasn't pleased. 'Yes, I have a key, Inspector. What about it? Does Mrs Razzle want it back now?

Doesn't she want me to work for her any more? Is that what it is?'

'No. No. It's nothing like that. Somebody entered the house the night Mr Razzle died. I believe that whoever it was entered by the front door, and must have used a key.'

She stretched herself up to her full height, looked him straight in the face and said, 'Well it wasn't me.'

'I didn't think it was. But I thought it might be possible that someone may have used your key . . . ?'

'Certainly not. How could they?'

'Without you even knowing?'

'Impossible.'

'Where is it now?'

She pointed to the open back door. The key was in the lock on a keyring with three others. She suddenly realized the possibilities. She put the tips of her fingers across her open mouth. Her eyebrows shot up momentarily, then returned to normal. She crossed to the door, and withdrew the key as she closed it. She selected the biggest one of the other keys and held it up. 'That's the one,' she said.

Angel breathed in heavily and said, 'And do you always keep the bunch in that open door . . . like that?'

She couldn't hide her discomfort.

'The door isn't *always* open, Inspector,' she said.

He sniffed. 'People may know that you work at the Razzles and suspect that you might have a key. If they watch you, they might wait for a moment when your attention is . . . somewhere else, and sneak in, and take the keys out of the lock. It only takes a few seconds, you know, to take a cast in a prepared bar of soap, pack of putty or Plasticene.'

Her face went scarlet. 'It's possible, I suppose.'

'Or have you had occasion to let someone else have your keys for some reason?'

'Certainly not,' she snapped.

'Have you ever been enticed out of the house for some reason, leaving the keys unattended? Might have seemed innocent at the time? Or have you ever misplaced them, maybe for a few minutes?'

'It's possible, Inspector,' she said.

'When was this?'

'I didn't say it had happened. I said that it was possible.'

'If you could recall a particular occasion, Mrs Dalgleish, it might be possible to put a name to the person who had that opportunity and that could lead to me arriving at the murderer of Mr Razzle. Don't you see that?'

'I can't say a particular occasion or a specific name. I get all sorts of friends and neighbours and visitors in to speak to me. I'm glad of their company. I live on my own. It would be very lonely without them. I'm just saying that my back might be turned . . . making a cup of tea or something . . . and I suppose it might be possible for some wicked person to . . . to do what you said.'

Angel rubbed his chin. He wasn't really satisfied. He wondered whether, if he persisted, he was likely to be successful in extricating a positive answer. He gave up and decided that he probably wouldn't. He moved on.

'Did you know Mr Razzle had a gun?'

'Yes. And I don't approve of guns. He kept it in a drawer at the side of the bed.'

'Was it loaded?'

'I don't know. I didn't ask. And I didn't touch it.'

'What colour was it?'

'I don't know. The usual.'

'If you saw it, you should be able to describe it. How big was it? It could have been black, silver-grey, brown or a blue colour.'

'It was blue and about as big as my hand.'

'And what was the writing on the barrel?'

'I didn't see any. I don't think there was

any. I can't remember.'

Angel was pleased that she was absolutely correct in every particular. 'When did you last see it?'

'I don't know. I don't want you to think that I go poking around in Mr and Mrs Razzle's things. Mrs Razzle asked me to bring down some hand-cream that was in the drawer at her side of the bed. Well I didn't know which was her side of the bed, did I?'

'You'll remember when you first saw it, surely?'

'I hadn't been going there long. Must have been three years or more ago.'

'And you haven't seen it since?'

She shook her head. 'I told you, Inspector. I don't go poking around into places that don't concern me. Once I seed it I didn't want to see it again.'

* * *

'There's no doubt about it, Flora,' Angel said, 'it would have been easy to have had a copy of it made. Mrs Dalgleish may have a lot to answer for.'

'Poor woman,' DS Carter said. 'You are not thinking that she was knowingly involved in the murder of Charles Razzle, are you?'

'No,' Angel said. 'But people should always

be more careful with keys.'

There was a knock at the door.

Angel glared at it. 'Come in.'

It was PC Ahaz. He was all smiles.

'What is it, lad?'

'I've just heard from 'Facial Recognition', sir, about that still I took from that overnight tape outside the jewellers'.'

'Ah yes,' Angel said. 'It's taken them long enough.'

'It confirms that the tall man in the black hat is Alec Underwood.'

'Aye. I thought as much. It doesn't progress us any, but it's good to have our thoughts confirmed.'

'And it illustrates what an accomplished liar Peter Queegley is,' Flora Carter said.

Angel nodded, turned back to Ahmed and said, 'But what about those tapes from Razzle's place that you were working on?'

'Oh, I've done that, sir. I've timed those tapes out, and the one focused on the workshop door would have been replaced at about eight minutes past nine, and the one by the front door at about ten or eleven minutes past nine.'

'That fits perfectly,' Angel said. 'Now we are getting somewhere. Great stuff. Thank you, Ahmed.'

Ahmed smiled and went out.

Carter said, 'That supports your theory, sir, but we are still no nearer knowing who actually murdered Charles Razzle, are we?'

'No. In cases like this, the spouse is often behind it. As you know, I am having her closely watched. That's what makes this case so — '

There was another knock at the door.

Angel glared at the door. 'Now what?'

It was Ahmed again. He was carrying a newspaper. He saw from Angel's face that the intrusion wasn't welcome.

'I'll come back, sir, if it's not convenient.'

'You're here now, what is it?'

PC Ahaz lifted up the *Bromersley Chronicle*. 'I thought you'd be interested in this, sir,' he said. 'Bought it this morning. Noticed this piece just now, while I was having my sandwiches. Thought you might know the man.'

He handed the paper to him, pointing to a heading of a short piece in the corner of the front page.

Angel frowned and took the paper.

It read:

BROMERSLEY MAN IN HORRIFIC MURDER

Skiptonthorpe police are concerned about the body of a man found behind a public house, the Two Widows, in the village of

Stallingon, yesterday afternoon. He died from a bullet through his heart at close range. Also after death, his tongue was torn out and left at the scene. There are no witnesses.

The man has been identified as Stefan Muldoon, 50, ex-bank robber, who had served eight years for armed robbery. He was originally from Bromersley, and after his release from Armley prison had been running his own small haulage business for the past twelve years as Muldoon Transport with his daughter and son-in-law.

A spokesman for Skiptonthorpe police said that it was a particularly horrific murder, and asked any witnesses or anyone with any information to phone them on 01302 969696.

Angel was subdued after he had read the report. He read the item again and then passed the newspaper to Flora Carter.

'I knew Muldoon,' Angel said. 'He was a particularly hard case. I've interviewed him a few times. It's not my patch, but I must give Skiptonthorpe a ring.'

The corners of Angel's mouth turned down as he thought more about the case.

Ahmed's eyes grew bigger. 'Does the report

mean literally what it says, sir?' he said. 'That his tongue was torn out?'

Angel shrugged. 'It would require a great deal of strength to pull the entire tongue out,' he said. 'Pliers or a similar instrument would be gripped round the tongue. Such a crude procedure would inevitably damage the underneath of the tongue which is particularly sensitive. I know that under the tongue is a place often used to administer drugs to stimulate the heart in emergency conditions, if intravenous means is not to hand. So you know that yanking at the tongue would have been quite horrific.'

Flora shivered. 'How awful. What a very uncivilized thing to do,' she said. Then she turned to Ahmed and handed him the newspaper.

Ahmed carefully straightened it, folded it up and put it in his pocket.

Then Angel said, 'You see what *that* was about, Flora? And *you* might take notice of this, Ahmed, also.'

Ahmed looked across at him. 'What's that, sir?'

'That report says that Muldoon died from a bullet to the heart,' Angel said, 'and that his tongue was torn out *after* death. Well, as it was after death, it wouldn't have mattered to Muldoon, would it? He wouldn't have known it was happening. He wouldn't have seen it or experienced any pain.'

'What are you getting at, sir?' Flora said.

'The savage pulling out of Muldoon's tongue like that was a means of putting the frighteners on somebody — or more than *one* somebody.'

'A gang, sir?' Ahmed said.

'Yes. And the only gang I am aware of round here at the moment is the country-house gang.'

Ahmed's face lit up. 'It would be great if we could catch them, sir,' he said.

Flora said: 'So the murderer was sending a message, sir. And the message was keep your mouth shut or this could happen to you.'

'Precisely. That's what this is all about.' He turned to Ahmed and said, 'Get on to the NPC and find out what you can about Stefan Muldoon's associates, recent and past, and anything known over the past twelve years. A hardened nut like him would find it hard to keep out of trouble. Go on, lad. Chop-chop.'

Ahmed rushed out.

'I know Skiptonthorpe force will be on to it, but I'm curious,' Angel said.

'Will Skiptonthorpe CID let you in on the case, sir?' Flora said.

'Not unless you're a good friend of the senior officer in charge, Flora,' he said.

'Coppers are just as possessive as any other creature on the planet. But I may not need to bother them.'

'Do you want me to fish around, see what I can find out?'

'Why? Do you know anybody on the force there?'

'No, sir. I meant in the pub and round the village?'

'No. Skiptonthorpe CID will have done that. There's something else far more important that I want you to do. I want you to ring Yorkshire CID Specialized Services at Wakefield, their CCC division . . . '

10

'Come in,' Angel said.

It was Ahmed Ahaz carrying an A4 sheet of paper. 'About Stefan Muldoon, sir.'

'Yes, Ahmed. What you got?'

'You asked me to look only over the past twelve years, sir. There's nothing since he came out of Armley. Plenty before: GBH, ABH, and armed robbery.'

Angel's eyebrows shot up. 'Nothing since he was released twelve years ago? Are you sure?'

'A clean sheet, sir. Seems to be a changed man. Proof, in this case, that prison works?'

'I don't know about that, lad,' Angel said. 'It could just be that he never got caught.' He bit his lower lip, shook his head and then said, 'His associates?'

Ahmed looked down at the A4 sheet. 'There were only two, sir. Sean Noel Riley, served three years in Strangeways for possession of a firearm. Came out 1987.'

'Never heard of him.'

'And Peter Amos Kidd, aka Peter Walters, aka Peter Waterstone, currently serving twelve years in Peterhead for armed robbery of Langsworth post office.'

Angel pulled a face like he was in the waiting room at the dentist's. 'Never heard of any of *them*, either.'

The constable frowned.

Angel ran his hand through his hair. 'All right, leave it at that. Crack on with what you were doing.'

Ahmed sighed and went out.

Angel reached out for the phone. A few minutes later he was talking to Detective Inspector Hubert Lord of Skiptonthorpe force. He was the man leading the inquiry into Stefan Muldoon's murder.

Angel introduced himself and said, 'I don't suppose that you are treating the murder of Muldoon as a 'domestic'?'

'All my options are wide open at this stage,' Lord said. 'Why?'

Angel knew that that was what he might have said in similar circumstances, especially if he didn't want to give any information away.

'An ex-con found shot with his tongue crudely pulled out indicates that it is almost certainly a gangland murder. The murderer showing the criminal fraternity what would happen to them if they didn't keep their mouths shut.'

'Possibly. Why, do you have some information?' Lord said.

'Don't want to intrude, but you may not

know that the 'Country-House Gang' is thought to be located on my patch.'

'Oh, really?' Lord said. 'No, I didn't know that.'

He sounded surprised, which pleased Angel. 'It's possible, nay likely,' Angel said, 'that Muldoon was part of that gang. So if you come across any recent associates of his that your SOCO might come up with, or that you might turn up on his SIM card or elsewhere, it might help me to build a case . . . '

'Of course,' Lord replied. 'I'll bear that in mind.'

'If you trip up over any names, I hope you'll let me know.'

Lord said, 'You could, of course, let me know if, in your travels, you hear anything at all about Stefan Muldoon.'

'Certainly will,' Angel said.

He guessed that Lord hadn't been a hundred per cent open with him. He wasn't surprised. There was no reason why he should be.

'Thanks for that,' Lord said.

Angel wished him luck and ended the call.

He replaced the phone, leaned back in the swivel-chair, looked up at the ceiling and blew out a long, tired sigh. He regretted being diverted by Ahmed's ill-timed, but well-meaning interruption with the report in the paper about the Muldoon murder. It might have been helpful. But *that* murder wasn't his case. And he didn't really expect Hubert Lord to break his neck to be helpful and come back with any names.

Angel resolved to stay with trying to solve the murder of Charles Razzle. From then onward it was to be his number one priority. All other cases would simply have to wait. He mustn't lose the momentum while the case was still hot.

He leaned forward in the swivel-chair to lower it just as, to his surprise, the office door was suddenly thrown open. It swung back and banged noisily on a wooden chair standing against the wall.

He sucked in air, leaned further forward and stared at the open doorway.

Standing there was the skinny frame of Superintendent Harker, his face scarlet and his small eyes red and shining. He was gripping a small sheet of pink paper so tightly that his hand was trembling. Angel recognized the paper as an expense voucher. He stood up.

Harker strode three paces into the little office and waved the voucher at him across the desk. 'What do you think this is, lad?' Harker said.

'Don't know, sir,' Angel said.

'I'll tell you what it is,' Harker bawled. 'It's a voucher for sixty-two pounds. It's been submitted by DS Crisp for room service meals and drinks at The Feathers Hotel.'

Angel frowned momentarily, then his jaw muscles tightened.

Harker said, 'I say to myself, who is this DS Crisp? I am sure that I have heard that name somewhere before . . . And when I look into it further, it turns out to be a charge for two days' snacks and drinks for Detective Sergeant Crisp's personal sustenance, while idling his time away in luxury at the taxpayer's expense at The Feathers Hotel.'

'He's on duty there, for me, sir,' Angel said. 'He's observing the movements of —'

'Is he? Why do your chaps never have to observe anybody in a tenement flat, the middle of a forest, a desert or a jungle?'

'He's observing Rosemary Razzle. It's all in my report. Her husband — '

'The woman off the television?'

'Yes, sir.'

'That doesn't mean to say that we have to adopt their lifestyle. Just because we occasionally have to look into the affairs of rich celebrities doesn't mean that we have to look like them and live like them. Where on earth does Crisp think he is? His expense chitties are more creative than our MP's.'

‘I instructed him to find out what he can about her activities, sir. Her husband has been murdered in unusual circumstances. He was enormously wealthy. She stands to inherit a considerable amount. She is the prime suspect. Her house was the scene of the crime so she was moved out. She elected to stay at The Feathers. Crisp monitors her from a small bedroom next door. What else can I do?’

‘I’ll tell you what you can do. You can tell Crisp the party’s over. If you still want him to shadow her, he’ll have to do it hiding behind a newspaper, or dressed as a waiter or a chambermaid. And he can live on home-made sandwiches and flasks of tea, like I had to, not caviar, smoked salmon and champagne at ‘room service’ prices.’

Angel shrugged. ‘I’m not sure that surveillance work can always be done efficiently or effectively in that way, but — ’

‘I’ll be the arbiter of what is efficient and effective. And on this matter of wining and dining out while on surveillance . . . let it be known that my officers can only charge for victuals if it is necessary to ingest them *with* the subject to make progress on the case. All right?’

Angel shrugged and said, ‘Right, sir.’

‘Otherwise they eat their own food and

drink, purchased and paid for, or prepared and brought from home. All right?'

Angel shrugged.

Harker stamped out. His footsteps could be heard stomping up the corridor. They continued until his office door was heard to open and then close.

Angel stood behind his desk scratching his head.

Ahmed appeared in the open doorway. He looked at Angel quickly then looked down. He came in and closed the door.

Angel sat down at his desk, sighed and rubbed his face.

Ahmed came up to his desk. He didn't say anything. He ran his fingertips over his lips and half-closed his eyes. After a few moments, he said, 'Do you want me to get DS Crisp on the phone, sir?'

Angel wrinkled his nose, sighed and said, 'No. Thank you, Ahmed. No. I must speak to DS Taylor first.'

Ahmed picked up the phone, tapped in Taylor's number and passed Angel the handset.

Angel took the phone, looked up at Ahmed, gave him a friendly nod, then said into the mouthpiece, 'Ah, Don. Have you finished sweeping Razzle's house?'

'Nearly, sir.'

'Anything interesting?'

'I don't think there's anything that you'd find interesting, sir. We've just a few drawers to finish looking into. Should be done by five o'clock, knocking off time.'

'Right, Don. Don't rush the job and overlook anything just to finish for the weekend.'

He ended the call, then tapped out Crisp's mobile number.

'Anything happening there, Trevor?'

'Nobody been, nobody phoned,' Crisp said.

Angel's eyes narrowed. 'You can close that obbo down now, lad. Rosemary Razzle will be moving back to her own house later today.'

'Oh?' Crisp was both surprised and disappointed. 'Right, sir,' he said.

Angel replaced the phone. It rang immediately. It was a young constable on reception. 'There's a young lady here asking to see you, sir. Says her name is Jessica Razzle.'

Angel's eyebrows shot up.

Three minutes later Ahmed showed a young woman in thick horned-rimmed glasses into Angel's office.

'I am Jessica Razzle. I was told that you were the officer in charge, looking into the murder of my father, Charles Razzle.'

'That's right,' Angel said gesturing with an open hand to a chair by the desk.

'Thank you,' she said. 'I want to report that I know the murderer.'

Angel's forehead creased up like corduroy trousers. 'Oh yes, miss?' he said.

'It was Rosemary Razzle, my stepmother,' she said. 'She engineered the whole thing. It was her idea . . . setting up the robot to make it look as if it had pulled the trigger of a gun pointed at my father by accident. She will inherit all his estate, including the complete control of my allowance.'

Angel blinked. 'There are several hundred witnesses that put your stepmother on a stage in London at the time of your father's murder,' he said.

'Yes, indeed. I don't mean that she actually pulled the trigger. As the murderer, she would obviously need a rock-solid alibi. I meant that one of her entourage of men would have actually done it for her. But she set it up, she organized it, told him how to get into his workshop, told him what to expect, where everything was . . . Dad's gun, the CCTV cameras, everything. She's the only one who could have done all of that.'

Angel rubbed his chin. There was nothing new there, unless Jessica knew something he didn't.

'How do you know this?'

'I know *her*, Inspector. She never loved

him. She told me so. He was her ticket to success in her career. It was Dad's money that financed her boob job, her hair, her wardrobe and her fabulous jewellery. Also his infallible advice and judgement about which roles would suit her, and which would not. Without her, she'd have been just another easy blonde, traipsing round the audition circuit, hoping to catch a director's eye.'

Angel pursed his lips.

'That's all very well, Jessica, but to follow up your accusations, I need names, addresses, places.'

'You don't believe me. That's it. She's fooled you like she's fooled everybody else. You don't believe me.'

Angel looked at her.

'She's too clever for you, Inspector,' Jessica said. She looked down and shook her head. 'Oh dear. How can I convince you?'

He pursed his lips.

'Before my father and Rosemary got married, she said how much she was looking forward to being a wife to my father and a close and loving friend to me. And I said — and I meant it — that I was looking forward to cementing that relationship with her. I knew it wouldn't have been — it couldn't have possibly been — anything like that with my own dear mother, but I hoped that it might have been like having a sort of big sister to love and laugh and confide in. But it never happened. In fact, the opposite happened. Shortly after they returned from their honeymoon, she said to me that she wanted me out of the house, and she talked my father into encouraging me to 'spread my wings', as she put it, and travel. I didn't want to go, but more and more I felt as if I was intruding . . . not welcome. I managed to stay around for a while longer, but she eventually got her own way, and I was pushed out. I am now travelling across the States, in no particular hurry, working my way. I was an assistant in a children's nursery when I heard of my father's death. I made my excuses, packed my bags and caught the first available plane out of Boston. I arrived in Bromersley this morning and went straight up to my old home, but the place was full of policemen. I spoke to one and was told you were in charge of the case, so I came straight here. I want to know what's happening.'

'I have a team making inquiries. Nothing conclusive has been arrived at yet.'

'Meanwhile, Rosemary Razzle can walk about free?'

'Afraid so.'

'Are you not afraid that she could just . . . disappear?'

'We have nothing on her. She is free to go wherever she likes. That's the law.'

Jessica Razzle's tortured face showed anger and grief and disbelief. 'But *she murdered my father*.'

Angel tried to think of something helpful and relevant to say.

Jessica Razzle said, 'Do you know where she is now?'

He hesitated. 'She's at The Feathers,' he said. 'But Jessica, if your accusations are true, they will need to be supported by proof. You can't go charging around making unfounded accusations, like that. To make a case stick, you need a name, a place and witnesses . . . and a motive. If Rosemary had an associate who murdered your father, to charge him, you'd need to have evidence. For a start, obviously, you'd need his name. Have you got a name?'

Her face hardened. 'No. But I'll get it. It will be somebody she's smiled at sweetly and promised — well, goodness knows what she might have promised.'

* * *

Angel yawned and threw back the bedclothes. He looked at the alarm clock. It said ten past eight. His jaw dropped open. He was going to be late. He leaped up. No. It was Saturday. He wasn't working that particular Saturday. Thank goodness. He sighed and scratched his head. He could hear Mary banging pots and pans about in the kitchen, but he couldn't smell anything cooking. He levered himself up, sat on the edge of the bed and stared at the Anaglypta.

He stood up, stretched, ambled round the end of the bed and glanced out of the window. It was a great day. It was sunny and dry. The sky was a beautiful blue. He looked down the garden. He saw the lawn . . . luxurious green. He looked at it closely. In places he could see that the grass was long and spoiled by a few dandelions. He wrinkled his nose. The hedge was rangy and untidy too. And the borders needed weeding. The garden needed his attention. It would have to be seen to. It was in that state because it had rained over the last three weekends. That Saturday the weather was perfect. He had no excuse this time. He knew there and then that this weekend the garden would need all his time to bring it back to a standard that would satisfy Mary. Therefore his time, that Saturday and Sunday, weather permitting, was completely committed.

A voice from the hall called out, 'Michael, are you awake? Breakfast's ready.'

'I'm coming, love,' he replied.

'That lawn needs cutting,' Mary said.

* * *

It was 8.28 a.m. Monday morning, 1 June.

Angel was walking briskly down the green corridor to his office. A uniformed police constable he didn't know dashed round the corner and almost bumped into him.

'Sorry, sir,' the constable said.

Angel stood back to let him pass. 'What's the rush, lad?'

'Triple nine call, sir,' said the constable as he raced off, his webbing rustling and handcuffs rattling.

Angel frowned. He continued his journey to his office, where he promptly picked up the phone and tapped in the single digit 7.

A voice said: 'Control room.'

'What's the triple nine, Sergeant?'

'Sounds like a domestic, sir. A man walking past a house on Creesforth Road heard a woman screaming.'

Angel's head came up. 'What was the house number?'

'No house number, sir. The man said it was The Manor House.'

That was the Razzle's place. Angel sucked in air. A lump in his chest began to beat like a drum. He banged the phone down and dashed out of the office.

He was at The Manor House on Creesforth Road in four minutes, about three minutes behind a police car. The patrolmen had gained access to the house and the front door was wide open.

As Angel approached the door he could hear a very stagey female voice. 'Get off me, you outsize gorilla!'

It was Rosemary Razzle.

'I'll report you to your superior officer,' she said. 'Hey! Just watch where you put your hands. I'm not one of your street girls. Let go. Let me go. Let me go!'

He followed the voice through the front door and then through the first door on the right, which led into the drawing room.

A constable was holding Rosemary Razzle's hands behind her back, attempting to put handcuffs on her. Her face was red and her eyes bright, wild and flitting from one direction to the other. Her mouth was open and moist, and she was panting. There was a satisfying click as the constable closed the handcuffs.

'Now behave yourself,' the patrolman said.

She made a last struggle to free herself. 'Hell. Do you know who you are talking to? Get these off. *Get these damned things off!*'

Another, younger woman whom Angel

recognized as Jessica Razzle was on the floor next to a broken china table-lamp. There was blood on her face, running from her nose on to her neck and her blouse.

He leaned over her.

She was motionless.

He reached into his pocket for his mobile and tapped in 999. 'Ambulance to The Manor House on Creesforth Road,' he said. 'Woman with head and face injuries.'

Rosemary Razzle, her eyes shining, her mouth open in disbelief, stared down at her stepdaughter, then up at Angel.

Jessica Razzle suddenly put her hand up to her face.

Angel sighed. 'She's moving,' he said and nodded towards the second constable.

The man came forward, moved the chair and got down on his knees. 'Are you all right, miss?'

Jessica moaned. She was holding her head.

There was relief around the room.

The constable then said, 'Can you stand up?'

From across the room, Rosemary Razzle yelled, 'There's nothing wrong with the little bitch. Keep her away from me or I'll give her another one.'

Angel's eyes flashed. 'Mrs Razzle,' he said.

The constable assisted Jessica to her feet.

Jessica's spectacles were on the floor by the lamp. There were spots of blood on the carpet around them.

Rosemary Razzle said, 'Call your gorilla off, Angel, before I stop him ever becoming a father again.'

Angel ignored her. He didn't even look at her.

The patrolman reacted. He had heard her loud and clear and, gripping the link between the wrists of the handcuffs behind her back, he stepped a pace back to avoid any contact with her foot or knee.

Angel glanced round the room. There were cushions on the floor, a table lamp damaged, and some chairs knocked askew, but the room seemed otherwise all right.

The constable settled Jessica Razzle on a sofa and sat next to her. She was holding her head in her hands, occasionally wiping her bleeding nose with a tissue.

Angel looked at Rosemary Razzle and said, 'What happened then?'

She shook her head vigorously a couple of times, then said, 'Nothing.' Then, changing her mind, she said, 'Plenty. The little bitch came for me, calling me all kinds of names and banging her fists into my face. I tried to reason with her, but it was no good. Eventually I lost my rag.'

'You hit her with that lamp?' Angel said. 'You could have killed her.'

'Unfortunately, I *didn't*,' she said. Then as an afterthought she added, 'She could have killed *me*. She was like a bloody tornado. She needs locking up. If you don't lock her up in a padded cell after this, I am going to need full-time protection.'

Jessica Razzle looked up. 'Yes, she is,' she said, calling across the room. 'Because I won't stop until I get the truth out of her. She murdered my father, and I promise you — '

Angel said, 'If you two cannot keep the peace — '

'She never loved my father,' Jessica Razzle continued. 'She told me so.'

'Ridiculous,' Rosemary Razzle said. 'I adored him and he adored me. You're talking through your backside.'

'You're a liar,' Jessica Razzle screamed and stood up. The constable pulled her back on to the sofa. 'If you can't see that she's guilty of murder, Inspector,' she said, 'then what sort of a detective are you? She's a thoroughly evil lot all the way through . . . just a common, jumped-up streetwalker whom God blessed with a beautiful body . . . '

Rosemary Razzle struggled with her handcuffs and said, 'Who are you calling a bloody streetwalker?'

‘If you two cannot keep the peace — ’ Angel said.

‘You’re the original tart — *without* the heart,’ Jessica Razzle said with a sneer.

Rosemary Razzle sucked air in noisily through her teeth. ‘Take that back, you little she-devil.’

‘Not one word. Not one syllable.’

‘Angel,’ Rosemary Razzle said, ‘you had better lock her up, good and quick, because I swear the next time I see this spoilt little cow I’ll tear her bloody tongue out.’

The two-tone siren of an ambulance could be heard approaching the house.

Angel blew out a slow sigh.

11

Two hours later, back at the police station, Angel went down to the cells.

'Now that you've cooled down, Mrs Razzle,' he said, 'I am conditionally releasing you, and I hope you will keep the peace. You'll be subsequently charged with assault and causing a public disturbance.'

'Thanks very much,' she said, twitching her nose. 'What was I supposed to do, let her kill me?'

'You can tell it to the magistrate,' Angel said. 'As it's your first offence, you will probably be fined. I strongly advise you to take control of your temper and keep out of your stepdaughter's way.'

'How can I do that? If she comes to the house — '

'When the doctor says she's fit she'll be released from the hospital, and she'll be specifically banned from approaching you and from being anywhere near The Manor House.'

Her jaw tightened. 'She'd better stick to it. She'd better not come anywhere near me.'

'By the same token, you must not approach

her or her living accommodation, wherever it might be, or you will be arrested.'

'I will have no reason to go to The Feathers, Inspector.'

'Good.' Angel said. 'I hope you mean that.'

Then he turned to the duty jailer, a constable who was standing in the cell behind him. 'Escort Mrs Razzle to the desk, lad. Let her pick up her possessions, and ask the duty sergeant if he can organize transport home for her.'

⋆ ⋆ ⋆

Angel drove the BMW down to Bromersley General Hospital and parked it outside the A&E entrance. He went through the automatic sliding door and straight into the ward. He looked round and saw PC Leisha Baverstock standing outside a cubicle at the far end. She caught his eye, waved, turned and pulled back the curtain to reveal Jessica Razzle seated on an examination bed. She had a plaster across her nose and various small contusions on her face. There was a small purple area round her left temple.

Angel walked down the length of the hall, into the cubicle, nodded at PC Baverstock and looked down at Jessica Razzle.

The young woman remained seated, looked

up at him and scowled.

He raised his eyebrows, then said, 'The doctor says you're OK, Jessica, you can leave.'

'What are you going to do about my stepmother?' she said.

He shook his head. 'I've told you, I can't do anything without evidence.'

'She's too clever. She will have covered her tracks by now.'

'You suggested that she had an accomplice — a man.'

'I'm sure she has.'

'You were going to give me his name.'

'Yes. It's proved to be more difficult than I thought it would be. I didn't expect her to attack me like that — so violently. I thought she would have had to tell me . . . boast about it, you know. Or that I would catch them together.'

He looked at her, nodded and said, 'You should leave these investigations to us, you know.'

'Huh. You'll never find the man who murdered my father.'

'You will have to be patient, Jessica.'

She sniffed. 'Oh yes. I had forgotten. You're *that* Inspector Angel, the detective who *always* gets his man, like the Mounties, aren't you? I read about you in a magazine in the plane coming back. I do hope that this is not the case that spoils your record.'

Angel blew out a foot of air. He hoped so too. There was nothing that he could say to her about *that*. He shrugged, then rubbed his chin.

'While you've been in this hospital, Jessica,' he said, 'you have been technically under arrest. You are now being conditionally released, but you'll be subsequently charged with assault and causing a public disturbance. In the meantime, you are not to go anywhere near Rosemary Razzle, nor The Manor House, also, you are not to leave Bromersley without notifying the police, understand?'

She was not pleased. 'Huh. Anything else?'

'About your conditional discharge, no. Those are the conditions, do you understand?'

She wrinkled her nose, looked at him, then turned away.

Angel clenched his fists. 'Do you accept the conditions?' he bawled.

Some nurses at their stations raised their heads, and two ambulance men looked in to the cubicle as they passed.

'It is necessary for you to accept the conditions so that you can be released, Jessica. All right?'

'Of course I accept the conditions,' she said. Standing up, she looked round for her shoulder bag. 'Can I go now? Is there anything else?'

Angel nodded. 'Yes, there is, as a matter of fact. Something that's still bothering me. There's a big safe in your father's workshop. It is empty now. Do you happen to know what he kept in it?'

Her eyes narrowed for a few moments, then she said, 'I think he kept his patents and important papers, books and stuff like that.'

'But you don't actually *know*?'

'I've been away two years, you know . . . things change.'

'It's all right, Jessica. Thank you. Now PC Baverstock will take you back to The Feathers.'

* * *

As Angel arrived back at his office door, PC Ahaz came rushing up to him. 'A sergeant from CID Specialized Services, Wakefield, CCC division has just been to see you, sir. He said he couldn't wait, so he's gone.'

Angel frowned and pushed open the door. 'Come in, lad. Did he go up to The Manor House?'

'Oh yes, sir.'

'Funny? I've been up there. I didn't see him.'

'No, sir. It must have been after you had brought Rosemary Razzle in. He said he had knocked on the front door up there, there was no reply, so he let himself in and checked round the workshop in the basement.'

Angel's fists clenched. 'He wouldn't have had time.'

'He left a message for you, sir.'

Angel raised his eyebrows.

Ahmed frowned and referred to a notepad. 'He said, 'One was in Preston and the other in Strangeways.' I hope that makes sense, sir. That's all he said.'

Angel thought for a moment, then realization spread across his face. 'It makes sense all right, Ahmed. It makes perfect sense, thank you.'

'Anyway, he'll be sending you a full report,' Ahmed said. He knew that the message must have been more significant than he understood because Angel's face looked brighter and happier.

Angel was still thinking about the message when the phone rang. He reached out for it. It was Hubert Lord, the DI of Skiptonthorpe force. Angel had never expected to hear from him again.

'Ah, Angel,' he said, 'I thought you might like to know that I've sewn up this Stefan Muldoon murder. Preparing it for the CPS. It was the son-in-law who did it. His wife is giving corroborative evidence against him. Singing sweeter than Katharine Jenkins. Didn't take long at all. Highly satisfactory, don't you think?'

Angel frowned and rubbed his chin. He wasn't certain how to reply. It sounded to him to have been far too easily achieved. 'Oh? Well, yes. I suppose.'

'Doesn't take us long once we get started, you know. And it had absolutely nothing at all to do with your country-house gang.'

'Right,' Angel said, though he wasn't altogether satisfied that Lord was right about that. 'Fine. Well, it was only an educated guess.'

'I don't believe in guessing, Angel,' Lord said. 'Just deal in hard facts, you know.'

We all do when we've got them, Angel thought, but he didn't speak it out loud.

Lord said, 'Now you said you would appreciate any evidence of Muldoon's recent contact with anyone *known*?'

'That's right,' Angel said, running his tongue over his lips.

'Well, there was a whole conglomeration of prints in the cabin in the yard where his lorries were kept. As well as Muldoon's, his daughter's, his son-in-law's, his drivers' and his customers' and neighbours', we found prints of a Sean Noel Riley. I thought you might be interested.'

Sean Noel Riley. Angel felt his pulse rate increase. He certainly *was* interested. And it was a starting point. He'd never before had as much as a sniff of a clue that could possibly relate to the country-house gang. That might be it.

'Are you there?' Lord said.

'Sorry,' Angel said. 'I was just . . . I was just finding my pen to write that down. Yes. Sean Noel Riley. Got it. Thanks very much.'

'There was a perfect thumb, first, second and third finger on an empty lager can in the rubbish. It would be very recent, because Muldoon's daughter emptied the rubbish every week.'

'Great stuff, Lord. Thanks very much. Have you interviewed this man, Riley?'

'No need to. I've got my man. Well, Angel, the best of luck.'

'Yes,' Angel said, 'and the same to you.' He thought he would need it. He also thought that Lord should have interviewed Riley to see if he could get any easy evidence out of him, but there you are. Lord had his methods.

Angel replaced the phone. His pulse was now racing. He turned to Ahmed. 'Get on to records and let me have everything they've got on Sean Noel Riley.'

'Right, sir.' Ahmed said and made for the door.

'And send Trevor Crisp and Flora Carter in.'

'Yes, sir.' Ahmed said as he dashed out of the office.

Angel was so pleased that, if Lord hadn't been so pompous, he might have popped out and bought the man a chocolate-covered ice-cream lolly.

* * *

DS Carter and DS Crisp arrived at Angel's office at the same time.

'Grab a chair each of you,' Angel said. 'Just waiting for Ahmed. Won't be a minute.'

Ahmed rushed in carrying a few sheets of A4. He put one of them on the desk in front of Angel, then turned back, closed the door and leaned against it.

Angel quickly began.

'I believe that we have a lead to the country-house gang,' Angel said. 'It's tenuous, but logical. The head of SOCA, Sir Miles Luckman, told the super that the gang must be from round here, and he gave the super a confidential twenty-four seven support-line phone number. I mention that solely to show

how confident Sir Miles is of that information. As to where the info originated . . . your guess is as good as mine. SOCA get up to all sorts of tricks. Anyway, this country-house gang is tightly run and highly successful at what it does. They've carried out five multimillion-pound robberies this year without leaving anything helpful behind for the respective SOCO teams to work on. Also the stolen items have not turned up anywhere even though many of them are easily identifiable antiques. Because of the style and method, I believe that the leader has adopted the Lamm method of operating.'

Crisp said, 'The Lamm method, sir? Hermann Lamm? I've heard of him. Fantastic man! Wonderful leader!'

'Don't glorify him, lad,' Angel said. 'He was an out-and-out villain.'

'I'm not doing that, sir, but it was fantastic how he always cased the target personally, built replica sets of the scene, trained and rehearsed his men, set a time limit that he considered safe in which to do the job, which had to be adhered to, and then planned their escape route in meticulous detail with permutations of optional escape routes and tactics in case anything went wrong.'

Angel blinked. 'Aye. That's right,' he said. 'Well, I was going to say all that.'

Crisp grinned and looked at Flora Carter, then at Ahmed.

'In addition,' Angel said, 'an important requirement of each gang member was that he could keep his trap shut. Now I don't quite know how Hermann Lamm would have reacted if he had found out that one of his gang had flashed big money about in a bar, or shot off his mouth to a girlfriend, but I don't expect it would have been friendly or that he would have reacted with sweet reasonableness. Now I think that Stefan Muldoon was a member of the country-house gang who *didn't* keep his trap shut and that the gang leader, whoever he is, took a gun and a pair of pliers to Muldoon and shut him up permanently. And he did it in such a way that there isn't a newspaper in the country — maybe the world — that didn't report his horrific death, which would be a lesson to the criminal world, not to mess with the leader of the country-house gang.'

Crisp and Carter nodded in agreement.

'You said you had a lead, sir?' Carter said.

'Yes,' Angel said. 'DI Lord from Skiptonthorpe told me — '

Crisp and Carter groaned unexpectedly, in unison.

Angel glared at them. 'What's that all about?'

'Do you think you can rely on anything DI Lord told you, sir?' Crisp said.

Flora Carter looked at Angel and nodded in support of Crisp. 'Yes, sir,' she said.

'He may be a bit pompous, but he's the source of our lead, and in the absence of any other, we have to follow it up. Now then, Lord told me that his team found prints of Sean Noel Riley on Muldoon's premises.'

He nodded to PC Ahaz, who handed A4 computer print-outs to Crisp and Carter. They were head-and-shoulders photographs, with a description underneath of a thickset man, six feet one, thirteen stone, aged forty-four, almost bald, with a scar across his left eye. The sergeants looked at the pics.

'He got the scar from a bottle fight in a quayside pub in Dublin in 1999,' Angel said. 'Not the sort of bloke you'd take home to Mother.'

Crisp and Carter frowned and exchanged sideways glances.

'We don't know much else about him. Served three years in Strangeways for possession of a firearm. Came out 1987. Before that only trivial stuff. 1986 accused of shoplifting, but released because the shopkeeper declined to give evidence against him. 1985, breach of the peace, throwing missile at moving police car, part of a park bench, got off with a warning. That's all. Associates, Stefan Muldoon. Well, I told you about him. And Peter Amos Kidd, aka Peter Walters, aka Peter Waterstone, serving twelve years in Peterhead for armed robbery. That's it.'

'You think that Riley murdered Muldoon, sir?' Carter said.

'I *don't* think so. I think the gang leader would have done that. I don't think that Riley is smart enough to be the gang leader. No, Sean Noel Riley is known to have been in the company of Stefan Muldoon sometime during the last week of his life. Riley's prints were on an empty can of lager found in Muldoon's waste bin. Now, there are a million reasons why he could have been there, but as they were both known crooks and, as both had not been found involved in any criminal activity for twelve years, I reckon the explanation could have been that they had learned their lesson, had gone straight and that they were busily engaged in some honest, wholesome endeavour such as planning to take the local old people on a day trip to Scarborough . . . or Whitby.'

Angel paused. Crisp, Carter and Ahmed looked at him with jaws dropped.

'Alternatively,' Angel said quickly, 'that Sean Noel Riley and Stefan Muldoon were both members of the country-house gang, and because of the new discipline they had learned from the gang leader, they had both kept out of trouble with the law for twelve years, and they had met on that day for a nefarious reason of some sort.'

'*That*'s very much more likely, sir,' Crisp said.

Carter and Ahmed nodded unthinkingly in agreement.

'Exactly,' Angel said. 'And that's what *I* think. Now it will be no good us trying to *lean* on Riley. We have no evidence that he's a member of the gang, and without proof, we'd never get a word out of him. He will be far more scared of having his tongue ripped out of him than of spending time in the poky. So I want a twenty-four-hour surveillance on him. DI Lord said that he'd not interviewed him, so Riley will not be alert to the fact that we are actively interested in him, which gives us a big advantage. He won't know he's in the frame. I want to know who he knows, who he visits, where he goes, where the gang meet and so on. Firstly, we need to know where he lives.' He looked across at Ahmed. 'What's the address the probation office gave you, lad?'

'26 Edward Street, sir.'

'Right,' Angel said. 'We're going to need all the cunning, thoroughness and discernment we can muster. This might be the only lead we'll ever get. Trevor, you nip down to 26 Edward Street now and find a strategic position, just in case he still lives there. Take a camera. See what you can see. Don't speak to anybody. Report back to me if anything happens. I'll be down there myself very soon.'

Crisp dashed out.

'Ahmed, get me the manager of Bromersley post office on the phone.'

Ahmed made for the door.

Angel called after him: 'And send Ted Scrivens in.'

'Right, sir.'

'Flora, I want you to make up a small parcel about seven inches by four inches by one inch and address it to S.N. Riley Esq., 26 Edward Street, Bromersley, South Yorkshire.'

* * *

An hour later, a red post-office van drove slowly along Edward Street.

Two men in an unmarked Ford car at the opposite side of the road carefully observed it stop outside number 26. The two men in the car were Angel and Crisp.

The driver of the van stopped, switched off the engine and sat in the cab slowly sorting through a stone-coloured bag. He eventually found a small parcel and got out of the van. He walked slowly up to the door of number 26 and banged the knocker.

It was DC Scrivens in an official postman's coat and hat.

The sound of the banging came through the earpiece in Angel's ear.

He turned to Crisp and said, 'I hope *someone*'s in, after all this.'

Eventually the door was opened by a middle-aged woman in an apron. She was wiping her hands on a blue-and-white tea towel.

'A woman's answered,' Crisp said.

'Yes, sssh,' Angel said.

'Registered packet for Mr Riley,' he heard Scrivens say.

'Right,' the woman said, 'I'll sign for it.'

'No, love,' Scrivens said. 'It's for Mr Riley, Mr S.N. Riley. He has to sign for it.'

'It's all right. I always sign for anything for him.'

'It's 'person to person', missis,' Scrivens said. 'Special. Sorry. He has to sign for it, himself. It's a nuisance, I know. You his wife?'

'No.' She hesitated, then said, 'His partner.'

'Pity. It must be valuable. It's insured for five hundred pounds,' Scrivens said.

The woman's eyes glowed like a 707's landing lights.

'I'll have to come back,' Scrivens said. 'When will he be in?'

'Might be in tonight, later,' she said looking longingly at the small package. 'But you know, young man, I've always taken things in for him in the past.'

'Yes love, but this is special. New service. 'Person to person' they call it. I can't come back tonight. I finish at four. What time will he be in tomorrow?'

She put a hand on her cheek as she thought. 'If I tell him tonight, he could be in at say ten o'clock tomorrow morning. How's that?'

'I'll come back at ten o'clock in the morning then, if the boss lets me.'

'Righto,' she said, then she swiftly withdrew and closed the door.

Scrivens got back into the red post-office van and drove away.

The muscles round Angel's jaw tightened. He snatched out the earpiece, looked at Crisp and said, 'Riley's not there, but she knows where he is.'

'We'll have to come back,' Crisp said.

Angel was about to get out of the Ford when he saw the door of number 26 open again. It was the woman. She was wearing a light mackintosh. She stepped out on to the pavement, turned back to the door, locked it and walked briskly along the road in the opposite direction to where Crisp's car was parked.

He watched her until she was out of sight. Then he turned to Crisp and said, 'Follow me. In the car.'

Angel got out of the car and walked quickly to the end of the street. He peered round the corner. The street joined Bradford Road which eventually led to the M1 motorway. He looked up the road. It was mostly terrace houses. There was the occasional public house, and a small frontage of shops 200 yards up. There were only a few pedestrians. He didn't see her at first, but then he spotted her light-coloured raincoat and black hair about 100 yards away on the pavement at the opposite side of the road. She was striding out determinedly. He crossed the road, carefully avoiding a Bromersley service bus and two heavy wagons. When they had passed, he looked back up the road for her. She was nowhere to be seen. He raced up to where he had last seen her, outside the frontages of five small shops. She could have dodged into any one of them. He bit his lip. He looked into four of the five shops and there was no sign of her. The fifth shop had a flowery sign painted on its window, number 129. It read: Alan Abelson. Picture framers.

Showing through the glass door was a card with the word CLOSED printed on it. Angel saw this and tried the door handle. It wasn't locked. He pushed the door, it opened and a distant bell began to ring. He walked in. He realized he was past the point of no return. He had no idea where he was going with this move. The woman he had been following might not have gone into that shop at all. There was just as much possibility that she could have gone into the newsagents, the post office, the butchers, or the Chinese takeaway next door (which also had a CLOSED sign on the door). The odds were against him, at five to one.

Anyway, he was in there now. He looked round at the countless samples of, picture-frame extrusions in different patterns, colours, sizes and textures, about fifteen inches long, fastened to display boards on the walls, also the many framed cheap prints of well-known pictures hanging above them. In between a collection of smaller pictures on the wall he noted a shiny piece of glass the size of the diameter of a policeman's whistle. It was the lens of a CCTV camera, photographing him and recording his every move.

It made him realize his possible dilemma. He couldn't admit to tailing a woman. That could blow the entire country-house gang surveillance mission.

He heard a shuffling noise. A person appeared between two display boards. The person stood there like a small stone pillar.

'We are closed, sir,' the person said. 'There is a sign on the door.'

Angel reckoned it was a woman. An old woman with grey hair. She had a gold cross with a figure of Christ on it in the form of a pendant on a gold chain hanging round her neck.

'I am sorry,' Angel said. 'I didn't see it. I have a painting I wanted framing.'

His acting wouldn't have won him any Oscars.

'We're closed,' she said.

'It's only a small painting. Are you open tomorrow?'

'Might be.'

'I'll call back when I can. I'm a policeman,' he said watching her face for a reaction. There was nothing. 'I'm with the Bromersley force, on Church Street station. I'll leave my card, if I may?'

She didn't say anything. She didn't do anything. She stood there like a letterbox.

He pulled a card out of his top pocket and held it for a second. She didn't offer to take it, so he placed it on the counter and came out of the shop.

He looked round for Crisp. He saw him in his car, fifty yards away, waiting at the side of the road with the engine running. He crossed the road, waved him up and got inside.

'Any luck, sir,' Crisp said.

He wrinkled his nose. 'I lost her,' he said. 'I don't know where she went to. Get back to that last address. Let's hope Riley turns up.'

Crisp drove the car back to the surveillance position on Edward Street, then Angel left him, walked to his car a few streets away and returned to the station.

12

Angel parked the BMW and dashed into the station by the back door, passing the cells and up the green corridor.

'Ahmed,' he called as he passed the CID room.

The young man came running to the door.

'Find out who owns 129 Bradford Road. It's a picture-framer's shop.'

'Right, sir.'

'And there's something else, lad. Sean Noel Riley served three years from 1986 to 1989 in Strangeways for possession of a gun. Find out if Peter Queegley was in Strangeways at the same time. We need to find as many links to the country-house gang as we can. I believe that Stefan Muldoon was part of that gang and Riley's fingerprints were found on an empty can of lager in his office. If Queegley and Riley also struck up a relationship then it is possible that Queegley is also a member of the gang, got it?'

Ahmed grinned. 'Got it, sir.'

Angel reached his office to find the phone ringing. He reached over and lifted it to his ear. It was the civilian woman on the station switchboard. 'There's a young woman on the line — at least she sounds young. She's a bit worked up about something. Will only speak to you. Says her name is Jessica Razzle.'

Angel wrinkled his nose. 'Put her through, please.'

'Is that Inspector Angel?'

She sounded angry.

'Speaking. What's the matter, Jessica?'

'Ah,' she sighed. 'She's gone, Inspector. Rosemary's gone. I thought she would. She's flown the coop and taken all sorts of things. The house is deserted. Most of her clothes, all her jewellery, everything of value. You know she's got all the bonds and the shares and everything.'

Angel blinked and said, 'How do you know? Where are you speaking from?'

'I'm at home, of course. At The Manor House.'

He frowned. 'What are you doing there? You're not supposed to be there . . . I'll come over.'

Angel replaced the phone. He was at The Manor House in five minutes. The front door was open and, as he reached it, he heard Jessica Razzle call out, 'Come in, Inspector. Come straight through. I'm in the kitchen. I've made you a cup of tea.'

The tea would be very welcome, but that

was not what he was there for. He closed the door, marched down the hall to the kitchen. She pointed to a beaker of tea and pushed the sugar bowl and a plastic bottle of milk towards him. He looked at the date on the milk. 'Use by Jun 1.'

'Was this in the fridge?'

'Yes. I'm sure it's all right, Inspector. I've had some.'

'No,' he said, shaking his head. 'I was trying to work out . . . Never mind.'

He poured a little in to his tea, stirred it noisily, put the spoon on the worktop and took a sip. It tasted good. He sat down opposite her, looked around then said, 'What are you doing here? Aren't you breaking the terms of your conditional discharge?'

'Oh *that*?' she said, wrinkling her nose, causing her spectacles to go up. 'I haven't been anywhere near *her* She isn't here. I have no idea where she is. Probably never ever see her again. And she's managed the perfect murder, and cleaned me out. It's not a bit fair.'

'Looks like you've got a house,' he said. '*And* the furniture. *And* a very big allowance.'

She nodded. 'But Rosemary's got absolutely *millions*.'

'And I keep telling you she could not have murdered your father. She has one of the best alibis anybody could have.'

'I know. She had an accomplice. Somebody who had a front-door key, who knew where . . .'

Angel peered at her. 'As a matter of fact, how did you get in here? The house was locked up, wasn't it?'

Her eyes flashed. 'I live here, for god's sake,' she said. 'Dad gave me a key when I was fourteen. I've had a key ever since we moved in here from the other house.'

Angel's forehead creased. He pursed his lips. 'Listen to me, Jessica. The murderer had a front-door key. Has your key ever been out of your possession? Have you ever loaned it to a friend, a workman, a deliveryman, to deliver or leave something, or pick something up or do some work on the house? Or did you ever lose it? These would have all been opportunities for a would-be intruder to take a cast and make a copy.'

'No. Not that I remember.'

He took another sip of the tea. It gave him time to think. 'You said that Rosemary had taken things. Her clothes, her jewellery, her bonds and shares. Has she taken anything that isn't hers?'

Jessica pulled a face. 'Yes. I am entitled to a proportion of the money.'

'I thought the terms of the will were that

your allowance could be increased if you were in need of it and Rosemary agreed. That's right, isn't it?'

'Huh. She was never going to agree to giving *me* an increase, was she?'

'So she hasn't taken anything that isn't hers?'

She glared at him. 'I knew you'd take her side.'

'I haven't taken her side. It's just the way it is.'

Jessica Razzle's lip quivered.

Angel said: 'Consider this, Jessica. I'm sure that if Rosemary was here, she'd accuse *you* of murdering your father.'

Her eyes shone like Strangeways' tower searchlights. 'Ridiculous. I adored my father.'

'I daresay, but *she*'d probably say that you could have sneaked into the house. You had a key. You knew where the CCTV cameras were located. You knew where your father's handgun was kept. You could have known how to set the combination on the security door.'

'Ridiculous. And what would have been my motive?'

'To steal the contents of the safe.'

'Outrageous. As if I'd put the contents of the safe ahead of the love of my father.'

Angel shrugged. 'I only said that that's

probably what your stepmother would say.'

'Huh. It's *her* I tell you. She has an accomplice somewhere.'

'So you keep saying.'

'Anyway, what was in the safe?'

'I don't know.'

Jessica finished her tea. She went to the sink, rinsed her beaker, put it on the drainer and turned back to Angel.

'What are you going to do about finding her, then?'

'I don't need to do anything,' he said, 'unless she fails to attend the court to answer the charge of assault on you and causing a public disturbance.'

'Huh. You'll never see her again.'

'We'll see,' he said as he passed over his empty beaker.

She took it, rinsed it and put it on the drainer. She turned back. 'Incidentally, I haven't heard anything more about that court case.'

'You will. You'll get a brown envelope from the CPS, giving you the date of the hearing. In the meantime, I hope you're not thinking of moving back in here.'

Her eyes flashed. 'Why not? It's my home.'

He licked his bottom lip and shook his head.

'Four reasons,' he said. 'One, it's against

your conditional discharge. Two, Rosemary might return and if she did there would be nothing but trouble if she found you here. Three, it isn't safe. There is still a murderer out there and we know he has a front-door key.'

Angel noticed that she shuddered as she turned and pressed her back against the sink.

'You'll be quite safe at The Feathers,' he said. 'There are always people around the hotel.'

'And what's four?' she said, looking up.

'And four, there are some further investigations I want my forensic team to make in your late father's workshop. It will be much more convenient for them if the house is unoccupied.'

⋆ ⋆ ⋆

It was ten minutes past five when Angel took his leave of Jessica Razzle and stepped out of The Manor House. He got into the BMW, started the engine, pointed the bonnet towards home and switched on the radio.

'More news is coming in regarding that gold and plaster statue of Dorothea Jordan,' a woman's voice said. 'We hear that the auctioneer's estimate has now reached a million pounds. Julia Weekes is at Spicers', the auctioneers for us on Royal Crown Road. A million pounds seems to be a lot of money for a plaster statue even if it is plated with gold, Julia?' she said.

'That's right, Marie. I am standing outside Spicers' imposing Georgian stone-pillared doorway where, earlier today, I collected a catalogue of the sale, and lot 1 — unusually the very first lot — is what all the fuss is about. It is described as, 'A plaster-cast recumbent statue lavishly coated in 24-carat gold of Dorothea Jordan, 1762–1816, actress and mistress of the future King William IV, and universally regarded as the most beautiful woman in the world. Estimate £1m to £1.5m'.'

'Is the public much interested in bidding for the statue?'

'It's difficult to say. The statue has been given pride of place on a dais in Spicers' entrance hall, so that everybody coming into the building has to pass it. I must say that hardly anybody goes by without giving it a look and reading the placard with all its intriguing past, historical significance and provenance. Earlier, I managed to speak to an American antique dealer from California, Abner Spiegel. I asked him what he thought about it.'

The recording of a man who spoke through

his nose was inserted here. He said, 'Well, gee. She looks absolutely fabulous. The provenance is right. It is obviously a highly desirable statue with historical, royal and erotic connotations. It will certainly sell. Whether one million sterling, is the market price, I don't know?'

'Will you be bidding, Mr Spiegel?'

'Depends how it goes, ma'am.'

'Thank you. Then I spoke to a bystander, a Mr Alec Underwood . . . '

At the mention of Alec Underwood's name, Angel blinked and his hold on the steering wheel tightened.

'Alec Underwood,' the radio interviewer said. 'What do you think to the Dorothea Jordan statue?'

'I find it extremely interesting. I expect it will fetch a lot of money. It is an item that is fascinating people from all over the world.'

'Why?'

'Well, it is historically extremely important, isn't it? I understand that at the time Mrs Dorothea Jordan was regarded as a strikingly attractive woman and that she bore the Duke of Clarence, later King William IV, ten children. The mould of the statue was actually taken from Dorothea Jordan's body, and the gold-plated life-size statue occupied pride of place on a couch in his bedroom at

Windsor Castle for twenty-one years, including the period of his reign from 1830 until his death in 1837. And then, there is this film coming out with Sincerée La More playing the part of Dorothea Jordan. With all this hype, this beautiful antique could hardly fail to command a high price.'

'And will you be among the bidders, Mr Underwood?'

Angel noticed that there was some hesitation, before Underwood said, 'I will have to think about that.'

The interview stopped there and the TV reporter said, 'Everybody playing their cards close to their chests, Marie.'

'Julia Weekes there for us at Spicers' auction house here in London. Moving on. The Footsie 100 fell again — '

Angel reached out and switched the radio off. He turned off the main road into Forest Hill Estate. He couldn't get away from that plaster statue. It seemed to haunt him wherever he went. He was positive Underwood was planning something bent.

'And will you be among the bidders, Mr Underwood?' he had heard the interviewer ask. Angel sniffed. Alec Underwood had never bought anything at the market price in his life. If he couldn't buy it cheap enough, he'd steal it. Angel pursed his lips. Was that his game? Was he planning to steal the statue? If he stole it, it would be the biggest scam he had ever pulled. The auctioneers had put a speculative million-pound-plus price-ticket on it, making it such a high-profile antique. And Underwood had been seen so near to it, interviewed about it. If he intended stealing the statue, Angel now had his address; at least he would know where to begin to look. He'd be an obvious suspect. He'd never get away with it.

What was happening out there in this wacky world, Angel wondered? A million pounds for that gold-plated plaster statue was ridiculous. He rubbed his chin, thoughtfully. Then again, so was his gas bill.

* * *

'Come in,' Angel said.

It was PC Ahaz. 'Good morning, sir. I have checked up on Peter Queegley's time in Strangeways.'

'Ah,' Angel said, eyebrows raised.

'Sean Noel Riley came out in April 1989, and Queegley didn't go in until January 1990. Sorry, sir.'

Angel shook his head and sighed. 'Right, lad.'

Ahmed said, 'My grandmother used to say

that disappointments were good for young folks, sir.'

Angel's teeth showed as his face muscles tightened. 'But your grandmother didn't have to deal with obnoxious oily ne'er-do-wells like Peter Queegley and Alec Underwood.'

'My grandfather was enough for her, sir. I have the owner of 129 Bradford Road, sir. The picture-framer's shop. It's a Mrs Aimée Podlitz, of the same address. She must live over the shop.'

'Oh. Podlitz? Foreign. Right. Find out if there's anything known.'

'Nothing known, sir. I knew you'd ask.'

Angel nodded. He was pleased. Ahmed was using his initiative. 'Who else lives on the premises?'

Ahmed's jaw dropped. 'Didn't get *that*, sir.'

'Do it now. You'll want the town hall.'

'Yes. I know how to find out, sir,' he said.

Angel said, 'And while you're about it, find out who lives at 26 Edward Street.'

'Right, sir,' he said and he went out.

Trevor Crisp came in.

'Good morning, sir.'

'Good morning, lad,' Angel said pointing to the chair.

Crisp sat down. 'That woman came back to 26 Edward Street at six o'clock last night, and Riley turned up there at nine fifteen.'

Angel looked up. His eyes locked momentarily on to Crisp's. 'Ah,' he said, pleased to hear some good news for a change.

'And I saw a light go on in the front bedroom at ten o'clock just before I knocked off,' Crisp said.

'And who is down there now?'

'Ted Scrivens.'

Angel rubbed his chin. 'I was thinking that it would be great to get a bug in there, but, you know, if the woman is not part of the gang, then he wouldn't talk such private stuff to her, would he?'

'I would have thought it worth the risk, sir.'

'If we make Riley suspicious, he'll go to ground and we may never get a lead again.'

'I could go in there as a meter reader.'

'It's been done so many times, lad.' He thought about it a few moments then said, 'We'll wait a day. See what else we can find out. We are monitoring his post and his landline. Are there any empty houses opposite? Any For Sale boards up anywhere?'

'Had a good look last night, sir.'

'Do we know anybody who lives in an odd number on there?'

'Don't know of anybody, sir.'

'No,' Angel said, running his hand through his hair.

The phone rang. Angel reached out for it.

It was Superintendent Harker. 'There's a triple nine. A dead woman with facial injuries found in long grass by a lay-by opposite Strawberry Reservoir between Sheffield and Bromersley.'

Angel squeezed the phone, his pulse racing. 'Right, sir,' he said.

'A man parking his car with the intention of going fishing found the body,' the superintendent said. 'He's standing by. Do you know where that reservoir is?'

'Yes, sir. I'm on my way.'

'Is it on Sheffield's patch?'

Angel realized that it was. He hesitated. 'Possibly,' he said.

There was a pause, then Harker said, 'I believe it is. Don't move until I get back to you.'

'I don't mind, sir. I can do it.'

Harker sniggered. 'You just love a good murder, Angel, don't you?' he said. 'Don't move a muscle. I'll check with Sheffield and get straight back to you. We've quite enough on here, and I don't want it going in our statistics unnecessarily. The figures are bad enough.' The phone went dead.

Angel put it back in its cradle.

Crisp stared at him.

'A dead woman with facial injuries,' Angel said slowly while rubbing his chin, 'found in long grass by a lay-by opposite Strawberry Reservoir.'

Crisp shook his head and frowned, 'As if we haven't enough on.'

Angel's eyes flashed. 'One murder case helps the others. Obviously takes more time. The initial routine is exactly the same. Gathering facts. After that, anybody with a tidy, methodical mind can assemble them and permutate them until out pops the answer.'

'It never works for me, sir.'

'It won't work for anybody if they haven't enough information.'

Crisp shook his head. 'You make it sound easy.'

'It *is* easy.'

'For you, sir, maybe.'

'With me, it's a habit.'

'With you, sir, it's a gift.'

The phone rang. Angel reached out for it.

It was Superintendent Harker again. 'Stand down. Sheffield are dealing with it.'

Angel's jaw stiffened. He wasn't pleased. He replaced the phone.

'I have to know who she was and how she died,' he said.

Crisp said, 'You're not expecting it to be Rosemary Razzle are you, sir?'

Angel hadn't realized that he had expressed his thoughts out loud.

'Eh? I don't know. It is a woman with facial injuries, and I need to know who she is, not who I expect it to be.'

Crisp frowned. 'You've lost me, sir.'

'Forget it,' Angel suddenly said and jumped to his feet. 'Have you got a camera?'

'In my desk, sir.'

'Get it quick. Come on. We'll go in my car.'

Angel raced out of the office. Crisp followed and called in to CID office for a camera. They met outside at Angel's BMW.

Angel knew exactly where the lay-by was and they were there in ten or eleven minutes. It was on an important fast road out in the country, opposite Strawberry Reservoir at the bottom of a long hill. There was a gathering of four men on the pavement by the lay-by leaning against their bicycles, each man had a fishing rod fastened to the crossbar. The men were standing there in the sunshine smoking cigarettes and expectantly watching every car that came near, hoping that it was a police car that would take over their self-appointed guardianship of a dead body.

As Angel and Crisp approached the lay-by, they could not see any signs of a dead body, but there was a lot of long grass everywhere, waving in the warm breeze.

As the BMW pulled up, it was besieged by the elderly fishermen, a curious, lined and tanned face at each window.

'The dead woman's over here,' one said, pointing ten feet away in the long grass. 'She's not breathing and as stiff as a board.'

'It's a dreadful sight. She looks awful,' said another, turning away and swallowing hard.

'I was the one what found her. I was the one what phoned up,' said a third.

'All her innards have come out of her mouth. Nobody should treat a woman like that.'

'Thank you, gentlemen,' Angel said getting out of the car. 'Please come away from the crime scene. The investigating team will not want you trampling over any possible forensic evidence.'

The men looked at each other in surprise.

'We want to go fishing. We've told you all we know. You can't want anything else from us.'

Angel said nothing. He stuck out his chest and walked a little way up the hill, the men following him, while Crisp sneaked out of the car and up the banking.

'Are you not the police, then?' the first man said.

Crisp easily found the mound of nondescript clothes in the long grass, and photographed it six times from different angles without touching it.

'We're just here to check that the integrity of the murder scene is being properly preserved,' Angel said to the men, as he saw Crisp running back to the car. 'Thank you very much. Please keep everybody away from it until Sheffield CID arrive.'

'How long will they be?' said one of the men.

Angel looked up the hill in the direction of Sheffield. He was surprised to see two police cars and a white van in procession, all flashing blue lights and approaching fast.

'There they are now,' he said, running back down the hill towards the BMW.

He climbed into the driver's seat, glanced at Crisp and started the engine.

Crisp looked pale.

'Everything all right?' Angel said.

'Got plenty of pics, sir,' Crisp said with a long sigh.

Angel pulled away from the crime scene only half a minute before Sheffield's SOCO's van wheels rolled to a stop on the very same grass verge.

'Who is it then?' Angel said. 'Recognize her?'

He put his hand to his forehead. 'No, sir. Pretty ghastly. Her own mother wouldn't recognize her.'

13

Back at the police station Angel and Crisp rushed into the theatre and transferred the pictures on to the viewing screen.

The photographs were horrible, but Angel had seen worse. The clearest photograph showed what seemed to be a bundle of rags with a grey ball at the top sparsely covered with grey hair, below that, red raw flesh with blue streaks. Beneath that, something shiny and yellow had caught the light of the sun. It confounded Angel for a while, until he enlarged the image up to the point at which the photograph dissolved into pixels, then brought it back a step. He could see that it was the profile view of a gold crucifix on a chain.

His eyebrows shot up. He nodded thoughtfully. 'We are rattling the big man's cage, Trevor,' he said rubbing his chin. 'We are in dangerous territory.'

Crisp frowned. 'You know this woman, sir?'

'She was the old woman in the picture-framing shop. Mrs Aimée Podlitz.'

He reached out for the phone and tapped in a number.

'*That* old woman?' Crisp lowered his eyes. His hands shook. Then he looked up at Angel. 'I wouldn't like to think that my mother suffered anything like that, sir.'

'It's a similar case to Stefan Muldoon,' Angel said.

'The woman you spoke to only yesterday?' Crisp said. 'And can you identify her from *that* picture?'

He nodded. 'He's had to resort to murdering an old woman fronting a picture-framing business to try to put the fear of God into anybody trying to get nearer to him.'

The phone was answered. Angel spoke into it.

'Ahmed,' he said. 'I want you to find out who owns the property, next door to, and at the back of, the picture-framing business at 129 Bradford Road, and phone it through to me asap.'

'Right, sir,' Ahmed said.

Angel replaced the phone.

'That was the country-house gang's HQ, sir?'

'Probably. I'm not sure of anything, lad, but what crook do you know who would murder anyone and leave a gold pendant and chain worth maybe two hundred pounds round the dead person's neck?'

Crisp's eyes narrowed.

'None, eh?' Angel said. 'Our man is way above risking being caught by being in possession of a two-hundred-pound necklace. He's playing for thousands. Must be him. The picture-framing shop might just be the way in, past the CCTV camera, so that all visitors — not that there'd be many — are clocked in, literally. He needed a place to store the loot and vehicles to transport it about the place. Maybe there are garages at the rear. They'll be in Aimée Podlitz's name, if they are. Anyway, whatever he was using there, he'll have cleared out of them by now. But we've got to have a look.'

* * *

'Come in,' Angel said.

It was Flora Carter. 'You wanted me, sir?'

'Yes. I want you to get together as many officers as you can to make an immediate assault on the 129 Bradford Road picture-framing shop and residential accommodation, and the lock-up garages and outbuildings at the back. I have reason to believe that the premises might have been the HQ of the country-house gang, and that they may have vacated them late yesterday or even overnight. An elderly woman who apparently worked at the shop, possibly a member of the gang, was found dead earlier today away from the house.'

'Is that the woman who has had her tongue pulled out, sir?' Flora Carter said.

'Well, yes. It seems to be the mark of the leader of the country-house gang to instil discipline. He's doing it to scare everybody.'

Her pretty mouth twitched. 'Yes. Well, he's . . . he's succeeding, sir,' Flora Carter said.

Angel looked at her a moment then said, 'Turn that fear into determination, Flora. Because we are coppers we can never run. We've always got to fight.'

She swallowed quickly, straightened up and said, 'Yes, sir. I know that.'

'Liaise with SOCO's Don Taylor. Treat it like a crime scene. If it's been abandoned in a hurry, you never know what valuable clues might have been left behind. That man might have slipped up for the very first time in his life.'

There was a knock at the door.

'Come in,' Angel said.

PC Ahaz came in, his eyes glowing. He looked at Carter and then at Angel.

'Excuse me, sir. I thought you'd want to know. Bradford Road is blocked. Traffic for the M1 is at a standstill.'

Carter said: 'Bradford Road?'

'Yes, Sarge.'

Angel's eyes narrowed. He wasn't pleased. 'Blocked? Why is it blocked?'

'Apparently there's a big fire, sir. I heard about it in the canteen. Inspector Asquith has summoned all his units to attend.'

Angel snatched up the phone and tapped in a 7.

It was soon answered by the duty sergeant in the control room.

'What's this about a fire, Sergeant?'

'Yes, sir. It's developing into a big one, sir. A Chinese woman reported the smell of fire in a picture-framing shop next door to her takeaway business on Bradford Road at 1128 hours this morning. Fire service were informed immediately. Logged in at 1129 hours.'

'I suppose the address is 129 Bradford Road.'

'As a matter of fact it is, sir. Fancy that. I have an update on that incident, just in, sir. It says, 'Fire has developed and spread to shops either side, and at storage premises and garages at the rear. Flames are ten metres high. Five fire tenders are now on the scene. Two more are coming from Rotherham. Residents of nearby houses have already been evacuated to Farr Street church hall. The road is likely to be blocked for at least six hours. Diversions have been set up.' I know that Inspector Asquith is out there with all the uniformed he could muster.'

'Right, lad, thank you,' Angel said. 'I've heard enough.' He replaced the phone. His face was like his mother's Yorkshire pudding, after the shilling in the gas had run out.

Ahmed said, 'Did it start in that picture-framer's shop you asked me about, sir?'

'Yes,' Angel said. He ran his hand through his hair. 'And there goes any chance of recovering prints, DNA or anything else useful from that damned place.'

'I also came in to tell you that Mrs Podlitz is the only person on the electoral roll at that address, sir. She is also down as the owner of the garages and outhouses at the rear. Also, I looked up 26 Edward Street. Mrs Violet Beasley is the only name down as resident on the electoral roll.'

Angel's eyebrows went up. 'Right,' he said, banging his fist on the desk.

'Also, there's nothing known about Violet Beasley or Violet Small, her maiden name, sir,' Ahmed finished with a self-satisfied nod.

Angel looked up at him. He was pleasantly surprised. 'Thank you, Ahmed,' he said.

Ahmed went out.

Angel rubbed the lobe of his ear between finger and thumb for a few seconds, then said, 'Flora, looks like we can't make any progress on the country-house gang for the moment. That clever man has got one over us again. Let's take advantage of The Manor House being unoccupied. There must be something we have overlooked in that cellar that would help identify Charles Razzle's murderer. I know you've already looked at everything, but did you actually move the stuff against the walls, the safe for instance?'

'No, sir.'

'Right. Withdraw the front door key from the stores. Take a few hefty lads from CID. Move what you have to. Same with the walls. I want you to take a final thorough look round the place. There must be something there we have overlooked.'

'Right, sir.'

'I'm going to visit that security specialist, Brian Farleigh.'

* * *

Farleigh smiled and looked around his showroom. There were no customers, only the pretty receptionist at the desk by the door.

'Shall we sit where we sat before, Inspector?' he said.

Angel nodded and flopped into an easy chair in a corner of the room.

'What can I do for you this sunny afternoon?' Farleigh said breezily. 'I assume that it is in connection with the murder of Mr Razzle.'

Angel sighed. 'Yes indeed. I just want to check on a few facts, Mr Farleigh. It is a mystery as to how the murderer managed to enter the house so boldly by the front door.'

'Must have had a key.'

'Oh yes. The windows and the back door were all closed and secure. So he certainly came in that way and he definitely used a key. I have accounted for all the official keys. So he must have used a copy . . . but I don't know how he might have come by it. Then he managed to dodge the two CCTV cameras, enter the cellar workshop, shoot Charles Razzle, set it up to look like it was the robot who had committed the crime, and then make his escape. Now, Mr Farleigh, I believe that there must be a way out of the workshop or at least a place where a man could have hidden down there, to make his escape at a later time . . . and I was just checking with you that you didn't come across such a possible hiding-place when you were fitting the security door for him.'

Farleigh grinned. 'You have already asked me that, Inspector?'

Angel hunched his shoulders slightly. 'Yes,

well, when we can't solve a crime,' he said, 'we go back over things. Maybe ask the same questions, hoping that we might glean a titbit of extra information that could provide another line of inquiry.'

Farleigh shook his head. 'No, Inspector. Sorry. I don't know of anything new or different. I just supplied and fitted the door. Charles Razzle wouldn't let me work on anything without him being there. He was very secretive.'

Angel wrinkled his nose.

'Sorry, I can't be more helpful,' Farleigh said.

Angel's mobile rang. He frowned, rummaged in his coat pocket, looked at Farleigh and said, 'Excuse me.'

It was Flora Carter. She sounded breathless. 'Sorry to bother you, sir. We're here in the cellar workshop at The Manor House.'

Angel turned away. 'Speak up, lass. It's a bad line. Did you say you were speaking from the cellar workshop at the Razzle's house?'

'Yes, sir,' she said. 'We've found a CCTV camera concealed in the wall.'

Angel's face brightened. 'Has it got tape in it?'

'Yes, sir.'

'Is it possible it was recording the night that Charles Razzle was murdered?'

'I don't know that for certain, sir,' Carter said, 'but that's what I was wondering.'

Angel nodded and looked at his watch. It was five o'clock exactly.

'We need SOCO to look at it for prints before we can actually view what has been recorded,' he said. 'You'll have to leave it where it is until morning. But be sure and lock the workshop door. It'll be safe there overnight.'

'Right, sir.'

Angel gave a big sigh and smiled. 'Great stuff, Flora. Well done. See you in the morning.'

Angel pocketed the mobile and turned back to Farleigh, who was thumbing through one of his own catalogues.

'Sorry about that, Mr Farleigh,' Angel said.

Farleigh looked up. 'That's all right,' he said closing the catalogue and tossing it to a table nearby. 'I'm sorry that I am not able to add to my original statement.'

'You only know what you know,' Angel said, getting to his feet. 'Well, must be off. Good afternoon.'

* * *

It was ten minutes past midnight. The sky was as black as fingerprint ink. The only sound to be heard was the nearby rustle of trees and bushes and the distant hum of traffic on the motorway a mile away.

A high-powered car whispered its way slowly past the front of The Manor House on Creesforth Road. It ran out of sight, then came back three minutes later with its lights switched off and drifted even more slowly past the big house. Then it speeded up and disappeared.

Twenty minutes later, the figure of a tall man in a black hat materialized from behind a laurel bush in The Manor House front garden. He was carrying a black canvas bag. He stood motionless. He was looking and listening. Then he suddenly darted across the lawn in the direction of the house and stood by a small bush four metres from the front door. Moments later he reached the front door, opened the canvas bag and took out a pair of earphones and a microphone. He put the earphones on and plugged them into a power pack round his waist. He pushed the microphone on a short wire through the letterbox on the front door, plugged the other end into the power pack, turned up the power and listened.

The listening system was so powerful that, reputedly at twenty metres, it could hear a mouse attempting to dislodge a sliver of mutton stuck between its molars. However, nothing was heard, so the man returned the microphone and earphones to the canvas bag, inserted a key in the front door and entered the house.

When inside he took a headband with a small handtorch fitted to it out of the bag, slipped it over his head, switched it on and adjusted the light beam to shine directly ahead. He made his way through the hall to the kitchen and down the basement steps to the security door to the workshop. There, he quickly secured a small processor to the door lock with magnets, connected it to a hand-held computer powered by the power pack on his waist and started a search for the lock combination. It soon connected, and in seconds the six digits were shown on the LCD. He tapped the number displayed on to the keypad on the door, there was a click and the door opened a centimetre. He pulled the connecting wires out of the equipment, put it in his bag, reached up the door handle, pulled open the door and went into the workshop.

No sooner had he entered the room than the light went on.

The intruder saw Crisp standing resolutely in front of him. He looked round to see Angel, who said, 'Strange place for you to be at this time of night, Mr Farleigh?'

Brian Farleigh's eyes flashed in every direction. His face glowed scarlet. His breathing was rapid. His head shook. He froze momentarily. Then with tremendous determination, he suddenly turned, brushed past Angel and made a run for the door. Angel reached out for him and caught his left arm. Farleigh turned back and lunged out at Angel's head with his right fist and missed. Angel hung on. Farleigh made another lunge and missed again. Angel improved his grip on Farleigh's arm, then, with a quick twist of his wrist and a push at his elbow, the man dropped to the floor with a scream. Angel followed him down and brought the big man's arm up round his back. Farleigh struggled like a madman. Crisp rushed over with the handcuffs and, putting his knee in Farleigh's back, the two policemen secured one wrist in them and then, after a struggle, the other. Then they rose to their feet, pulling Farleigh up between them.

When Farleigh's shining big eyes met Angel's, he yelled, 'It was a trick, you bastard! A filthy trick.'

Angel nodded and said, 'Rather good, wasn't it?' He turned to Crisp and said, 'Search him. Then charge him.'

Crisp said, 'Spread your feet.'

Farleigh did so grudgingly and Crisp began

patting him down.

Over his shoulder Farleigh looked at Angel and said, 'What are you charging me with?'

'The murder of Charles Razzle. What did you think?' Angel said.

'Ridiculous. What motive could I possibly have for murdering him?'

'Robbery,' Angel said as he dusted down his suit with his hands.

There was a pause.

Crisp began emptying Farleigh's pockets.

'Robbery of what?' Farleigh said.

'The contents of that safe.'

'How would I know what was in his safe?'

'You saw the contents when you fitted this door and you've been wanting to get your sticky fingers in there ever since.'

'That's not true. What proof have you got that I knew what was in there?'

'The fact that it was found empty after his dead body was found.'

'That's not proof, and it's not proof that I murdered him.'

'Robbery was the motive, and *you* stole the stuff. We've plenty of proof of the murder. Firstly, rather obviously, what are you doing here now, and don't say you fancied a midnight stroll. You've already acknowledged you were tricked.'

'No comment.'

'Exactly. You were worried in case a CCTV camera, which doesn't exist, had film showing you murdering Charles Razzle and ransacking his safe.'

'No comment.'

'And where did you magic a front-door key from in a matter of six hours? It was the same key you used to break in here on the twenty-fifth of May to murder Charles Razzle, wasn't it?'

'No comment.'

'No matter. We shall find it.'

Crisp took something out of Farleigh's jacket pocket and handed it to Angel.

Angel looked at it. It was a strangely shaped key. He nodded and said, 'Well, well, well. Here it is. Obviously home-made from the cast of an original. The jury will love that.'

Farleigh glared at it and said, 'It's a plant. I've never seen it before.'

Angel shook his head. 'You're a terrible actor, Farleigh. But what really brought you to my attention was the fact that it took you over two hours to open that door for Rosemary Razzle with your modern combination lock equipment the night you murdered him, while three days later, the police sergeant at the head of the CID Specialized Services, Cyphers, Codes and Combinations division, opened it in one minute and forty seconds, which was about the length of time it took you tonight. So why did it take you so long on the night of the murder?'

'No comment.'

Angel looked at Crisp, nodded and said, 'Get on with it, lad. I've a bed to go to.'

Crisp said, 'Brian Farleigh, I am arresting you on suspicion of murder. You do not have to say anything but it may harm your defence if you do not mention, when questioned, something . . . '

14

'Come in,' Angel said.

The office door opened. It was Ahmed, his eyes like two fried eggs in a frying pan. 'Good morning, sir. Is Mr Farleigh locked up for the murder of Charles Razzle?'

'He is, lad. Why?'

'Mmm. That's great, sir. He's making a lot of noise.'

'He can make as much noise as he likes. He'll get tired before we do.'

'He's saying he didn't do it sir, and he wants to see his solicitor.'

'Well, he can see his solicitor, but he'll have to give the poor man time to finish his kedgeree and devils on horseback. Find out who he is and tell him he has a client screaming out for his services.'

'Right, sir.'

'And there's no soap again in the washroom, Ahmed. When we've finished here, will you see if you can catch the cleaner before she goes and get a bar put in there?'

'Right, sir.'

'Now we've a lot to do this morning, Ahmed. I've no time — '

The phone rang. Angel reached out for it. It was Harker.

'Yes, sir?' Angel said.

Harker coughed several times into the mouthpiece, causing Angel to screw up his face and hold the phone away from his ear. When Angel thought he had finished the racket, he brought the phone back to his ear and had to endure another ear-splitting episode. Eventually, between the coughing, he managed to hear Harker say, 'Come up here, Angel. This is a very serious matter.' It was followed by more coughing.

Angel wrinkled his nose as he replaced the phone. He stood up. He looked across at the young constable. 'It's the super,' he said. 'I have to go.'

'Right, sir. I'll see if I can find the cleaner,' he said and went out.

Angel thought about what the 'serious matter' might be. There were quite a few peripheral matters and corners he had cut over the past two weeks, but he couldn't bring anything to mind that might be described in such terms. Of course, he had never adopted the HOLMES method of investigation, which in the UK was highly regarded and applied by most of the forty-three police forces. It had nothing to do with the fictional character, Sherlock Holmes.

The name was an innocent coincidence. HOLMES was an acronym for Home Office Large/Major Enquiry System, the UK mainframe police computer system.

Angel had never attempted to adopt this thorough and extreme system and he hoped that Harker hadn't suddenly realized that it should have been in use and that he intended to compel Bromersley force to embrace it.

He arrived at the superintendent's door. He took a deep breath, knocked, and walked in.

Harker glanced up from his overloaded desk. His eyes seemed more bloodshot than usual, his sparse grey/ginger/brown strands of hair even sparser than before, and his potato-shaped nose more purple than the red colour he usually showed.

He sniffed. 'Ah, yes. *You*, lad.' He reached out for a letter in one of the wire baskets on the desk in front of him. He read it, put it back, pulled out another, read that, looked up and said, 'You were assisting Sheffield CID last Tuesday?'

Angel blinked then he said, 'No, sir.'

Harker glared across at him. 'Your BMW was seen driving away from the crime scene at Strawberry Reservoir just as Detective Chief Inspector Pimm and his team were arriving. You took statements from the four witnesses and instructed them on how to behave at a crime scene.'

Angel's eyebrows shot up. 'No, sir. Not really. I — '

'Didn't I tell you to stand fast because the crime was in the Sheffield area and was nothing to do with us?'

'Yes, sir, but I needed to know whether the victim was who I thought it was.'

Harker was angry. His heavy eyebrows fluttered. 'Have you stopped taking orders from your superiors, then?'

'No, sir. You didn't order me not to *look* at the victim. I understood that you simply didn't want me to undertake the investigation of the case.'

'You did not only *look* at the victim, you had . . . DS Crisp, I suppose it was . . . take photographs. And you interviewed the four witnesses.'

'I didn't interview them, sir. I merely spoke to them, or rather they spoke to me.'

'Are you quibbling with me, lad? Did the witnesses impart any information to you about the dead woman or not?'

'Well, yes. I suppose . . . They sort of . . . volunteered it.'

'And did you have someone take photographs at the scene?'

'Well, er — yes. That was entirely at my instigation, sir.'

'DCI Pimm is not favourably impressed with this interference, lad. He is quite right to call it professional trespass. The matter will have to be reported to the chief constable. It will be up to him how far he wants to take the matter. We must retain a good professional relationship with all other forces, particularly those with whom we share a common boundary. Also, there's the matter of the taking of photographs of corpses that are not your case.'

Angel suddenly had an idea. 'Does DCI Pimm know the identity of the dead woman, sir?'

'Of course not. That's what's made him so angry. He says that he may never find out who she is.'

Angel ran his hand slowly across his mouth and said, 'That's true, sir. That's very true.' Then he added, 'I can send him the photographs if — '

'What's the point of that? He's got the body. He can take as many bloody photographs as he likes, can't he?'

'Just trying to put matters right, sir. If he feels hard done by — '

'I should think he does. Right. Get back to your desk. This complaint against you is far too serious for me to deal with. I shall pass it upstairs. The chief can make the decision what to do with you when he gets back.'

Angel didn't like that. If it was upheld, it would go on his record and might be referred to endlessly by Harker. He might have a stoppage of pay. He didn't want any of that, either.

He came out of the superintendent's office and stormed down the corridor. He felt as if he had been force-fed three helpings of Strangeway's fish pie and it wouldn't drop down his stomach.

PC Ahaz saw Angel coming towards him. He stopped and said, 'Excuse me, sir. The radiator in the corridor outside the CID office is making a funny noise.'

Angel kept on walking. 'Tell me later, lad. Tell me later,' he said, not caring if the radiator exploded into a thousand pieces. He reached his office, immediately reached out for the phone and tapped in the number for the South Yorkshire Police.

'Detective Chief Inspector Pimm, please.'

After a few seconds a crisp, efficient sounding voice said, 'DCI Pimm.'

Angel bounced straight into dialogue with him. He had absolutely nothing to lose. He could only gain or stay as he was. He began very quietly. 'I believe you are trying to determine the identity of a body found near Strawberry Reservoir yesterday?'

'Indeed I am,' Pimm said. 'Who is this speaking, please?'

'I am the driver of the unmarked police car you saw leaving the crime scene.'

'Oh yes, the BMW,' Pimm said.

'I would like to point out that I didn't interview *any* of the four men. They approached me and told me where the woman's body was and how appalling it looked. I am pretty sure that they were fed up of waiting. They were anxious to tell their story so that they could leave and get on with their fishing. I didn't ask them any questions. There was no interview. I didn't even say I was from the police.'

'That's all right,' Pimm said. 'What is your name?'

'My sergeant, under my instructions, took some photographs because I thought the dead woman probably had a bearing on a case I am working on. Accordingly, we put them on the computer, blew them up and I discovered that I was able to identify the woman. I also know where she lived.'

'Right,' Pimm said. 'That's great. How *could* you recognize her? Her mouth had been mutilated, and the rest of her face had been — '

'I know that her tongue had been pulled out with some sort of — '

'Oh. You knew about that?'

'I have another case, similar. *He* was shot in the heart, before the — '

'Yes, this woman had been shot in the heart before the mutilation.'

Angel was relieved to learn that the old lady hadn't been alive to experience the savagery. 'I identified her from a piece of jewellery . . . a gold crucifix on a chain I had seen her wearing recently.'

'Ah yes. Good. Well, who is she?'

'Hold on a minute,' Angel said. 'Now, I am in trouble with my super because you have written complaining — with some justification, I admit — of professional trespass.'

'Oh, that's what's bothering you? Forget that, old chap. I was peeved because I thought you would turn out to be some cheeky sprog copper, treading heavily over my crime scene to get ghoulish photos of yet another corpse to enlarge his scrapbook collection and sell to the *Daily Bugle* for some outrageous sum of money.'

'Not at all. Nothing like that. I will let you have all the photographs my sergeant took if you wish. And my sergeant was very careful approaching the body, and, after all, the crime scene *was* out of doors.'

'Are you going to give me your name?'

'My name is DI Angel and the dead woman's name — '

'Just a minute. DI Angel, did you say? Not Michael Angel, the cop who they say, like the Mounties, always gets his man?'

Angel's cheeks felt hot. He knew his face would be red. It always embarrassed him. 'Yes, sir,' he mumbled at length. 'That's me, I'm afraid.'

'Well. Well, well. Pleased to meet you — well *speak* to you — Michael. Call me Archie. Well, well, well. That's all right, Michael. I understand perfectly well. I wish I had *your* record. You say you know the dead woman's name and address? Well, I forgive anybody anything who knows that. She's not known on the NPC, there's nothing on her clothes, only sawdust, no distinguishing marks on her body, she's not been reported missing, there's nothing. No *that*'s all right. I will immediately contact my super, straighten all that out and quash the whole thing. He'll be delighted to have the dead woman's ID. He'll be on cloud nine. Wait till I tell him it was Michael Angel who told me. Well, well, well. Meeting Michael Angel at last.'

'Thank you very much, Archie.'

'It's a pleasure, Michael.'

* * *

Angel told Pimm what he knew about Aimée Podlitz, the huge fire on Bradford Road of her shop and home, and that he had just heard that the buildings at the back were all in her name and had been burned out the previous day. He told him that he believed that the property had been the HQ of the country-house gang, that she had probably been a lowly pawn, murdered because, in the eyes of the gang leader, she had become a security risk, following the visit by Angel to the shop, and that he assumed the gang must now have established themselves in other premises.

Pimm and Angel parted good friends and Angel was clearly much happier. The three unwelcome helpings of Strangeway's fish pie on his chest seemed to have swum away just as quickly as they had arrived.

Angel then rang for PC Ahaz.

'You wanted me, sir?' Ahmed said.

'Yes, lad. Who is on surveillance of Edward Street?'

'Ted Scrivens, sir. Been there since 0600 hours.'

'Is Riley in the house?'

'Unless he went out in the night, sir, yes.'

'Any post? Any phone calls?'

'Only the electric bill and a mail-order catalogue, sir, both addressed to Mrs V. Beasley. No phone calls yesterday, not even a wrong number.'

'Right lad. If there's any change, let me know.'

Ahmed made for the door.

'And find DS Carter and ask her to see me.'

'Right, sir,' he said, then dashed out.

Angel phoned Don Taylor and told him that Brian Farleigh had been caught and charged with the murder of Charles Razzle. He instructed him to search Farleigh's premises on Abbeydale Road, also his home address. He also told Taylor that he was looking particularly for anything valuable and compact that Farleigh could have stolen from Razzle's safe.

He then rang Mr Twelvetrees at CPS and had a long discussion with him about the case against Farleigh. Angel wasn't too pleased with the outcome. He was returning the phone to its cradle when there was a knock at the door. It was DS Carter.

'Come in, Flora. Sit down. I've just been talking to the CPS. There are a few snags. Mr Twelvetrees says he needs to know how Farleigh came by the gun that he used to murder Charles Razzle. He's happy about the fact that it *was* Razzle's gun all right, and that Rosemary Razzle said it was kept in the drawer of the table on her husband's side in their bedroom. But Twelvetrees thinks there needs to be some explanation as to how Farleigh actually came to possess it to commit the murder. Twelvetrees also said he needs to know how Farleigh managed to get hold of the key to the front door of the house from which a cast was made. He says the case needs those points strengthening, or some additional compelling evidence is required, such as whatever Farleigh stole from Razzle's safe being found in his possession, before he'd be satisfied in taking the case to court.'

Carter frowned. 'I thought you had enough, sir.'

'So did I.'

'Well about the keys, sir,' she said. 'There were four keys to the front door, weren't there?'

Angel nodded. 'Charles Razzle, Rosemary Razzle, Jessica Razzle and Elaine Dalgleish each had one. I can't see Charles Razzle parting with his to anybody easily. Jessica was abroad up to the time of the murder, so she's way out of it. That leaves Rosemary and the housekeeper. I wish I knew where Rosemary was . . . we can't ask her until she turns up.

That leaves the housekeeper, Elaine Dalgleish.'

'Do you want me to see her?'

'No, I'll see her,' he said. 'I've got used to her.'

'Well, didn't you want me for something, sir?'

'Yes, Flora. I'm concerned . . . very concerned. We've only one lead to the country-house gang.'

'You mean if we find Sean Noel Riley with a bullet through his heart and his tongue pulled out, we've been the cause of another death and we're no further forward.'

Angel blew out a metre of breath and ran his hand over his chin. 'I didn't mean to be as graphic as that, but, yes.'

'Sorry,' she said with a slight shrug. 'What do you propose to do, sir?'

'We've got to get a bug in there somehow. We've got to know what's happening.'

* * *

It was an hour and a half later when Angel came out of the station and drove the BMW down through town on to Park Road, where he parked. He walked round the corner to Edward Street and joined DC Ted Scrivens, who was in his car parked in a line of other cars. He had an unhindered view of the front door of 26 Edward Street.

'Any movement?' Angel said as he opened the door to get in the seat beside him.

'Nothing, sir. Nobody been out. Nobody been in. No outgoing phone calls. No incoming phone calls. It's all very boring.'

Angel squeezed the lobe of his ear between finger and thumb. 'Are they both in there?

'I believe so. Saw her at about ten minutes past eight. She was opening that bedroom window. I haven't actually seen *him* this morning.'

'Let's hope he is in there or this whole set-up is a waste.'

Scrivens's face hardened. 'He's *in* there, sir.'

Angel knew that it was wishful thinking, but he thought Scrivens was probably right.

'Sergeant Carter is on her way. She's going to plant a bug in there. She's wearing a wire.' Out of his pocket he took a small black plastic box that looked like a mobile phone, pressed a button and put it his ear. 'I'm going to monitor her.'

Scrivens grinned. He was pleased to see that things were moving.

'She's here now,' Angel said. He felt his pulse quicken.

A small car turned the corner, past

Scrivens's Ford which they were in, and stopped at the opposite side of the road outside number 26 Edward Street. DS Carter in the uniform of a NHS sister stepped out of it, carrying a black bag.

The two men watched her knock on the door of number 26.

She very much looked the part in the navy-blue raincoat, black stockings and white cap. Scrivens thought she looked very sexy.

Angel heard the knock through the receiver.

The hot, throbbing pain in his chest began. He'd had it for years. It was part of the job.

It was a while before the knock was answered. The door was eventually opened by Mrs Beasley

'National Health Service,' Flora Carter said. 'Mrs Beasley?'

The woman's jaw dropped. 'Yes?'

Flora Carter flashed an ID card made up by Ahmed on his computer twenty minutes earlier, using an NHS logo and a recent head-and-shoulders photograph of Flora from her police record, but Mrs Beasley was hardly interested in it.

'Well, what do you want?'

'It's a swine flu check.'

'Swine flu!' Mrs Beasley exclaimed. Alarm showed in her eyes. 'I haven't got swine flu.'

'I don't suppose you have, Mrs Beasley,' Flora Carter said. 'Need to go through a check list of symptoms with you and take a sample of water from your cold tap. That's all. Only takes a minute.'

Mrs Beasley put her hand on her chest. She knew there was something very unusual about this National Health Service visit, nevertheless she was looking forward to having it confirmed that she hadn't caught swine flu, also that the supply of water to the house was as pure as it should be.

Mrs Beasley stepped back and pulled the door open wider.

Flora Carter swung the black bag in front of her and swept into the house with a flourish of confidence.

Angel saw the back of her raincoat disappear past the doorjamb, then saw the door close. His jaw tightened. He rubbed his chin. He hoped this was all going to work. Ideally she'd need the woman out of the room for a few minutes, but a few seconds would suffice.

'Is there just you living here, Mrs Beasley?' Flora said.

Unexpectedly, through the receiver, Angel heard a deep, man's voice say, 'No. There's me an' all. Now what's this all about? You're not calling at *every* house?'

Angel held his breath. The owner of the voice had to be Sean Noel Riley.

'Certainly not,' Flora Carter said. 'One in every fifty. It's a survey. I'm working fourteen hours a day as it is. If you don't want to take part just say so and I can easily go next door.'

'No. No. It's all right,' Mrs Beasley said quickly.

'You said it only takes a minute?' the man said.

'That's all,' she said breezily.

Angel was worried. There were now two people in the room with Flora. How could their attention possibly be diverted?

Angel heard the click of Flora's, ball point. 'Can I have your name, please?'

'What me?' said the man's voice. Then he said, 'Sean Noel Riley.'

'Date of birth?'

'December the twenty-fifth, 1967.'

'Thank you,' Flora said.

Angel felt a drum beating in his chest. He turned to Scrivens. Very quietly he said, 'He's in there. Riley's in there.'

Scrivens nodded.

Flora said: 'And your name is Violet Beasley . . . date of birth, Mrs Beasley?'

'May the third, 1971.'

'Thank you. Now has either of you any of the following symptoms. Fever, cough, shortness of breath, sore throat, tiredness, aching muscles, sneezing, runny nose or loss of appetite?'

'No.'

'That's good,' Flora Carter said.

There was a sigh. It sounded as if it was from Violet Beasley. Riley didn't reply.

'Now I just need to take a sample of water from your cold tap,' Flora Carter said.

Angel's eyes suddenly flashed. 'She's stuck with both of them watching her,' he said. 'I'll have to give her a chance.' He dropped the receiver into his pocket, opened the car door, dashed across the street and up to number 26. He banged hard on the door. He wasn't sure what he was going to say.

The door opened. It was Violet Beasley. 'Yes?' she said.

'Ah yes,' Angel said. 'Could you direct me to the . . . to the abattoir, please?'

Violet Beasley frowned. She wasn't pleased. 'The abattoir? I don't think I know where *that* is? Just a minute,' she said. She turned and called back into the house. 'Sean, can you direct this young man to the abattoir?'

'What?' Riley said.

She shook her head and gritted her teeth. 'Come and have a word with this young man,' she snapped.

There was the muttering sound of

dissension from Riley as he thrust his way up to the front door.

Angel's heart began to beat like the drums at the end of the *1812*.

Riley looked down at Angel as if he was looking in the slop bin at Strangeways.

'He wants the abattoir,' she said, pointing at Angel, then she turned and went back in the living room.

Riley said: 'I'm a stranger round here myself, lad. I don't know where it is. Sorry.' He closed the door.

Angel reckoned that that had given Flora Carter about six clear seconds to hide a sticky bug somewhere in the room. Six seconds wasn't long, but it was long enough. He only hoped that in the process Riley hadn't suspected anything.

* * *

It was one o'clock exactly, only sixty minutes after the successful placing of a listening device at the back of a picture on the wall in the sitting room at 26 Edward Street. Flora Carter had gone back to the station, changed out of the nursing sister's uniform, and returned it, and the bag, to her friend at the hospital. Don Taylor had set Scrivens up in the white unmarked surveillance van outside the house with earphones to monitor the bug, and Angel had set off down to 22 Canal Road to interview Elaine Dalgleish again.

'Come on through, Inspector,' she said, a little breathless. 'Just back from the shops myself. Sit yourself down there. I'll just put these bits and bobs away in the fridge; if you don't mind.'

She quickly pulled groceries out of two shopping bags. She slotted some purchases in a cupboard, put some in the fridge and left some on the worktop, then squeezed up the empty plastic bags and dropped them in a waste bin underneath. She washed her hands under the tap, wiped them on a towel by the sink, then slid on to a stool, dragged off her headscarf and said, 'Now what is it, Inspector? Have you heard from Mrs Razzle?'

'No I'm afraid not.'

She pulled a face. 'I'm worried about her, Inspector. Her husband shot dead. Tried to make it look like that robot. The murderer might be . . . looking for *her*.'

'Why? What has she done? Do you know something I don't, Mrs Dalgleish?'

'No. No I don't. But I just . . . I just wish she'd come back. Besides, if she doesn't come back soon, I think I'm going to have to look round for another job.'

Angel knew how difficult it was getting

employment of any sort in Bromersley at that time and nodded sympathetically. 'I'm sorry.'

She shrugged then smiled.

'I came to ask you a couple of questions,' he said. 'Small matters that need tidying up. Firstly, about the gun that was in the drawer in the bedside table at the Razzle's house.'

Her lips tightened almost imperceptibly. 'I thought we had been through all that.'

'I need to know who you *told* about it.'

'I didn't tell *anybody* about it,' she said staring coldly at him. 'It was the Razzles' business. I wouldn't tell anybody anything about the Razzles that was private.'

He maintained the stare she had started.

'All right,' he said. 'Now, that was the actual gun used to murder Mr Razzle. The murderer took that gun out of the drawer the night of the murder, or earlier. Or someone took it from there and gave it to him or left it somewhere for him to collect. But however he came by it, he would need to know that it was there in the first place, wouldn't he? Now only you, Mr Razzle and Mrs Razzle knew of its existence. I have this problem, you see. I can't understand how the murderer knew it was there.'

She blinked. 'I have no idea.'

Angel rubbed his cheek. 'Is it possible that

Mr Razzle might have innocently told somebody? Maybe someone he trusted . . . while talking about his security arrangements.'

'I suppose so. He was a nice man, a gentleman. He would talk to anybody. I suppose it's possible.'

'But you never heard him . . . telling anybody about the gun?'

'I told you, Inspector, no.'

There was suddenly a banging against the back door. And then another tattoo.

Elaine Dalgleish jumped up from the stool, snatched a bunch of keys off the worktop, charged across to the back door, selected a key, unlocked the door and opened it wide. The sounds of transistor music, a baby crying, the thump of a ball being kicked and children squealing excitedly flooded into the kitchen.

She leaned out of the doorway. 'Was that you, Kevin?' she said.

'Sorry,' a voice from outside said.

'You're ruining the paintwork on my door,' she said. 'Take your ball up the yard, please. There's much more room up there. I've paid out a fortune to have this house painted. Go on. Off you go. All of you.'

She came back in, closed the door, locked it, stared at Angel who was now standing by the sink. He was holding the bar of soap from the soap dish in his hand. He pointed to the soap. It had the indentation of a key in it.

'This is a mould of Razzle's front-door key taken just now from the bunch that was hanging in the lock of your back door. From this bar of soap, I could now have made a serviceable key that would open their door. Taking the mould has only taken me a few seconds . . . the time you were talking to those boys. I took the keys out of the lock, pressed it into the soap, then replaced the keys. That's all it takes.'

Her mouth dropped open.

Angel returned the bar of soap to the soap dish at the side of the sink, rinsed his hands and wiped them on the towel.

'The murderer of Charles Razzle used your key to take a mould to make a key to gain access to the house. We have arrested the murderer and he actually had the home-made key on him. But the legal boys need to be able to illustrate just where and when he had the opportunity to make a mould of it.'

Elaine Dalgleish blinked. 'You've got the murderer?'

'A man has been charged.'

'Who is it?'

'All in good time.'

She sat quietly and looked at him for a few seconds, then said, 'There are three other keys, inspector, and if my key was the one used — and I am not saying it was — I have no idea when or how it *could* have been.'

Angel knew she could be right, but that wasn't going to satisfy the CPS. He thought a moment. He couldn't see how he could sensibly press her any further, so he stood up thanked her and left.

15

Angel arrived back in his office and immediately reached for the phone.

'Mr Twelvetrees? Michael Angel here. Regarding those two points that needed clarification.'

'Yes, Inspector?'

'I've just spoken to Elaine Dalgleish. It wasn't very productive. I daresay that if she knew how her key might have been borrowed she wouldn't have admitted to it. On that other matter, is it not unreasonable to suggest that Charles Razzle, being a decent, friendly, approachable man, might very well have talked over his security arrangements with an ostensibly friendly so-called security expert and revealed to him that he owned a firearm and where he kept it?'

Twelvetrees said: 'Maybe, but I may have to try to convince a cynical jury of it.'

'Well, with it, or without it, do you think you have enough to get a conviction?'

There was a delay before Twelvetrees replied. 'I'm not sure, Inspector. These details would not be at all significant to the outcome of the case if there was an incontrovertible motive that the defence had to try to explain away.'

Angel understood the point well enough. He was disappointed because it meant more work. 'Very well, Mr Twelvetrees. I'll see what I can do. Goodbye.'

He replaced the phone. He knew that Twelvetrees was right. He only hoped that Don Taylor was able to uncover something at Farleigh's house that would be useful in constructing a motive.

The phone rang again. He reached out for it. It was a young PC on reception.

'Sorry to bother you, sir, but there's a strange, foreign man here by the name of Van Hassain. Said he wanted to speak to the chief of police. I spoke to the super and he said to pass him on to you.'

Angel wasn't pleased. His face creased. He had enough to do. 'What does the man want, lad?'

'He wouldn't say, sir. He's seems to be very . . . posh. Arrived in a chauffeur-driven car.'

'All right. Bring him down.'

Minutes later the constable arrived and ushered the visitor into Angel's office.

Van Hassain stood at the door, adjusted his monocle, stared at Angel, smiled and said, 'Ah, Inspector Angel, *you* are ze chief of police?'

'The chief constable is away at a conference, Mr Van Hassain. I am afraid you will have to put up with me.'

The smile on Van Hassain's face vanished. 'No. I will speak only with ze chief of police,' he said. He turned towards the door, then turned back. 'When will he be available?'

'Monday morning.'

Van Hassain grunted and looked thoughtfully round the office. He was clearly undecided. Then he reached into his mustard-coloured waistcoat pocket and produced a card about the size of a playing-card. He handed it to Angel. 'This will introduce me to you, Inspector.'

It was gold-coloured lettering on black.

Angel blinked as he read it.

It said:

Moses Van Hassain.
Secretary of State to Omanja, Omanja State Offices, PalaceRoad, Koolali,
Omanja, Africa.
Telephone (private line) 229.
email <goldenmistress@omanga.af.com>.
Also principal of Hassain Oil, Hassain Antiques and Hassain Gold Mines.

Angel read it again. He had never heard of a country called Omanja. It must be very small. He had never heard of Moses Van Hassain either. What could this man want in downtown Bromersley? Angel wanted to send him on his way as quickly as he could manage. He had a lot to do.

He offered the card back to Van Hassain, who waved a hand indicating that Angel should retain it. Angel placed it on the desk in front of him.

'Well, Mr Van Hassain, I am the most senior officer available. I regret that you must deal with me or make an appointment with the chief constable's secretary for some time on Monday.'

'No. No. No. Dis matter cannot wait until Monday, kind Inspector.'

'Very well,' Angel said, and pointed to a chair.

Van Hassain sat down, removed his straw hat and placed it lightly on a chair close by, then put his bamboo cane with the carved ivory head of a tiger in front of him and rested his hands on it.

'This is a delicate matter for me to talk about, Inspector. You see, it is a personal, commercial matter. Being Secretary of State for Omanja, answerable only to King Moogli, which is a very great honour, and a vocation which I gladly undertake and for which I accept no remuneration whatever, necessitates that I earn my livelihood by way of business. I had a gentleman's agreement with Charles Razzle, to purchase his collection of twenty-eight gold snuffboxes. I am aware that Mr Razzle was tragically murdered on the twenty-fifth of May. Nevertheless, I assume that the transaction will still be honoured. I have been to the Razzle's house, but the dear, honourable, beautiful Mrs Razzle was out, so I am here to see the chief of police, who I assume will be dealing with Mr Razzle's affairs.'

Angel said, 'Well, it's true that I am the police officer dealing with the murder of Mr Razzle . . . '

Van Hassain smiled and said, 'Good. Good.'

'But I have to say that no gold snuffboxes have been found among Mr Razzle's effects.'

Van Hassain's face hardened. He looked down at the floor, then gripped the ivory-headed cane tightly and banged it on the terracotta-coloured tiles angrily several times. 'May the curse of our gods be upon all thieves.'

Angel watched. He silently rubbed his chin.

Then in an even tone, Van Hassain smiled and said, 'Vell, Inspector, would you locate them for me and I will happily pay the price agreed plus, in these circumstances, ze usual 'finder's fee' of twenty per cent. That's one hundred and twenty thousand pounds in cash, English sterling. I am on my yacht, the *Golden Mistress* anchored outside your port of Bridlington for another day only. Then I must leave for home . . . state business, you understand?'

Angel looked him straight in the face. 'Mr Van Hassain,' he said. 'I have no idea where the snuffboxes are. I said that they were not in Mr Razzle's effects. They have not been found.'

'According to him, they were in his possession the day he was murdered, Inspector. I had an email from him that morning to zat effect. They could surely not be far away, nor hard to find, eh?'

Angel suddenly realized that the snuffboxes could have been in Charles Razzle's safe. There would be the motive for his murder . . . the motive he had been searching for. It followed then, that they should be found in Farleigh's possession.

'Have you found ze murderer?' Van Hassain asked.

'We have charged a man.'

'He is here, in your cells?'

'Yes.'

Van Hassain's eyes glowed. 'Where the murderer is,' he said, 'surely there you will find ze gold snuffboxes.'

Angel hoped he was right.

'Do you know the Razzles well, Mr Van Hassain?' Angel said.

'No, Inspector. I have never met Mr Razzle. My contact with him is through the Internet only, and the beautiful Rosemary Razzle, through the medium of the television and the film. I am such an admirer of feminine beauty, Inspector. I am hoping to meet the lady before I leave your lovely city. You will find for me the twenty-eight gold snuffboxes, Inspector. I have the cash upon my person. I regret I cannot pay more.'

'If we do manage to find them, Mr Van Hassain, they would be evidence and therefore they would be an exhibit, and needed for the trial.'

Van Hassain sucked air in noisily. His nostrils flared. His face flushed up scarlet. He rocked backwards and forwards over his stick five or six times, his hands clenched tightly round the ivory tiger's head. 'One hundred and thirty thousand pounds, Inspector Angel,' he spat out through clenched teeth. 'That is absolutely my top figure.'

Angel shook his head. 'I'm sorry, Mr Van Hassain. The price is nothing to do with me. I am not in a position to negotiate with you about them. If we do come across the gold snuffboxes, and it is established that they are part of Charles Razzle's estate, then any disposing of them would be a matter for you to take up with Mrs Razzle.'

Van Hassain stopped rocking and looked up in surprise. 'Of course. Of course,' he said quickly. He tapped his cane several times on the tiles and closed his eyes for a moment, then he looked up and said, 'And where would I find the beautiful Mrs Razzle, Inspector?'

'I wish I knew,' Angel said.

The monocle dropped from Van Hassain's eye. He caught the ribbon. 'You do not know?'

Angel shook his head. It worried Van Hassain. It was beginning to worry Angel as well.

Van Hassain adjusted the monocle and said, 'One more thing, kind Inspector Angel, then I will leave you in the peace of your god to complete your investigations. May I speak with the man who is charged with this murder?'

'I'm afraid not,' said Angel rising to his feet. 'Now, if there is nothing else I can assist you with Mr Van Hassain . . . ?'

* * *

As soon as Van Hassain had closed the door, Angel tapped the number of the Feathers Hotel into his phone.

'Put me through to Miss Jessica Razzle, please.'

'I am so pleased to hear from you, Inspector,' she said. 'It is so boring here. I don't know anybody. I shall leave for the States as soon as the funeral is over. You have some news for me? Has my *dear* stepmother turned up?'

'No, sorry, Jessica. I have not heard a word. I just want to ask you a question. Do you know anything about a collection of gold snuffboxes belonging to your father?'

'Snuffboxes? He used to collect them . . . last I heard he had about a dozen. Quite nice, but very expensive, and boring. When you've seen one you've seen them all.'

'You say expensive; how expensive?'

'I can't remember, say — oh, I don't know — say a hundred pounds each. I might be wrong about that. Might be only twenty pounds. Can't remember. I know it seemed a ridiculous price at the time. But that was quite a few years ago.'

'And where did he keep them?'

'In a drawer in his desk. Wrapped in tissue paper in a little cardboard box. He used to bring them out and show visitors. I used to show my doll. He used to show his snuffboxes. I know that some were seventeenth-century. He was very proud of them. Have you any idea where Rosemary is?'

'No, I haven't heard from her.'

'You know, Inspector, I hate her, but not as much as I hate Farleigh, and I'm ever so worried about her.'

'I know,' Angel said. He tried to hide his concern. He didn't want Jessica to know *how* worried. There was no point in her worrying needlessly. She would still be grieving the loss of her father. That was more than enough to bear, especially without a family member to share it with. He wanted to say something that would cheer her up.

'You know what they say,' he said, 'no news is good news.'

There was a pause. 'Yes,' she said. 'I suppose so.'

'Thank you very much, Jessica. Goodbye.'

He ended the call and immediately dialled a London number. It was his good friend, DS Matthew Elliott at the National Police Antiques and Fine Art squad.

After the usual warm courtesies, Angel said: 'Matthew, can you give me a ball-park value of twenty-eight gold snuffboxes? I am working on a case where they seem to constitute the motive for the murder of a man, and I don't know anything at all about them.'

'Well Michael, of course it depends. They *are* still pretty rare. Sir Jack Prendergast had his mansion stripped of antiques last month by the country-house gang and among the items stolen were twenty gold snuffboxes. Now they were on his insurance valuation at over a million quid. The dates of some of them went back to Elizabethan times. But there are late Georgian examples you can occasionally buy in country auctions for around two hundred pounds or so if in reasonable condition. I hope that's helpful. Sorry I can't be more precise. I would be able to say more if I saw them.'

'Could add up to a lot of money then? Well, thanks very much.'

He replaced the phone and leaned back in the chair, looking up at the ceiling. He squeezed the lobe of his ear between thumb and forefinger. Rosemary Razzle would be able to tell him so much more about the snuffboxes if he only knew where to contact her. Her running off like that was very unhelpful. It was worrying when there was so much crime about. He wished that he could find her. He *could* enlist the help of the newspapers. They'd enjoy making a story about the beautiful actress/heiress who had gone missing. He visualized the headlines and then changed his mind. She had only been gone three days. It was hardly long enough to make it into a mystery. It could all be a hullabaloo for nothing. She might turn up giving some innocuous explanation, and there'd be so many red faces, and his would be the reddest. He considered the matter a little while longer and considered that it might be worthwhile circulating the police service. Her famous face might be spotted and recognized somewhere in the course of a policeman's day-by-day work.

He picked up the phone and tapped out PC Ahaz's number.

'Ahmed. Come in here.'

The young man duly arrived.

'Get a photograph of Rosemary Razzle, Ahmed. Put her description under it and email it to all forty-three forces. Mark it 'Confidential — wanted as a witness.' Don't let it look as if she's a suspect.'

'Right sir,' Ahmed said, then turned towards the door. He turned back. 'The prisoner in cell one, sir, Farleigh. Is it all right if he has a tin of shoe polish and a duster? Says he wants to keep looking smart.'

Angel frowned. He'd never had a request like that before. In his experience, prisoners never seemed to consider the cosmetic appearance of their footwear. He had to consider whether there were any ulterior reasons for which Farleigh might require the polish and duster. Suicide was common in prison, so he had to take the prisoner's disposition into account. But there would be easier ways than eating a tin of polish or choking on a piece of duster.

'Anybody with him at the moment?'

'He's with his solicitor, sir, I think.'

'Anybody we know?'

'Haven't seen him before.'

Angel didn't like that. Could be some slick young lawyer from the city, trying to make a name for himself.

He rubbed his chin. 'I hope his visitors are properly searched and cautioned,' he said.

Ahmed didn't reply. The searching wasn't up to him.

'Who seems to be doing most of the talking?'

'Farleigh does, sir.'

'Aye. Well let him have the polish and the duster then.'

'Right, sir,' Ahmed said, and went out.

The phone rang. It was Scrivens from the listening van on Edward Street.

'Riley's just left the house, sir. I heard him tell Violet Beasley he was going to the garage.'

'What garage?'

'Didn't say. I'm going to leave the tape running, sir, and follow him.'

Then the line went dead.

Angel thought a moment, closed the phone, jumped up, ran out of the office and out of the station. He got into the BMW went down Park Road almost to the corner of Edward Street, where he stopped the car, picked up his mobile and dialled Scrivens.

'Where are you, lad?'

Scrivens answered breathlessly: 'Bradford Road, sir. I lost him. I'm on my way back to the van.'

Angel grunted and rubbed his chin. Then he said, 'Did he say anything more than that he was leaving for the garage?'

'No, sir.'

'All right, lad. Not to worry. I'll send you some company . . . that mustn't happen again.'

Angel returned to the office, found DS Flora Carter and dispatched her to join Scrivens in the van. Then he phoned Twelvetrees at the CPS. He told him about the possible value of the twenty-eight gold snuffboxes and the fact that they were missing following the murder of Charles Razzle. Twelvetrees said that if the twenty-eight gold snuffboxes were found in Farleigh's house or showroom, or if they could be positively linked to Farleigh, then the case against him would be solid and the CPS would proceed and set a date for the case to be heard.

Angel smiled as he replaced the phone. There was progress indeed. All he had to do was find twenty-eight gold snuffboxes in Farleigh's house or showroom and the case was sewn up.

He picked up the phone and tapped in Taylor's number.

'How's it going, Don?'

'All right, sir. Almost done. Nothing incriminating here.'

'Tell me about it.'

'Well, the house is well-furnished for a bachelor. Games room and small gymnasium. Swimming pool. Two cars in the garage. One is a Ferrari, the other a Bentley. Everything of the best. No signs that a woman has had any influence in the planning, designing or running of the place, and no embarrassing things under the bed or anywhere else. Although certainly small traces of face powder and long brown hairs in the en suite bathroom indicate that he has entertained women or a woman here recently. But no drugs, jewellery, gold bars, pornography, cash, weapons or stolen property.'

The muscles in Angel's face tightened. This

was not what he wanted to hear.

'I'm looking for a collection of twenty-eight antique gold snuffboxes,' he said, 'individually wrapped in tissue paper and kept in a small cardboard box. They are worth a small fortune and finding them there, or at his shop in Sheffield, will wrap it up.'

Taylor pursed his lips. 'Oh. Right, sir,' he said resolutely. He understood Angel's concern and the pressure on him.

'Now he was a security man,' Angel said. 'So he might have some smart, hidden safe somewhere where we least expect it.'

'Don't worry, sir. Now that we know, we shall be especially thorough. If the snuffboxes are in this house, our detectors will find them.'

Angel replaced the phone. He rubbed his chin. There was nothing more he could do with that until SOCO turned up the booty.

There was a knock at the door. It was Crisp. He bounced in and said, 'I've a message from Maintenance, sir.'

Angel wrinkled his nose. He was hardly likely to be very interested in anything the station lavatory man had to say. 'What?'

'That radiator in the corridor outside the CID office that was making a funny noise has been fixed.'

'Good.'

'Apparently a tiny control knob had been completely unscrewed and was missing. It's been replaced, adjusted and it's all right now.'

'Good. Are you monitoring what is happening down at 26 Edward Street?'

'Yes, sir. There's nothing happening. Just come off the phone to Flora.'

'Wish we could speed things up a bit.'

The phone rang. It was the civilian woman on the switchboard. 'Mr Hargreaves to speak to you.'

'Is that Inspector Angel?'

'Yes, Mr Hargreaves. What can I do for you?'

'I was wondering how you were getting along finding the person or persons who stole those three coffins from my premises last month. You see, you will have heard that the former town clerk, Samuel Freeby has died. His widow has entrusted me with the care of his last remains. It will be a big funeral and she has expressed the desire of a mahogany casket. I wondered . . . ?'

'I am afraid that we have not managed to catch the thieves yet, Mr Hargreaves, but I am still working on it.'

'The funeral is next Wednesday, Inspector.'

'I doubt that we could promise anything definite by then. I am sorry, Mr Hargreaves. Please pass on our condolences to Mrs Freeby.'

'Very well.'

Angel replaced the phone looked up at Crisp. 'Anything heard about those three stolen coffins?'

'No, sir.'

Angel pulled a face.

This hanging around in the office waiting for other people to report in and fielding queries and inconsequential questions from all and sundry was driving him crackers. There was an ever increasing pile of post, circulars and reports on his desk that needed his attention, but even reading and dealing with every piece of the stuff, would not solve any of the cases in hand, nor result in the catching of one single murderer. He suddenly stood up.

'Come on,' he said to Crisp. 'Let's see how Don Taylor is getting along.

They went in Angel's car to Farleigh's house.

Taylor saw them arrive and headed them off at the front door. He produced a big brown envelope with the word EVIDENCE printed in red across it.

'There's a pile of accounts and bank statements and papers from here, sir,' he said. 'Do you want to go through them yourself or do you want me to do it?'

Angel took it. 'I'll do it,' he said. He put the

envelope in the boot of his car and locked it.

Then Taylor said: 'We've just finished inside the house, sir,' he said. 'We've been over all the walls, along all the floors and even the ceilings. The only metals detected were constituents of electric circuits and gas-carrying pipes. I've also had a team measuring the external walls and then the internal measurements, searching for false walls, hidden rooms, or secret cupboards. There weren't any. There's nothing here, sir. I'm certain.'

'Does this house have a cellar, Don?'

'Yes, sir. Had a good look down there. Three interconnecting areas, which have obviously not been used for anything.'

'Let's have a look,' Angel said. 'Just to be sure.'

Angel took a hand torch out of his car and followed Taylor down thirteen steep steps into a dank, cool place where the floor consisted of polished flagstones and the walls were stone and brick, whitewashed over. He flashed the torch around the edges of the flagstones to see if any had been disturbed recently or to see if there was anywhere that had been freshly dug. There was nothing. They trudged up the steps.

'Must be outside in the garden,' Angel said. He strode round the grounds. They were bigger than they had first appeared, comprising lawns, a tennis court, a copse, outbuildings, a summerhouse and a tool shed.

He and Crisp looked for areas that seemed to have been recently disturbed. There weren't many, but SOCO checked them out with their metal and heat-sensitive detectors. They had machines sensitive to changes in temperature, which detected buried human or animal remains, because the process of flesh decomposing actually produces heat. They found part of an ancient plough which they pulled out, and the skeleton of a large dog which they reburied carefully.

The clock raced round to 5.04 p.m.

Taylor said, 'We've finished here, sir.'

Angel wrinkled his nose. He wasn't pleased. He ran his hand through his hair. It looked like Brian Farleigh was Snow White in trousers.

'Right, Don. Well, start searching at Farleigh's office and showroom in Sheffield, tomorrow, first thing. Those snuffboxes have to be somewhere.'

16

It was 8.28 a.m., the following morning, Thursday, 4 June 2009.

Angel drove the BMW straight from home through Bromersley town centre straight down to the bottom of Park Road, where he stopped, parked and walked down to the corner of Edward Street and up to the observation van. He looked round, then tapped on the door. Crisp opened it carefully and let him in.

Flora Carter was seated in front of a reel-to-reel tape-recording machine, wearing headphones. She looked up at Angel, smiled and nodded.

'Anything happening?' Angel whispered.

'They are arguing about money,' Carter said. 'She says she hasn't enough to pay the gas bill.'

Angel nodded. 'I know the feeling.'

Carter said: 'He said he hasn't a job. He doesn't know when he'll be able to give her any money now that the boss is away.'

'What's he mean by that? Angel said.

'Maybe the gang leader's on holiday, sir,' Crisp said.

Carter put a finger up and said, 'She's crying.'

Angel sniffed. It wasn't out of sympathy. 'Why can't somebody say something incriminating? Or put a name to the boss — whoever he is? Or why can't Riley trot off and lead us to their new HQ?'

Carter reported more words between Riley and Violet Beasley, but neither said anything critical and nothing interesting happened.

After forty tedious minutes Angel came out of the van with a face as long as the padre's sermon.

He trudged back to the BMW and drove up to the station.

He phoned Taylor, who was then in the process of searching Farleigh's business premises in Sheffield.

'Nothing yet, sir,' Taylor said.

Angel replaced the phone and reluctantly began to tackle the pile of bumf that had accumulated on his desk. He kept his head down, ploughing through it all that Thursday and the morning of the next day hoping for a vital phone call from one of his sergeants that would progress his investigations.

At one o'clock on Friday, the phone rang. Angel snatched it up. It was DS Taylor. 'Yes, Don?' he said.

'We've finished these premises, sir, and it

seems to be just what it looks like, a sales and service centre for safes and security systems. We've checked it out for concealed areas. There weren't any. And we've run the metal-detectors along the floors, walls and ceilings. There's nothing untoward.'

Angel rubbed his chin. He recalled that the property was a converted Victorian residential house.

'The cellar?'

'Done that, sir.'

'The garden or land at the back . . . have you gone over that?'

'There are some waste bins and the remains of empty packing cases close to the property wall under the back windows, sir. We've checked through those. Beyond there is a bit wild. Looks like it was once a garden . . . been neglected . . . just overgrown grass and weeds.'

'Check it out, Don. It's our last chance.'

'Right, sir.'

Angel replaced the phone.

There was a sound of hopelessness in Angel's voice. Taylor knew it, and although finding the snuffboxes or anything incriminating out there seemed unlikely, it made him more determined to be thorough and scan every square metre of Farleigh's land with great care.

Meanwhile, Angel kept his backside on the swivel-chair and his head down midst the paper jungle and was reading the last report off his desk when Ahmed arrived with a small pile of additional post from Superintendent Harker's office.

Angel sighed and continued the marathon. At half past four, he looked up and phoned Crisp to check up on the latest news on Sean Noel Riley. He wanted to know if had let anything useful slip yet, or if he had ventured out of the house.

'Nothing's happened here, sir,' Crisp said. 'Do you want to keep this obbo going over the weekend?'

'Of course. It might just be the time he might let something slip or do something enlightening. Work out a rota with Flora, Ted Scrivens and whoever else wants overtime, and you supervise it, all right?'

'Right, sir.'

'If anything vital happens, contact me immediately on my mobile.'

'Right, sir.'

He replaced the phone and tapped in Taylor's number.

'Just finished, sir,' he said, 'and I'm sorry to say there's nothing concealed in the garden area that we're interested in. Just weeds and worms.'

'Right, Don. Pack it in. See you on Monday.'

To say that Angel was disappointed was an understatement. His face dropped like a guillotine. He began to wonder whether his powers as a detective were on the wane. Neither of the cases was unravelling. Both seemed to have reached an impasse. Maybe the murder and the stealing of twenty-eight snuffboxes from Charles Razzle was the first and only serious crime Brian Farleigh had committed. Didn't seem likely, but it was possible. And maybe, because gold snuffboxes were collectors' items and in great demand, he had already sold them. Maybe there had been an ardent collector out there somewhere, waiting, holding out his sticky hands laden with cash and the exchange had already been made.

Angel wrinkled his nose.

It was certainly possible . . . again, not likely, but possible. He considered that option for a little while, then he thought, if that *had* taken place, then Farleigh would have been in possession of a pile of cash. Taylor and his team had looked everywhere and had been unable to turn up anything incriminating. If there were cash or snuffboxes, where had Farleigh hidden them? The main evidence Angel had against him was his possession of a hand-made front door key to Razzle's house. If Farleigh simply said that he found it and the jury believed him, he could get off. After all, there was nothing known: he didn't have a police record. Then Angel recalled the long-winded way Farleigh had taken to find out the six-digit code to open the cellar workshop door, which later, when he thought there was the possibility of CCTV film of him in the camera, he cut down to less than two minutes. Yes. Now that *could* be proved. There were plenty of witnesses. Angel's confidence was returning. The murderer *was* Farleigh. He was very clever. But the murderer was definitely Farleigh. All Angel had to do was find the snuffboxes, link them to him, and he'd go down for life.

* * *

The weekend came and went quicker than two Senokot.

Mary had kept Angel busy in the garden between the showers. He had cut the lawn, weeded the borders, dead-headed the roses, trimmed the hedge and generally tidied round. He didn't much care for gardening, but it got him into the fresh air and was a change from the smell of fingerprint ink, formaldehyde and button polish.

Mary reckoned that it kept his mind busy and stopped him worrying about his job. Its success was limited, because like the showers, it was only effective intermittently.

Anyway, he had been known to say that he really expected a certain amount of stress in catching murderers. It was what made the job worth doing.

He was back at his desk that Monday morning 8 June at 8.28 a.m., riffling through his post.

The phone rang. He reached out for it.

It was Harker. 'Come up here, lad. Smartly.'

Angel groaned. He didn't want to start a new week with a rollicking from the superintendent. He replaced the phone and rushed up the corridor to Harker's office. He tapped on the door and pushed it open.

Harker was sitting at his desk looking like a man who had just discovered that he was holding a lottery ticket only one digit away from being the winner.

'What's this?' Harker said, waving the paper at him.

Angel couldn't read it, but it was pink and therefore almost certainly an expense voucher.

'Looks like an expense chitty, sir,' he said.

Angel scoured his memory to think who in his team had incurred any out-of-pocket expenses over the past few days. He couldn't think of anybody.

'Correct,' Harker said, then proceeded to read it out loud as if it was a salacious extract from a novel by DH Lawrence. 'One cod, chips and peas, four pounds eighty, portion bread and butter, fifty p. Egg custard, one pound eighty. Total seven pounds and ten p.'

He then looked up at Angel. 'Who was *that* for?'

'Don't know,' Angel said with a shrug.

'You don't know?' Harker said.

A ball of fire from Angel's stomach burned fiercely up into his chest. His face burned like a sunlamp. He clenched his fists and made himself breathe in and out slowly. He couldn't reply.

'Well, I'll tell you,' Harker said. 'It was for a man you have put in the cells called Brian Farleigh.'

Angel realized what he was getting at. 'Yes, sir.'

'Had you forgotten about him, lad?

'No, sir. He is *my* prisoner.'

'I understand that he has not been charged.'

'He *has* been charged, and cautioned.'

'I don't understand,' Harker said. 'The CPS say they haven't enough evidence to build a case against him. I presume you know about that?'

'Yes, sir. But the missing piece of evidence is only very small, and, anyway, I am working towards producing the actual motive, which I expect to be irrefutably conclusive.'

'Nevertheless, according to Farleigh's solicitor, you have not built a case against this citizen who he claims is totally innocent, and who can and will produce evidence in court to prove it.'

'Well, he would say that, wouldn't he? He wants to be set free. What do you want me to do about it, sir?'

'You must play the game by the rules, lad. You can't arrest a man and charge him until you have a pretty watertight case.'

'I *have* a pretty watertight case. With the evidence I have already given him, Mr Twelvetrees believes that he can *possibly* get a guilty verdict, but he also said that if I could get the motive, it would be a certainty.'

'And what's the motive?'

'The stealing of a collection of twenty-eight antique gold snuffboxes.'

Harker blinked.

Angel said: 'DS Elliott of the Antiques and Fine Art squad, confirms that they are worth a fortune.'

'Really? I see. And you have searched Farleigh's home and place of business?'

'Yes, sir. And the grounds attached to both

places, and both his cars.'

'Does he own any other properties?'

'No sir. Not that we have been able to find out.'

'So what is your plan now?'

Angel knew he was in trouble. He could see the question coming and he didn't have an answer. 'I shall keep scratching around, sir. I am hopeful that — '

'I knew that you hadn't a plan, Angel,' Harker said. 'You are just bumbling along, as usual. Had it occurred to you that Charles Razzle could have disposed of the snuffboxes before he was murdered? I mean do you know for a fact that Farleigh took them?'

Angel pulled a face. 'No, sir, but it seems very likely that he did.'

'In your searches of Farleigh's house and business premises, did you find anything there that was incriminating?'

'No, sir.'

'Doesn't it strike you as odd?'

'Not odd, sir. A bit unusual. Maybe he's a clever man.'

'Maybe he's innocent. He has reached the age of thirty-nine and he has no police record, not so much as a parking fine.'

'He knows about security matters, sir. He might be a clever man, too clever to be caught.'

'And you are trying to wrap a murder-for-robbery charge around him with insufficient evidence.'

'I have a lot of evidence to show his guilt. For one thing, he had a home-made key to Razzle's house in his pocket. Also, he opened Razzle's security door in less that two minutes when he thought there was a CCTV camera in there with film of him murdering Razzle.'

'Well, we can't keep him locked up for much longer. You'll have to find that necessary evidence or I'll have to release him.'

'You can't do that, sir.'

'Tell that to Twelvetrees, lad. He's the one you have to convince.'

Angel couldn't think of a suitable reply.

'Can't hold him longer than Thursday,' Harker said. 'Then he *must* appear in the magistrate's court and the CPS *must* declare what evidence they have. If it isn't enough, they'll have to let him go. You know the drill. You've two days.'

Angel came out of the superintendent's office and wearily closed the door. He made his way down the corridor as if he had a hundredweight sack of law books lashed to his back with red tape. He shuffled down the corridor to his own office, glad to reach his chair. He dropped into it, leaned back and contemplated the ceiling. Two days wasn't long, especially as he had nowhere else to search and he hadn't an idea in his head. Angel thought it would make him ill if Harker released Farleigh after all the trouble he had taken to get him in a cell. He couldn't think what to do next.

The phone rang. He reached out for it. It was Crisp from the observation van. Angel's face brightened. He sat upright.

'Hello, yes? Yes, what's happening?' he said.

'Nothing, sir. It's DS Carter and me, just checking in.'

'What do you mean, 'Just checking in'? Nobody checked in at all over the weekend.'

'Nothing happened over the weekend, sir. We thought you would enjoy not being disturbed.'

'Nothing at all?'

Crisp said: 'Riley and Violet Beasley have been surprisingly cool and uncommunicative towards each other, sir. It is probably a carry-over of the row they had on Friday about bills and lack of money.'

'And nothing was said about where he worked, his boss or other premises or workplace anywhere?'

'Nothing at all, sir.'

'And did either of them go out?'

'She never left the house all weekend, sir.

He went out to the Rising Sun, just round the corner on Bradford Road, yesterday lunch-time on his own. It was ten past twelve. I followed him. He had one glass of lager, which he swallowed in one gulp. Came back straightaway. Didn't speak to anybody, only the barman.'

Angel growled, then said, 'You could have told me.'

'There was nothing to tell, sir. We were back here before you could say Frankie Dettori.'

Angel recalled that at that time, that day previous, he had been trimming the hedge. If Crisp had only phoned him, it would have got him out of that. 'Next time I tell you to keep me posted about anything, you bloody well keep me posted, understand?'

'Yes. Right. Sir.'

'Now poke out your ears. Keep your mind on the job. You can remind Flora Carter, Ted Scrivens and John Weightman what this obbo is for. We are still trying to find the leader of the country-house gang, who is a very clever thief and murderer. He guards his own and his gang's privacy and security and liberty in the manner of Hermann Lamm. Also, he murders anybody who talks about him, or who might have talked about him, or might be about to talk about him, by pulling out their tongues with a hefty pair of pliers. He's sly, cunning and brutal. He's not your average uneducated villain, so you need to be on your toes. Got it?'

'Oh yes, sir. I've got it.'

'I want him locked up.'

'Yes, sir.'

'The man we are looking for probably has no criminal record, therefore his fingerprints won't be on file anywhere. And presumably when he is out murdering and stealing, he always wears gloves. Summer and winter alike. They will keep his hands warm in the winter, but . . . '

Suddenly Angel's voice petered out and his eyes glazed over.

'Hello. Hello,' Crisp said.

Angel's thoughts were in another place. He was recalling the picture of seeing a mangled black glove coming out of a washing machine on one of the hottest days of the year. His heart was pounding. His eyes opened. He blinked several times, saw the phone in his hand, frowned, quickly said, 'Goodbye,' into the mouthpiece and closed it down.

Then he came out of his office and made for the BMW. He drove it along Wakefield Road, turned left on to Canal Road and pulled up outside number 22. He got out of the car, raced round the bonnet and banged on the house door. He stood impatiently on the step . . . it seemed a long time before it was answered.

Elaine Dalgleish eventually appeared.

'Oh. Inspector Angel. Whatever's the matter?' she said.

'I must see you,' he said.

She pulled the door open further and he pushed past her into the little sitting room and through the internal door to the kitchen.

Elaine Dalgleish closed the front door with shaking hands, and came up behind him. He stood in the centre of the tiny kitchen and looked up to the ceiling at the clothes' rack. It was empty.

She watched him and said, 'What is it you want, Inspector?'

'Where is that washing?' he said pointing in the direction of the ceiling.

She swallowed. 'What washing?'

His eyes flashed. 'Do you do washing for other people?'

She didn't answer immediately. 'A woman has to make a living, Inspector, in these hard times.'

'I'm not criticizing you, Mrs Dalgleish. Work is virtuous. I want to know who you do washing for?'

'Why?'

'Can't you answer a simple question? A week last Friday, I came here to see you. The place was flooded. A washing-machine repair man pulled a woollen glove out of the thing. He said it had been causing the trouble. Remember?'

She could hardly deny it.

'Of course,' she said. 'It was one of *my* gloves.'

Angel's jaw dropped open. He stared at her. 'There was enough wool in that one glove to knit you four jumpers. Whose glove was it?'

'I've told you, mine.'

'And the five sets of overalls on your rack, were they also yours? Be careful how you answer, Mrs Dalgleish. I could lock you up this instant for obstructing me in the execution of my duty.'

She licked her lips, twice. 'What do you want to know for?'

Angel shook his head. He was surprised at his own patience. 'It is very likely that your customer is a murderer and the head of a gang of thieves.'

She shook her head. 'No, Inspector. Not this man.'

Angel's eyes were nearly popping out of his head. 'I want his name and address.'

'I don't know his address. He drops the

dirty clothes off here, I wash them, then he picks them up a couple of days later. His name is Lucan, Arthur Lucan.'

Angel sighed. 'Arthur Lucan. Mmm.' He thought the name rang a bell.

'And you have no idea where he lives? Do you have his telephone number?'

'No.'

'How does he pay you, cash or a cheque?'

'Cash. Are you sure you're not from the Inland Revenue, Inspector. You can tell me now.'

'Certainly not. Why?'

'Well, you see, I don't declare my washing money to anybody.'

'Well it's nothing to do with me, Mrs Dalgleish. Is that why you didn't want to tell me about it?'

She hesitated. 'Well, yes.'

'Nothing to do with me. That's entirely up to you. Tell me, have you done washing for this man, Lucan, before?'

'Yes. About five times. He says he wants them thoroughly washing and drying but not ironing.'

'And what exactly do you wash?'

'Five overalls, five woollen hats, five balaclavas, five pairs of gloves.'

'You'd better come back to the station with me and make a statement.'

Elaine Dalgleish frowned and reached out for her coat.

On the journey back to the station, it came to Angel that Arthur Lucan was the name of a music-hall comedian who played the part of an Old Mother Riley character early in the last century. He wondered if Sean Noel Riley had adopted the alias.

He led her through the cell entrance into his office, and instructed Ahmed to bring in the laptop and the memory stick with the up-to-date 'rogue's gallery' on it.

'I want you to look through these photographs, Mrs Dalgleish,' Angel said. 'See if you can spot the man.'

Ahmed set up the laptop on Angel's desk.

After only a couple of clicks of the mouse, she pointed to one of the photographs and said, 'That's him.'

Angel looked across at her choice.

It was Sean Noel Riley.

He nodded and said, 'Thank you, Mrs Dalgleish.'

He looked at Ahmed and jerked his head towards the door. 'We'll organize a lift for you back to Canal Road.'

PC Ahaz nodded and showed Mrs Dalgleish out.

Angel was only moderately well pleased that Elaine Dalgleish had picked Riley out. It confirmed that Riley was a member of the gang, if not the leader, but it didn't broaden the inquiry at all. A different face would have provided Angel with an entirely new line of inquiry. Nevertheless, he promptly phoned the observation van. Scrivens answered and said that there was nothing to report. Angel updated him about Elaine Dalgleish laundering the crook's kit and the fact that she had picked Riley out of the rogue's gallery. He told him to tell the others on that watch. He thought it would encourage them. He ended the conversation and replaced the phone.

He leaned back in the chair again and gazed at the ceiling. There was nothing more he could do to speed up the listening operation at Edward Street. Riley's mail was being intercepted; his phone calls and all his conversations downstairs were being monitored. Something had to break soon. Angel accepted that he would simply have to be patient.

Regarding Farleigh, things were more difficult. He really needed to find those twenty-eight gold snuffboxes. Farleigh's house and office, land and cars had been thoroughly searched. There simply was nowhere else to look. Angel desperately hoped that the CPS would be able to make a case with the evidence he had already provided. He could think of nothing else he could do to drive that inquiry along.

He looked down at his desk. There was another pile of mail and reports needing his attention and on top of it was the big EVIDENCE envelope of balance sheets and bank statements gathered by Don Taylor from Farleigh's office. He wrinkled his nose and opened the big envelope. He pulled out the balance sheets for the past five years and spread them across his desk. They made pleasant enough reading. Brian Farleigh had apparently been running a very prosperous security business. Both the turnover and the profit had been maintained at approximately the same ratio each year, and both increased handsomely each year. It all seemed satisfactory as far as it went, and justified Farleigh's sumptuous lifestyle. Angel then turned to his bank statements. Throughout the five years, they were always in credit which was also a very comfortable position to be in. The debits could usually be understood from the tiny, hand-penned notes against each entry, but the credits were sometimes large sums with only the words 'sales and labour' scrawled against the entry. He reckoned that Farleigh must be working on a high hourly rate for his labour. Angel frowned, shook his head and moved on.

The bank did not seem to charge Farleigh excessively for their services. It could have been because he always maintained a high credit balance in the account. The only direct bank entries he could see were 'S & S' charges of forty pounds a quarter which were debited from the balance, which Angel considered had not been at all excessive.

He heard the church clock chime five o'clock. He leaned back in the chair, yawned and rubbed his chin. He was ready for home. He closed the file of bank statements, stuffed it and everything else to do with Farleigh in the envelope and locked it in his desk drawer. He would try and come back fresh to the job and finish the statements tomorrow.

He then made for his car and home.

Mary was pleased to see that he was on time. He could see that she was. He gave her a peck on the cheek, opened the fridge, took out a beer and went into the sitting room. He threw off his coat, loosened his tie and flopped into the easy chair. He had a sip of the beer and switched on the TV.

When the picture and sound came up, it was the tail-end of the news. There was a picture of the front of Spicers', the specialist antique jewellery and work-of-art auctioneers, and their imposing Georgian stone-pillared doorway on Royal Crown Road,

London. It quickly cut to the statue of Dorothea Jordan in the entrance hall, and a voice-over reporter was retelling the history of the statue and the fact that a TV documentary programme was to be shown on that channel very shortly. Angel noticed a tall man in a black hat worn Gestapo fashion. He peered at the screen. The man turned and looked direct to camera. Angel's eyes opened wider. It was Alec Underwood again. He seemed never off the television, and never far away from that statue.

The voice-over reporter finished by saying that the actual auction of the statue was tomorrow morning at ten a.m., and that it would be transmitted live on their channel and asked viewers not to miss it.

Angel thought that he probably would.

Then up came the local news, which led with a piece about a local fishing trawler from Bridlington, which had been involved in an accident in early morning mist in the North Sea forty miles east of Flamborough Head. It had been badly holed by a huge foreign container ship. The coastguard at Flamborough Head had been aware and an RAF rescue helicopter from Leconfield had been dispatched. No lives had been lost, and, 'In the tradition of the Navy,' the news reporter said, 'the captain refused to leave the badly listing trawler.'

Angel thought you could take bravery too far.

He leaned back in the easy chair, took another sip of the beer and closed his eyes. Next thing he knew, he felt the beer can being whisked out of his hand. He looked up and saw Mary going out of the room with it. He blinked a couple of times. She returned after a few seconds with the remainder of the beer in a tumbler, and held it out to him. He took it. She stared at him and said, 'You're not in the back of a bus going to Blackpool, you know, Michael.'

He looked at her in a vague sleepy fog, sipped the beer again and closed his eyes.

17

The following morning, Angel came into the office at the usual time and was met by an excited Ahmed who had an unusual twinkle in his eye.

'Isn't it a hoot, sir?' he said with a grin. 'About that gold statue. After all that ballyhoo.'

Angel frowned. 'The auctioneers are selling it today, lad, then it'll all be over.'

'Oh no, sir. Haven't you heard? It's disappeared. It's gone. Unless they find it very soon, they *won't* be selling it. They can't. They made a point of saying that. Spicers are worried about losing faith with their customers. They expected a big crowd attending the auction because that statue was to have been there . . . and now it won't be.'

Angel looked at him, almost closed his left eye and pulled his head back on to his neck. 'What do you mean, lad?'

'It's been on the news, sir. The statue disappeared last night.'

'Really? Was it stolen?'

Ahmed hesitated. 'Yes, sir.'

Angel pursed his lips. 'What about our

friend, Alec Underwood? What's happened to him?'

'Don't know, sir. He doesn't seem to be anywhere around the auctioneers now. I saw the TV news this morning. I saw a live shot of the pedestal where the statue had been in Spicers' entrance hall, and Spicers' spokesman being interviewed . . . and Alec Underwood wasn't anywhere about.'

Angel squeezed the lobe of his ear between finger and thumb. 'Did anybody say what time the statue was taken?'

'All the man said was last night, sir.'

'Really?'

Angel rocked on the swivel-chair for a minute, then said, 'Get me Spicers' auctioneers on the phone.'

Ahmed found it and Angel was on the phone within a minute or so. He had to hold on a few minutes before he got through. A weary voice said, 'Spicers' Auctioneers. Melanie speaking. How can I help you?'

'This is Detective Inspector Angel of Bromesley Police. I want to speak to Mr Alec Underwood please.'

Angel heard the girl gasp, then say meaningfully, 'So does Mr Oberon.' Then she changed her tone. 'Here, are you having me on? You know that Mr Underwood doesn't work here.'

'No, miss. I really am a policeman. So Alec Underwood is not there?'

'Nobody knows where he is.'

'And Mr Oberon — is he the boss?'

'Yes. He's absolutely livid. The gold statue will *not* be offered for sale today. The management is very sorry. Now, this phone line is extremely busy, sir. If you don't want anything else, sir, I'm afraid you must hang up.'

'Thank you,' Angel said and replaced the phone.

He suddenly turned to Ahmed. 'I think I know where Underwood and the statue will be. If anybody wants me, I'm going to his place, 29 Bromersley Road, Cadworth.'

'Right, sir.'

Angel then went out through the back entrance, passing the cell where Brian Farleigh was being held. He looked though the food hatch in the door and saw him with a big tough-looking man in a dark suit and sunglasses. They were seated on the bunk and seemed to be whispering together intensely about something.

Angel turned to the constable on Jail duties. 'Who is in there with Farleigh?'

'His barrister, sir. Mortimer Selmer.'

Angel blew out an imaginary candle. He thought he looked more like a bouncer from the 'Red Devils' night club.

'Did you search him?'

The constable looked insulted. 'Of course.'

Angel wrinkled his nose, then rushed off.

It was only a two-mile drive to Underwood's and it took him only five minutes. As he approached the bottom of the drive he was amazed to find it filled to the gate with cars, and then more cars on the highway. He stopped the BMW where he could at the side of the main road and made his way on foot along the pavement and up the drive.

Much to his surprise he saw a crowd of a dozen or so men and a couple of women outside Underwood's front door, peppering him with questions and, at the same time, taking his photograph. He was looking somewhat forlorn, hanging on to his front-doorknob and saying, 'I've answered all your questions. I've nothing more to say. Thank you so very much, now please would you go? Thank you so much. No. I've nothing more to say. Absolutely nothing. Thank you so much. Please go, and don't damage the hollyhocks. Please walk round them. Thank you so much. Good day.'

They were filtering away, but some watched Angel curiously as he walked straight up to Underwood.

Angel and Underwood didn't exchange

words, just looks. Underwood quickly opened the door wider, and Angel nipped into the hallway.

Shirley Vance came into the hall, saw Angel and screamed.

Underwood promptly shut and locked the front door, then looked back to see what the scream was all about.

'You've let one in, Alec,' she said looking at Angel suspiciously.

Angel pulled out his warrant and said, 'I'm a policeman, miss. You've nothing to worry about.'

She didn't look comforted. She turned away quickly, reached for her handbag and began ferreting about in it.

Underwood looked at Angel and, with a look of distaste said, 'Now, what is it *you* want, Inspector?'

'Where is it, Underwood?' Angel said. 'What have you done with it?'

'What are you talking about?'

'The gold statue.'

Shirley Vance said, 'Oh that. That's what all those newspaper men want to know.'

'What's your name, miss?' Angel said.

She smiled sweetly. 'I'm Shirley Vance, I'm a moggle.'

Underwood said, 'Shut up, Shirley. I'll handle this.'

She pulled a face, found a packet of cigarettes in the bottom of the bag, took one out and lit it.

Angel said: 'Come on, Alec. Don't mess me about. Where is it?'

'I haven't got it,' he said.

Shirley Vance stared at Angel, her fingers twitching as she took a draw from the cigarette.

'You know where it is?' Angel said.

'No,' Underwood replied. 'It could be anywhere.'

Angel turned to Shirley Vance. 'What do you know about it?'

She looked at Underwood who shook his head.

She pulled the cigarette out of her mouth and said, 'Nothing. But he hasn't done anything wrong.'

Angel said: 'All right, Alec, is that your last word?'

Underwood stuck his chin out and said, 'My first and my last.'

'You give me no choice,' Angel, said. 'Alec Underwood, I am arresting you for the robbery — '

Underwood pulled back his shoulders and said, 'No, you're bloody well not.'

Then Underwood aimed a powerful punch with his right hand at Angel's head. Angel quickly bobbed down and Underwood's hand went straight into the doorjamb. He yelled and put it in the other hand to nurse it.

Shirley Vance screamed.

Angel then swung behind him and jabbed the back of Underwood's legs with his foot, causing him to drop down on to his knees, then Angel clapped Underwood's head between his forearms, causing him a dizziness he didn't expect. Angel followed this with a knee in his back to send him forward on his face. When Underwood became fully alert six seconds later, he found that he was on the floor, his arms behind his back and his wrists in handcuffs.

Shirley Vance rushed over, crouched down, showed a lot of thigh, grabbed his arm and said, 'What's happening, Alec?'

Underwood's face was scarlet. His eyes glowed like searchlights. 'Help me up,' he said.

Angel was on the phone. 'Tell Ted Scrivens, Leisha Baverstock and Don Taylor and the SOCO team I want them down here asap.'

* * *

When DC Scrivens and WPC Baverstock led Alec Underwood and Shirley Vance respectively out of 29 Bromersley Road, Cadworth, to a police car outside, the press corps had doubled. Four TV news companies' transmitting vans had arrived, had set up their aerials and the camera mechanisms were making their humming sound. Commentaries in Spanish, German, French and English could be heard jabbering competitively against each other.

Reporters surged up successively to everyone who came out of the house.

'Sorry. Can't say anything,' was the reply from the police personnel.

Underwood had a lot to say. 'This is a wrongful arrest,' he said. 'I have done nothing wrong. No. I have no idea where the statue is. I've never touched it. It's all down to the auctioneers, Spicers. They were responsible for the security of the statue, not me. Yes, I was interested in it. Who wouldn't be? It was so beautiful. This is a wrongful arrest. Don't worry. I'll soon be free. They've nothing to hold me on.'

PC Baverstock brought Shirley Vance outside; she was hanging tightly on to Underwood's arm. She was overwhelmed by the reception. Her big frightened eyes looked in all directions and when asked anything, said, 'I don't know nothing. I'm with him.'

When the police car had sped away, the press corps took very little time to pack up and leave. They knew they weren't likely to find out anything from SOCO or Angel, who were still searching Underwood's house for the statue. It didn't take them long to discover that the gold-plated statue was not there.

When Angel arrived at the station, there was a group of national and local reporters hovering round the front door and reception area. He drove directly round to the back, let himself in with his swipe card and went straight to his office. He had Shirley Vance brought to his office. She looked nervously round the little room. He invited her to sit down, then he said, 'Now then, Miss Vance, what is Alec Underwood to you?'

She looked serious and afraid. 'He's my man, you know. We're going steady.'

'Do you want to go to prison?'

'No, of course not.'

'Well, tell me all you know about this gold-plated statue.'

She shrugged. 'I don't know nothing.'

'The statue is reputedly worth millions. If you have been in any way co-operating with Alec to steal the statue you could finish up spending a long time in prison. If you know where it is and you tell me now, you might be saved a long time behind bars.'

'I haven't been to prison, Inspector, and I

don't want to go there, but I don't know nothing about stealing the statue. And Alec hasn't stolen it either, I'm sure of that. He wouldn't steal anything. He's a lovely, proper, decent man who wouldn't take nothing that wasn't his.'

Angel knew different but he didn't enlighten her. He rubbed his chin. He wondered where they could have hidden it.

'Whereabouts do you live?'

'I live with Alec, of course.'

'Where did you live before that?'

'I was a chambermaid at the Feathers Hotel in town for two years, I lived in there.'

'Where did you live before that?'

'I shared a room with a girl in Dublin. I was chambermaid at the Dublin Schooner Hotel in Ireland for four years. That was another living-in job.'

'Do you have a car?'

'No. Can't drive, Inspector.'

'Does Mr Underwood have another garage or lock-up besides the one at the house?'

'Not that I know of . . . shouldn't think so.'

'Right. Thank you very much, miss. You can go.'

She breathed a sigh of relief. 'I can go? What about Alec? Are you letting him go?'

Angel shook his head. 'I'm afraid not. I need to know a lot more from him yet, miss.'

* * *

The following morning, the radio, television and newspapers were full of pictures of Alec Underwood being dragged into Bromersley police station accused of stealing the missing statue. The pictures were accompanied with columns of copy about the case and the searching of his house at Cadworth.

As soon as Angel arrived at the station, he was summoned into Harker's office.

'Don't like all this publicity, Angel. I don't know what you've been doing to create all this hullabaloo. There's a photograph of Underwood in every UK paper, and I even heard it on CNN this morning. It's only a gold-plated plaster statue that's missing, isn't it?'

'It's not anything I've created, sir. Intrinsically it *is* only a gold-plated plaster statue, but it is an important antique surrounded by a lot of authentic royal history. They say it's worth millions.'

Harker wasn't impressed. He wrinkled his nose then said, 'Well get him charged, in court, bailed and out of the station asap. I don't like this place being turned into the X-Factor.'

Angel agreed. It would suit him fine. He nodded. 'Right, sir.'

He went out of Harker's office rather surprised. It wasn't often he was in agreement with the superintendent, in fact he couldn't recollect *any* previous occasion. He returned light-heartedly to his own office and phoned the CPS. He wanted to make sure that there wouldn't be any difficulty in presenting Underwood before the magistrates' court that morning for bail to be set and a date for a hearing to be fixed. Apparently Twelvetrees was engaged with somebody else and he sent a message back to say that he would phone back in a few minutes as soon as he was free.

Angel wasn't pleased but there was nothing he could do about it. He busied himself looking through the morning's post. As usual, most of it was inconsequential bumf. He was in the middle of shredding a letter when the phone rang. He reached out for it. 'Angel.'

It was the superintendent.

He was coughing noisily down the phone before he managed to say, 'That chap Underwood, I want you to withdraw the charge, set him free and get him out of the place asap.'

Angel's face creased. 'What's that, sir?'

'You heard. There's no case to answer. Just . . . discharge him and let him go.'

'What do you mean, there's no case to answer?'

'Don't argue with me, lad,' Harker said. 'Withdraw the charge and do it *now!*' Then he slammed the phone down causing an uncomfortable and annoying click on Angel's eardrum.

Angel banged down his own phone, got to his feet and charged up to Harker's office. He didn't bother to knock. He simply barged in and went straight up to the skinny man's jumbled desk.

Harker looked up at him, absolutely furious. His face was as red as a lobster's belly and his lips and eyebrows twitched as if they had been connected to each other by invisible wire.

'What are you doing here? I have told you what to do, lad,' he bawled, waving a skinny arm. 'Now get on with it.'

Angel forehead creased into a dozen lines. 'Are you all right, sir,' he said. 'You're not being got at, are you?'

'No. Go and do it.'

'I am at least entitled to some explanation, sir.'

'I don't recall where it says *that* in your terms of employment.'

Angel stared at him for a moment, still hopeful of an explanation as to why he should release Underwood. When he realized that none was forthcoming, he shook his head, ran his hand through his hair, stormed out into the corridor and back to his own office.

PC Ahaz was there. 'Can I have a word, sir?'

Angel was too angry to speak. He waved him away.

'Can I get you anything, sir?'

Angel shook his head.

Ahmed didn't like leaving him. He knew something was wrong. He hesitated but went out and closed the door.

After five minutes, Angel went down to the cells. He took the key to cell number 3 off the board and unlocked it.

Underwood was reading a newspaper when Angel went in.

He looked up. 'Ah, the mountain has come to Mohammed,' Underwood said. 'What can I do for you?'

'I'm letting you go.'

Underwood frowned then sniggered. 'Couldn't find the evidence, eh?'

'Something like that.'

'When can I go?'

'Now. Push off. We probably haven't finished with you. Wasting police time, assaulting an officer in the course of being arrested. There will no doubt be more.'

Underwood smiled. His lips twisted cruelly. 'What's that worth?' he said. 'Twenty hours community service? Congratulations.'

Angel pulled the cell door open wide for him.

'What about transport?' Underwood said.

'What about it? You can organize that when you get your personal stuff back at the desk. Follow me.'

Angel led him up through the green corridor to the desk sergeant and asked for his possessions to be brought out of the safe in the stores.

The desk sergeant looked surprised at Angel releasing the man without charge after all the trouble they had had bringing him in. He remembered that three officers had had almost to drag him down to that cell, accompanied by newspapermen and photographers.

The desk sergeant began filling in the release form, and addressed one of the questions to Angel. 'Am I putting you down, sir, as the officer authorizing the discharge of the prisoner?'

'No. Detective Superintendent Harker,' Angel said.

'And are you signing him out, sir?' the desk sergeant said.

Angel had no choice. 'Yes,' he said and signed the sheet.

Underwood picked up the contents he had had in his pockets on admission, signed the receipt and curled his lip in cruel pleasure as he turned away from the counter and noticed Angel watching him.

'Goodbye, little man,' Underwood said.

'You'll be back,' Angel said. 'And I'll be waiting for you.'

Underwood curled his lip again, then immediately made for the pay phone on the wall in the reception area.

Angel slowly walked through the security door and along the green corridor. He turned left and along to the superintendent's office. He knocked on the door.

'Come in,' Harker said.

When he saw it was Angel, he wasn't pleased. 'Have you come here to argue some more, lad?'

'No, sir. No.'

'Have you let Underwood go?'

'Yes, sir. All the documentation is done. I left him phoning for a taxi. I've come to say that we should inform the press. Tell them our side of the case. We can charge him for wasting police time. Resisting arrest. Can't let him make monkeys out of us.'

'No. The one you'll embarrass is the chief constable,' Harker said. 'Just shut up and that's an order. The stolen item, if it was stolen, has been returned. No offence has been committed. Let's keep it like that.'

Angel's mouth dropped open. His eyes darted about as he tried to make sense of what he had been told and what it implied. *What was happening?*

'Now buzz off, lad,' Harker said. 'I've a lot on. Last quarter's figures have to be finished by Friday.'

Angel came out of the superintendent's office in a daze. He walked slowly down the corridor to his own office for a bit of quiet to try and sort this mess out. He arrived at his office and slumped down into his chair. PC Ahaz followed him in. He was touching his lips and blinking intermittently.

Angel wrinkled his nose. He wanted to send him away.

Ahmed sensed it. He came up to him quickly. 'I've something I *must* tell you, sir,' he said. 'I tried to tell you before.'

Angel pulled a pained face. 'What is it, lad? Make it quick.'

'Well sir, you know that I went to school with Clive Exham. His father is the chief constable's driver and handyman.'

'Yes. Yes,' Angel said.

'Well Clive told me that early this morning a big crate was delivered to the chief constable's house by a man in a hired van. The crate was so big it had to be put in the garage. When it was unpacked it was found to be the missing gold-plated statue that all the fuss is about. Well the chief was furious, and Clive's dad got a rocket from him for accepting delivery of it. Anyway he was told to pack it up again, which he did, and half an hour later it was collected by Express Carriers to be transported to Spicers' auction house in London.'

Angel could hardly believe what he had heard.

'Are you sure, Ahmed?' he said.

He nodded.

Angel rubbed his chin. So the statue had not been stolen. But if so, what was the point of the exercise? What *was* happening?

'Well, thank you for that, Ahmed,' he said.

Angel began to rub his earlobe.

The phone rang.

It was the desk sergeant. 'Thought you'd like to know, sir. Underwood hasn't yet left the premises. His girlfriend has arrived, and a dozen news reporters — national and local — have turned up from nowhere. They're asking why he has been released. Nobody has an answer.'

Angel shrugged. He didn't know either.

'He's giving interviews and posing for photographs at the front of the station, sir,' the desk sergeant said. 'Just thought you'd like to know.'

Angel frowned. He was intrigued and curious. 'Yes, Sergeant,' he said. 'Thank you. I'm coming up straight away.'

He replaced the phone, turned to PC Ahaz and said, 'Come on. Let's see what's going on.'

As the two men rushed up the green corridor to reception he told Ahmed about the reported activities there. By the time they arrived, the gathering had moved outside to the bottom of the front steps. Alec Underwood and Shirley Vance, surrounded by reporters with flashing cameras, were climbing into the back of a large estate car like a couple of Hollywood film stars who have just been awarded a shelf-load of Oscars.

Angel observed that in the driving seat was his sidekick, Peter Queegley.

In all the clamour, Angel didn't miss the opportunity to note and write down the registration number of the estate car. He knew he hadn't finished with Mr Underwood.

18

Angel returned to his office, opened his desk drawer to take out the EVIDENCE envelope containing Farleigh's bank statements and balance sheets intending to finish his inspection of them, when the phone rang.

It was DS Mathew Elliott of the Antiques and Fine Art squad, London.

'I thought you would like to know, Michael, that at last, something stolen on a raid by the country-house gang, has turned up. Actually it was from the gang's last job in Buckinghamshire on the sixteenth of May. It's been identified as a huge painting by Rubens, *Girl in Red Robe*, more than twelve feet by five feet five inches, oil on canvas. Worth millions.'

Angel's face brightened. 'Where was it found?'

'On the rocks at Whitby in North Yorkshire.'

'Huh. I know where Whitby is. How did it get there? Is it damaged?'

'No. In perfect condition, or so I am told. It was found very early this morning by some joggers. The painting was very carefully wrapped in several layers of heat-sealed waterproof paper. It appears to have been floated in by the tide. It is now safely locked up in a cell at Whitby station. I wondered if you wanted to retrieve it and hold it for the time being, seeing as though you already have an involvement in the case?'

Angel had always liked Mathew Elliott. It was a most generous suggestion, coming from another copper.

'Well, thank you, Mathew. Do you think there'll be any DNA on it?'

'Yeah. Probably a couple of hundred holidaymakers and half a dozen North Yorkshire coppers.'

Angel knew what he meant. 'Anyway, I'll send my SOCO team up to collect it tomorrow. They'll have a close look at it. You never know.'

'Right, Michael. I'll advise Whitby to expect them.'

Angel replaced the phone and leaned back in the chair. *There* was progress. None of the loot stolen by the country-house gang had ever been recovered before. It had always seemed as if it had disappeared off the face of the earth. He wondered why it had come in on the tide.

He phoned Taylor and instructed him to go to Whitby the following day to collect the

Rubens from the station there. He also said that he wanted him to treat the painting and its packaging as evidence, and see what prints or DNA he could recover from it.

He replaced the phone, then looked down at the EVIDENCE envelope containing Farleigh's bank statements and balance sheets, which was still on his desk. He had intended clearing them that day. He began to finger them. His eye caught the clock. It said five past five. He looked at it again. He had been right the first time. He checked his watch. That also said five past five. He wasn't in the mood for fussing with figures at that time in the afternoon, anyway. He quickly rammed the stuff back in to the envelope, put it in the desk drawer, locked it and went home.

* * *

The following morning was Thursday, 11 June 2009.

Angel entered his office at 8.28 a.m., exactly. He was determined that this was the day he was going to solve the puzzle of the gold-plated statue.

He picked up the phone and dialled Spicers', the auctioneers. He was surprised that, at that time, he was immediately put through to Mr Oberon.

'Good morning, Inspector. If you are phoning about that wretched gold-plated statue, I can tell you that yesterday afternoon it was delivered here, and I gave immediate instructions to my staff to reject it and return it to the vendor.'

Angel blinked. He thought for a moment.

'Because, of course, it's a forgery?' he said.

Angel heard a gasp.

'Certainly not,' Oberon said. 'It's the genuine article all right. But we have a reputation to maintain here at Spicers', and we can do very well without this sort of publicity. We have returned the . . . the item to the vendor by Express Carrier and informed him that he and his wares are no longer welcome at Spicers'.'

'I see,' Angel said, 'and what is the vendor's name?'

'Ah, Inspector, you know full well I cannot tell you *that*.'

'Where a crime has been committed, Mr Oberon, you cannot withhold vital information from the police.'

'But a crime *hasn't* been committed. Therefore I am not under that particular obligation. But thank you for your good intentions, Inspector. Goodbye.'

Angel frowned and slowly replaced the phone.

He pursed his lips and eased the chair backwards. Oberon said that no crime had been committed. There was no robbery, and he had said that the gold-plated statue was genuine and was being returned to the vendor. Who was the vendor then? Of course. There was only one person it could be. Alec Underwood. He must have been the purchaser, the maiden bidder, the only bidder. He'd bought it at Pinsley Smith's little auction in that marquee in Jubilee Park. Now that put an entirely new complexion on the case. He could see that as far as Spicers' was concerned, there had been no crime. There had been plenty of wrongdoing, misuse of their services, but nothing actually illegal. Underwood had used Spicers disgracefully to publicize the statue but, true enough, it seemed that there was nothing Angel could charge him with.

He sat there thinking for a few minutes, when suddenly an imaginary cog fell into place between two non-existent sprockets, the mechanism turned causing a metaphorical chime of bells to ring. His face brightened and he rubbed his hands together like an undertaker at a nonagenarian's birthday party.

He leaned forward and picked up the phone.

'Ahmed,' he said. 'I want you to withdraw a night camera from the CID stores, and then I want to speak to DS Crisp and DS Carter.'

'Right, sir. And do you want DS Taylor as well?'

'No. You won't get him anyway, Ahmed. He's gone to Whitby on a job.'

'Right, sir. Is this a night surveillance job to do with Alec Underwood, sir?'

'It is, lad,' he said. 'It is.'

'Well, sir. If you don't mind me mentioning . . . I can't see exactly what you can get him for?'

'It will all come clear tonight, I hope, Ahmed.'

* * *

It was 1.50 a.m. early Friday morning, 12 June. The night sky was as cloudy as prison-made gin, which allowed the moon, briefly, to illuminate Angel, Crisp and Carter crouching behind gravestones at the furthest point from the church gate. Everything was still. The constant humming of traffic on the M1 a mile or so away was the only sound to be heard.

Crisp took out the compact video night camera and removed the lens cover. He turned to Angel on his right and said, 'How certain are you that they'll come, sir?'

Angel rubbed his nose with the back of his hand. 'Keep your voice down, lad. In this stillness, your voice might carry.'

'Right, sir.'

'Pretty certain. Spicers returned the statue to Underwood by Express Carriers late on Wednesday afternoon. He must have received it yesterday, sometime. Therefore, tonight is the first opportunity Underwood will have had. They'll be here. When they were seen here before, it was two o'clock, so I thought that this would be the most likely time they would return.'

'Sounds solid, sir,' Crisp said.

Angel looked at his wrist trying to see his watch. The cloud across the moon beat him. 'What's the time?' he said.

'Two minutes to two.'

Flora Carter said, 'While we are waiting, sir, can I ask about Brian Farleigh? . . . I see he hasn't been to court yet. I thought it was all sewn up.'

'So did I.'

'I thought you said you had enough for the CPS?'

'I thought I had, but Twelvetrees wants it easy. He's expecting me to produce Razzle's collection of twenty-eight gold snuffboxes in Farleigh's possession, but they're evidently not there. Don Taylor and I have looked everywhere for them. If I could find them, the case against him would be complete,' Angel said, brushing his hand through his hair. 'And I fear that the super is going to ring me up tomorrow, that is today now, and demand that I release Farleigh because of insufficient evidence.'

Crisp nodded knowingly.

Flora's eyes opened wide and her jaw dropped. 'Surely not,' she said. 'He wouldn't do that, sir.'

'He *would*,' Angel said.

Trevor Crisp leaned over, looked at Flora Carter in the moonlight and said, 'Can't hold a suspect with insufficient evidence.'

'I know *that*,' she said.

'Sshh!' Angel said.

All three bobbed down behind the gravestones.

There was the sound of a car engine close by.

Angel peered from behind a stone. 'A big car with its lights extinguished has pulled up by the church gate,' he said. 'It's an estate car, towing a trailer . . . looks like a horse box. They are here . . . getting out of the car. The tall one in the big black hat . . . it's Alec Underwood. The driver is Peter Queegley.'

Angel then ducked down.

'They're looking round,' he whispered. 'Don't move a muscle.'

His heart banged like a Salvation Army drum.

The three pressed themselves hard against the cold grey stones and stayed stock-still. After a minute or so, they heard the rattle of machinery from the direction of the church gate.

Angel straightened up and peered between two gravestones across the churchyard again.

'What's happening, sir?' Flora Carter said.

Angel turned to Crisp and said, 'They've got a little tractor, Trevor. Get that camera running.'

'Right, sir,' Crisp said. He raised the little video camera, looked through the viewfinder and squeezed the trigger. 'It's the sort of tractor you can hire to dig trenches,' he said.

'Or graves,' Angel said.

'Or plant telegraph poles,' Flora said.

They saw Queegley driving a small-track vehicle down a ramp from a horse box attached to the back of the car. Underwood and Queegley then together uncoupled the empty trailer and pushed it back down the lane several yards. Underwood then opened the tailgate door of the estate and Queegley drove the tractor right up to it. The two men huddled round the tractor and the estate car for several minutes so that it was not possible to see what they were doing. However, in due course, Queegley got in the driving seat of the tractor, reversed it away from the estate car. The police could then see that the little tractor now had a thick arm sticking upwards and a big sling arrangement suspended from it. In the sling, swinging slightly to the movement of the tractor was a large box in the shape of a coffin.

'Bloody hell,' Crisp said.

Flora Carter said, 'They're not going to bury somebody, are they?'

Queegley turned the tractor towards the church gate being held open by Underwood. He went through it, into the churchyard.

Angel glanced at Crisp. 'You getting all this, Trevor?'

'Oh yes, sir,' Crisp said, not taking his eye from the magnified viewfinder.

Queegley drove the little vehicle along the front of the church along an uneven path among gravestones, almost to the end. Underwood followed, sometimes reaching out to steady the coffin as it swung at precarious angles. Queegley stopped when he arrived adjacent to an old sandstone box grave. He moved a lever and the coffin lowered slowly on to the path. Underwood unhooked the sling fastening, took some steel cords out of a box on the tractor, fastened them on to the hook, then set up corner pieces that fitted neatly over each of the corners of the box grave. When he had finished, Queegley moved a lever that took the strain, then slowly lifted up the old box grave top and lowered it safely on the grass at the side. Then they reversed the procedure and put the coffin into the stone box grave and replaced the stone lid on top.

'They've buried something or somebody,' Crisp said.

Angel quickly dipped into his pocket, pulled out his mobile and tapped in a number.

'Trevor, forget the camera now,' Angel said. 'Climb up that wall and go round on the outside to the gate and head them off, in case they try to make a break for it.'

Crisp's face creased. 'Oh. I shall get my suit all muckied up. I thought you were sending for help.'

'Hurry up,' Angel growled.

Crisp began to scale the wall.

Into the mobile, he said, 'DI Angel here. Send two cars to St Mary's church immediately to rendezvous with me to arrest two men and take possession of some vehicles.'

He closed the phone and returned it to his pocket.

Meanwhile Queegley had turned the tractor round and was following Underwood along the path.

'Come on, Flora,' Angel said. 'If they don't come quietly, I'll take Underwood. You take Queegley. Trevor Crisp should be at the gate by then to assist you.'

They broke cover, ran the length of the churchyard and were almost upon the two crooks when Angel in a loud voice said, 'Stop where you are, Underwood. This is the police. You are both under arrest. Get off that tractor, lad.'

Underwood gasped. His eyes flashed. He glanced at Flora Carter, then at Angel, then said, 'I don't think so.' He began to run towards the church gate.

Crisp saw him coming and stood in the gateway to block him.

Underwood saw him, turned round and made a straight line in the opposite direction, which was towards the entrance to the church.

Angel immediately gave chase after him.

Meanwhile Queegley had got off the tractor and was looking round wondering whether he could make a run for it. Then he saw Crisp approaching from the church gate and Carter from the direction of the church door, and he knew he was sunk.

Underwood had reached the church door.

He tried the handle but it was locked. He punched and kicked at the door. It didn't budge.

Angel caught up with him.

Underwood turned and saw him. His evil eyes stared hard at him.

Only four yards of churchyard flagstones separated them. 'You're under arrest, Alec,' Angel said. 'You can't get away. You might as well come quietly.'

'You can't arrest me,' Underwood said, and he made gestures with his hands inviting him to come closer.

'Come on. Take you on, any time, Angel. Come on.'

Angel shook his head. 'Turn round and put your wrists together,' he said, and he went up to him.

Suddenly Underwood's fists closed and he lunged out a hard right which grazed Angel nastily on the chin. The expected follow-through left hook was deftly caught by Angel with both hands. He gave Underwood's wrist a quick twist and a jerk. Underwood let out a loud yell and landed in a heap on the church path.

Then Angel heard a noise from behind. He turned to see two uniformed constables running up to him.

'Want, any help, sir?' one of them said.

He pointed to Underwood on the ground. 'Cuff that, search it, arrest it and drop it in a cell.'

Angel inspected the underside of his chin carefully with his fingertips and let out an unintentional groan.

* * *

It was 1005 hours, Friday morning, 12 June, 2009. Assembled in interview room 1 were, Alec Underwood, Mr Bloomfield his solicitor, DI Crisp and Angel. The spools in the recording machine were rotating.

'I have to tell you, Mr Underwood,' Angel said, 'that we have opened that stone box grave that you and Queegley adopted as your own secret hiding-place and found that in there was not only the original famous antique gold-plated plaster statue of King William IV's mistress in a mahogany coffin, but two other gold-plated plaster statues of a similar but different young woman, also each in a mahogany coffin.'

Underwood raised his head and with a sneer said, 'So what? I didn't steal any of the statues.'

'No. You bought the original at Pinsley Smith's auction. And you made the other two copies from a mould of another woman. I suppose Queegley mixed the plaster and did all the hard work.'

'There was nothing dishonest about that.'

Angel pursed his lips. 'Wasn't there? Spicers' tell me that they don't want to see you or your wares ever again.'

'I don't owe them a bean. My account with them is clear. They should thank me. I brought them a lot of publicity.'

'No, Mr Underwood. You brought them a barrel load of notoriety. It was *you* who got the good publicity. That was what the stunt was all about, wasn't it? Whenever the statue was mentioned or photographed, and you made sure that it happened often, there you were, right up close to it.'

'There's still nothing there you can charge me with, Angel.'

'So that when it went missing, you also went missing. So that all the crooks who knew that you were a crook would naturally think that *you* had stolen it.'

'You can't blame me for what people think. Anyway, how could I have stolen it? I own it.'

'Exactly. But they didn't *know* that, did they? So that all you had to do was go home and sit by the phone. Wait for the rich crooked punters with more money than sense to phone in and make you an offer. Having three to sell, the original and two fakes, and a worldwide market in which to sell them, you expected to clean up triple the going price of, say, one and a half million — that's four and a half million quid!'

Still apparently unmoved, Underwood said, 'Even if this nonsense is correct, you still can't charge me with it.'

'No, I can't charge you with that, but I can, and I will, inform every national newspaper and all the TV and radio news offices today, that you not only own the original statue but that you have two other home-made ones that you and Queegley intended passing off as the real thing. Then I think the market price will drop considerably.'

Underwood's face hardened. 'You can't do that.'

'You'll find that I can. I would only be telling the truth.'

'That's monstrous,' Underwood said.

'In the meantime, we will be charging you, jointly with Queegley, with attempting to pass off two statues as if they were antique, stealing three coffins from Hargreaves Funeral Directors, trespassing on church land, illegal use of church property, illegally opening a grave, forging a work of art with a view to obtaining money by false pretences, resisting arrest, assaulting a police officer and anything else I can think of.'

19

'Great stuff, sir,' Flora Carter said. 'Congratulations.'

'Thank you, Flora,' Angel said.

'What I don't understand, sir, is how the statue became worth so much so quickly.'

'The statue was sold to Alec Underwood by phone for a thousand pounds so nobody knew *he* owned it. If they *had* known, honest people would have run a mile. After that he kept putting it into more important auctions, one after another, secretly selling and buying it back himself, by private arrangement with the auctioneer, gathering publicity all the way until the item had an apparent value of more than a million pounds. No capital had to be paid to the auctioneer. He owned it, so it only cost him the auctioneer's commission at each sale. His activities also brought the true romantic story of the love of Dorothea Jordan and the eventual William IV to a TV company. You know how the public loves true romances, especially if they are royal and a bit spicy, so that added to the hype.'

'He *was* lucky, sir.'

'We were luckier. I am glad to get shot of

those two. Now I've got to find these snuffboxes, get this Razzle case sewn up and Farleigh permanently behind bars, then find the leader of this country-house gang. Who is manning the obbo on Edward Street?'

'Ted Scrivens and John Weightman, sir.'

'Is anything happening down there? I can't keep that going much longer. We are going to be sussed.'

'All I hear is that she wants money from him for housekeeping and board. He says he has nothing. She says when is the next job. He says he doesn't know. She is turning nasty and he gets angry back. The rows get more frequent and louder.'

'Doesn't either of them go out to the shop or the pub or somewhere?'

'No, sir. No money.'

'Anything in the post or on the phone?'

'Only people selling stuff or chasing money. Nothing helpful to us.'

'We'll stick with it another day. Something might give.'

'Right, sir,' she said and made for the door, then she stopped. She came back up to him with a fetching smile. She didn't know it, but a smile like that from a pretty face always put Angel on his guard.

'Now what?' he said, his eyes narrowed.

'You were going to tell me the significance

of that date you used as the code number you put on Razzle's workshop door. Number 130864, thirteenth of August 1964.'

He wrinkled his nose. 'There isn't time now,' he said.

'*Please*, sir,' she said.

Against his better judgement he relented and said, 'Well, all right. Briefly, it was supposed to be the date that marked a turning point in British people's attitude to criminals in this country. Instead of dealing with brutal murderers in this so-called civilized society by hanging, a serious attempt was instigated to discover the causes and try to improve conditions. And the date of the hanging of the last two men in this country for the joint murder of a man was on the thirteenth of August 1964. The two murderers were Peter Anthony Allen in Preston and Gwynne Owen Evans in Strangeways. They were hanged at the same time, 8 a.m.'

Flora Carter looked at Angel, her mouth open. She didn't say anything. He thought he must have shocked her.

'All right?'

'Yes, sir.'

'Right now,' he said. 'Crack on with that job.'

She hesitated. 'Yes, sir,' she said, and went out.

Angel shook his head and shrugged. He now had the opportunity to finish looking at the Farleigh papers. He would like to get them finished that day. He opened up a desk drawer and took out the envelope marked EVIDENCE.

There was a knock at the door. 'Come in.'

It was Taylor.

Angel looked up. He pulled a pained face. 'What is it, Don? Enjoy your day at the seaside?'

'Hardly saw it, sir. I've brought that painting back, and had a good look at it.'

'Yes?' Angel said, looking at him expectantly. 'Anything of interest? Tell me, quickly.'

'It had been wrapped very carefully in several layers of corrugated waterproof paper, sir, heat-sealed so that the painting and frame were bone dry. It is in perfect condition, even though it was recovered from the rocks and had been in the sea.'

'It was hanging on a wall in a house in Buckinghamshire until the sixteenth of May, so it could have been in the water any time up to a month. Anything else?'

'Hadn't been in the sea long, sir. There are quite a few smudged fingerprints. I have taken some of them off, but there are none that can be matched. And I found a pungent smell of diesel oil in the wrapping. I think for whatever reason, after it had been sealed, it had been sprayed with diesel oil.'

Angel pulled at his ear. 'Diesel?'

'But I couldn't find anything else that might be useful, sir.'

'Right, Don. Thank you.'

Taylor went out and closed the door.

Angel thought a few moments about the careful wrapping of the painting and the strong smell of diesel surrounding it, then he picked up the phone and tapped in Trevor Crisp's number.

'DS Crisp,' came the answer.

'Ah, Trevor,' Angel said. 'Don Taylor is back, and he reports that the wrapping round the Rubens painting reeks of diesel. Now the painting is huge. A fishing trawler's diesel tanks are also surprisingly huge. That's because they might be away from a diesel supply pump for weeks or months at a time. Now, Trevor, I think the country-house gang steal the antiques. Waterproof them and pack them in the fuel tank of a fishing trawler. It meets up way out of the English Channel with a boat, possibly a large private yacht. The treasures are transferred. Big money changes hands, and some millionaire or president of an oil-rich country acquires irreplaceable treasures that can only increase in value. That's why we never — well, hardly ever — recover the property. On Monday, a fishing trawler from Bridlington was involved in an accident in early-morning mist in the North Sea off Flamborough Head. It had been holed by a huge foreign container ship. Now the trawler's fuel tank may have been damaged and some of the illicit cargo spilled out into the sea, including that very valuable Rubens that floated up to Whitby. Anyway, go to Bridlington. Clear this with the North Yorkshire police then speak to the coastguard. Find that trawler. Look in the fuel tank. Insist that the top is removed. Then, wrapped in waterproof under the diesel level, I am confident that you will find various antique treasures from the house of Sir Jack Prendergast. Anyway, the timing fits. You've got the list. Then interview the skipper.'

'Right, sir,' Crisp said. 'Can we do anything about the boat the antiques are transferred to, sir?'

'I don't know. I suspect the offending yacht will be the *Golden Mistress*, owned by that chap, Moses Van Hassain, Secretary of State of Omanja. He'd be taking them back to Africa, possibly to curry favour with his president. If you get anything out of the trawler skipper, it might need Interpol or the Foreign Office to intervene. If we can get the skipper banged up then that line of traffic will come permanently to an end, which could only be good.'

'Right, sir. I'll start that on Monday?'

'*What?*' Angel yelled. 'No. You'll start right away. The evidence might have disappeared by Monday.'

'But it's Friday, sir. It'll probably take me over the weekend.'

'It probably will. Now crack on with it.'

He replaced the phone.

He sighed and reached out for the EVIDENCE envelope and the Farleigh papers when the phone rang. His face creased with annoyance. He reached out and picked it up. It was the civilian on reception. 'There's a young lady on the phone asking to speak to you, Inspector. Her name is Jessica Razzle.'

He sighed. 'Put her through, please,' he said.

'Hello, Inspector. I have received that summons this morning, and I have to attend the magistrates court in a fortnight regarding that assault on the first of June.'

'Yes, Jessica. What about it?'

'I wondered if I could get out of it in some way. I mean I don't want to have to say anything unkind in public about Rosemary. It's bound to be reported in the local paper . . . and because of her celebrity status, it might hit the nationals. And I don't think she was entirely to blame. Also I want to return to the States and continue my life where I left off. There's no way in which I can persuade you to drop the case, is there?'

Angel rubbed his chin. 'Have you been talking to her?'

'She phoned me up. She sounded genuinely concerned as to how I was. We had a good long serious talk. It was a surprise, I must say.'

'Has she put you up to this?'

'Certainly not. But I was thinking. Dad would be very upset if he knew we were fighting like alley cats. If it's a matter of a fine, or something, can we not pay it, apologize and get on with our lives?'

'Where is she now?'

'She doesn't want me to say. She doesn't want the newspapers to find out.'

'If she's not broken the law, Jessica, she has nothing to fear from me.'

'Well, she's drying out in a clinic in Zurich, but for professional reasons, she doesn't want that to become common knowledge.'

Angel nodded. He had suspected that she was on the bottle. 'Her secret's safe with me, Jessica. I'm afraid there's no simple way I can drop the case, but the police will not be vindictive in this case, you know. I simply want the best thing to happen for all concerned. I advise you to talk to your solicitor, and get Rosemary to speak to her solicitor. They'll advise you the best thing to do.'

'All right, Inspector. Thank you. Goodbye.'

Angel replaced the phone, sighed and reached out for the EVIDENCE envelope and the Farleigh papers again. He hoped for no more interruptions. He looked again at Farleigh's bank statements with the tiny handwritten appendages to all the entries. He recalled noticing the only direct bank entry of forty pounds a quarter for 'S & S' charges. Although he didn't think the charges unreasonable, he didn't understand the debit and decided to look further into it. It was probably unimportant. He found the bank telephone number from the top of the statement and tapped it into his phone. He was soon speaking to the assistant manager.

'The two letters, 'S & S,' simply stand for storage and service, Inspector. It will mean that the client has a deed box or a package being stored in the bank vault for him. That's all.'

Something in the bank vault stored for him? It could be the twenty-eight gold snuffboxes and the end of a long road, or it could simply be another dead end.

Angel felt as if he had a belly full of toads.

Ten minutes later he was at the bank counter. He had had to give half a dozen signatures and prove his identity and authority before the clerk would hand over a locked metal box about twenty-four by sixteen by six inches, with carrying handles at each end. It had a simple blue label with the name 'Mr B. Farleigh' and an account number handwritten on it.

Angel slid it off the counter top. It was quite heavy, and as he walked towards the door of the bank, he felt a tingle of excitement across his chest down his arms to his fingertips. He couldn't get to the station quickly enough to get the box open. He arrived in his office, put the box on his desk, looked at the keyhole with the brass surround and picked up the phone.

'Ahmed, go to the stores and ask for the envelope containing Brian Farleigh's personal possessions on being admitted. There is a bunch of keys in there. Sign for them and bring them to me.'

'Right, sir.'

Angel sat at his desk looking at the deed box, hoping that the collection of snuffboxes was in there and that it didn't contain old account books. He wasn't at all certain that there was a key on Farleigh's bunch that would unlock the box, but he thought that there very likely was.

Ten long minutes passed before Ahmed arrived with Farleigh's bunch of keys.

Angel took the bunch from Ahmed, found the only a key that might fit and inserted it in the lock.

Both men stared at the box.

The key went in easily. Angel then tried to turn it. It turned first try. There was a click. He lifted the lid. It appeared to be filled to the top with twenty-pound notes wrapped in £1000 bundles.

He stared at it, speechless. He had never been so close to so much money. He looked at Ahmed. He was also staring at the money. His eyes were bright, his mouth open.

After a few moments, Angel's face changed to disappointment. He had been hoping for a box or a bag of twenty-eight gold snuffboxes. Though all this money might have been stolen, if he couldn't prove positively that it came from Razzle's safe, he would have to let Farleigh go free.

Eventually Ahmed was able to speak. He grinned and said, 'Wow, sir, what are we going to do?'

'Count it,' Angel said and he began to unpack the box by taking out bundles, four or five at a time, and tossing them into the lid. He also wanted to check that the notes were all twenties and all wrapped in bundles of £1000. He was about halfway down when he felt something different. It was a cardboard box. He brushed away the bundles of notes from the top of it and pulled it out. It was about as big as a shoe box.

Ahmed stared at it.

A small powerful engine began to bang away in Angel's chest. His face was red. His fingers were tingling.

The box had an elastic band round it to keep the lid secure. He sprang it off and opened the box. Inside were some old leather boxes about twice the size of a ring box; underneath them were similar shaped items in small linen pouches with drawstrings. He reached in, snatched at a box and opened it. Inside was a beautiful yellow shiny gold container with diamonds and sapphires on the lid.

Ahaz said, 'A snuffbox, sir.'

Angel's eyes glowed.

He reached in for another and opened that. It was a beautiful gold box decorated with seed pearls and turquoise. He opened more . . . They were all snuffboxes in the shoe box and they were all magnificent.

He sighed with relief. At last. *There* were the snuffboxes from Razzle's safe. *There* was Farleigh's motive for murdering Charles Razzle.

Angel left the counting and repacking of the deed box to PC Ahaz, and leaned back in his chair deep in thought. Now the charge of murder against Farleigh was absolutely safe and the CPS could move on that without delay. He must phone Twelvetrees.

'Excuse me, sir,' Ahmed said. 'Didn't you say there should be twenty-eight snuffboxes, sir?'

Angel's eyes flashed wide open. 'Don't tell me there are any missing.'

'Oh no, sir,' Ahmed said. 'There's none missing. But there are forty-eight snuff boxes, not twenty-eight.'

Angel jumped to his feet. 'Forty-eight? Show me, lad.'

Ahmed opened the box and put the snuff-boxes in eight rows of six on the desk top.

Angel quickly opened each box and each bag to be sure that there was a snuffbox in every container. Ahmed was indeed correct.

Then Angel sat down slowly and said, 'You know what these means, Ahmed.'

'No, sir.'

'The extra twenty were stolen from Sir Jack Prendergast's house last month. It means that Brian Farleigh is not only the murderer of Charles Razzle, he is also leader of the country-house gang, and murderer of Stefan Muldoon and Aimée Polditz.'

Suddenly Angel's door was thrown open

causing it to bang noisily on the chair against the wall. Standing motionless in the doorway was the constable who had been acting as duty jailer. He looked strangely uncomfortable. His hands were down by his sides but his shoulders were hunched up. His face seemed inexplicably paralysed. Only his startled eyes moved. They traversed jerkily from left to right.

Angel's pulse began to pump faster. He rose to his feet.

'What do you want, lad?' Angel said.

The constable didn't reply. He just stood there, frozen to the spot.

Angel and Ahmed looked at each other, then back at the constable.

Then Brain Farleigh's head bobbed from behind the young man's head. His eyes were staring, his head jerky, his hair dishevelled. '*There* you are, Angel. I've been looking for you.'

Angel's heart began to pound.

Farleigh pushed the constable into the office. 'Go inside, lad,' Farleigh said. 'Hurry up. The Inspector wants to know how I got out of the cell. Shall I tell them or will you?'

Then Angel saw that he was holding something in his hand that looked dangerously like a Glock G17 handgun. That model had a magazine that held seventeen rounds. It was fast, accurate and could kill at sixty yards. Farleigh waved it around dangerously in every direction.

Farleigh then quickly closed the door and turned the key. 'That's cosy. Just the four of us.' He prodded the constable from behind and said, 'Well, tell him, lad.'

'I don't know how he got the gun, sir,' the constable said. 'I took him in a cup of tea and he pulled it on me. Then made me tell him which was your office.'

Angel sighed and said, 'All right, Constable.'

Angel had been worried for some time that prisoner's visitors had not been adequately searched. It seemed his fears had been justified.

Farleigh suddenly saw the deed box, the money and the snuffboxes on Angel's desk. His eyes nearly popped out of his head. 'Here, Angel, that's mine.' He was going to come forward to get a better look, but stopped. 'Well, that's fine. You've saved me a job. It's amazing, Angel. You've already been into *my* deed box and *my* money. Were you going to share it out among yourselves?'

He turned to PC Ahaz and said, 'Pack all those snuffboxes up, lad. And all that money. Quickly. Put it all back in the box and lock it up.'

Ahmed hesitated. He glanced at Angel.

'Do as he says, Ahmed.'

Farleigh blinked when he heard the name.

Ahmed began to repack the deed box.

'You wanted to see me, Farleigh,' Angel said. 'What do you want?'

'I want a fast car and a tank of fuel.' Farleigh glanced at Ahmed and said, 'The lad would like a day out of the office, with me, wouldn't you, Ahmed?'

Ahmed winced.

'No,' Angel said. 'I can do the car and fuel, Farleigh, but Ahmed stays here.'

Farleigh's face hardened. He looked Angel up and down and said, 'You're hardly in a bargaining position, Angel.'

Angel pursed his lips then said, 'Take me. I'll be your hostage. Just leave these two lads alone.'

'No. You might try something brave, and I would have to kill you.'

'You're the one with the gun, aren't you?' Angel said. 'You've already murdered three people, a fourth would hardly make any difference.'

Farleigh smiled and waved the gun at him triumphantly. 'I like the way you think, Angel. I put the fear of God into anybody I thought might be getting too close for comfort. I tried to keep everything secret. There's security in secrecy, you know.'

'You managed that all right, Farleigh. Tearing out people's tongues tends to frighten everyone who knows them. Tell me, did you steal to order, or would any genuine valuable antiques satisfy your customer?'

'You are asking questions, Angel.'

'You're surely retiring now. It hardly matters what you tell me.'

Farleigh sighed, then said, 'If the pickings looked good and plentiful enough, and there were at least two ways of escaping in the event of being surprised by the owners or the cops, I would consider it.'

'Interesting,' Angel said. 'That's the Hermann Lamm method.'

Farleigh looked at him thoughtfully for a second. He looked as if he was going to reply but changed his mind. Instead he turned to Ahmed. 'Come on, lad. Hurry up.'

Ahmed glanced at him, finished pushing the bundles of bank notes into the deed box, lifted over the deed box lid, but it wouldn't close. He opened it again and began to rearrange the bundles.

Farleigh watched him for a few seconds. 'Hurry up,' he screamed, then he looked at Angel. 'Help him lock that frigging deed box.'

Angel pulled out a couple of bundles of the bank notes. 'These won't go in.'

Farleigh snatched them from him and

stuffed them in his jacket pocket.

Angel finally lifted over the deed box lid, applied his weight to it and Ahmed turned the key. It was locked. Farleigh dragged the box off the desk and put it by the door. 'I'll take my keys, Angel, thank you. Throw them. Very carefully.'

Angel did so.

Farleigh caught the keys and, with a satisfied nod, bounced them in his hand and dropped them into his pocket. Then he turned to the constable and said, 'Show me your handcuffs, lad.'

The constable hesitated, looked at Angel, who nodded. He took them out of the pocket on his belt and held them up.

Farleigh said, 'Right. Show me the key.'

The constable dug into his pocket and produced the key.

'Throw it,' Farleigh said, then with a menacing stare added, 'very carefully.'

Farleigh caught it and put it in his pocket. 'Now put your right wrist in one cuff. Fasten it. Tight. *Tighter*. Now go over to that radiator. Thread it round the securing bracket.'

The constable obeyed. There was nothing else he could do.

'Now then, *you*, Angel,' Farleigh said. 'Go over there and put your left wrist in the other cuff.'

Angel didn't move.

Farleigh glared at him. 'Move it.'

Angel glared back at him and said, 'No. You're not taking any of my officers with you as hostage.'

Farleigh's face went scarlet. He breathed very deeply. 'Put your frigging wrist in that frigging cuff.'

Angel's chest burned like an open furnace. He didn't move.

'I'm telling you,' Farleigh said, 'if you don't put your hand in that cuff before I count to — '

Suddenly the phone rang.

All eyes turned to look at it.

It kept ringing.

Farleigh screamed an expletive, reached over the desk and, with one hand, snatched at it, gave it a sharp pull, tearing the wires out of the connection box on the wall, and threw it into the corner of the office. He turned back to Angel, his hand pointing the weapon at him, his eyes flashing like a madman's, perspiration running down both his temples and said, 'You have five seconds to put your hand in that cuff.'

'I'll go as your hostage,' Angel said quietly. 'But leave my men alone.'

Angel's self-control made Farleigh angrier. He pushed Ahmed roughly out of the way and came right up close to Angel, grabbing him by the collar of his suit.

Angel's chest was heaving.

Farleigh said, 'If you don't put your frigging hand in that cuff in three seconds, I will kill you. And you know I can do it.'

Ahmed could stay silent no longer. 'I'll be the hostage, sir,' he yelled. 'Do it, sir. I'll be the hostage. Honestly, sir. Willingly.'

The constable turned from the radiator and said, 'Don't be a fool, sir.'

Angel indeed knew that Farleigh could kill him. He had already murdered three people, another murder would make little difference to his sentence when he was caught. He looked into his eyes. They were the eyes of a madman.

Farleigh stuck the gun into Angel's chest and said, 'I'm counting up to three. *One*.'

Ahmed screamed, 'Sir! Sir!'

Farleigh's eyes flashed as he jabbed the weapon deeper into Angel's chest.

Angel looked down at it. He sighed. A smile developed across his face.

'It's all right, Ahmed,' Angel said. 'He's not going to kill me.'

Farleigh's face muscles tightened. 'I assure you that I will,' he said through gritted teeth. '*Two*,' he bawled.

'*Please*, sir!'

'You have one second to live, Angel,' Farleigh said.

'I don't think so,' Angel said. He made a grab for Farleigh's left hand, gave it a twist, pushed his knee into Farleigh's stomach. Farleigh groaned and bent forward, causing his jaw to come in contact with Angel's left fist. The weapon dropped on to the floor. Farleigh went down on his knees. Angel put his knee and all his weight on to his back and Farleigh was on the floor on his face.

'Ahmed,' Angel said, 'there's some handcuffs in the middle drawer of the desk.'

Ahmed quickly found them, dashed over, dropped on to his knees and closed them round Farleigh's wrists as Angel held on to them.

Angel and Ahmed then stood up, breathing heavily.

Farleigh stayed on the floor, wriggling and shouting every obscenity he knew, and he knew plenty.

The constable turned away from the wall and said, 'Bloody hell. That was damned risky.'

PC Ahaz nodded and said, 'Why didn't he just pull the trigger and kill us all, sir?'

Angel bent down and picked up the weapon. 'Simple. It wasn't a bit risky, lad, or else I wouldn't have done it. When he came up close to me and pushed this thing into my chest, it didn't have the cold, hard feel of steel. Then I remembered. He was a follower of the Hermann Lamm method. The gun was not made of steel at all. Then it brought to mind all the soap that had been disappearing in the station this last three days? Also I asked myself, why was he so keen to have a tin of black shoe polish to keep his shoes polished? And where had the missing part of the radiator outside the CID office disappeared to? Farleigh had been accumulating these bits to make himself a lookalike gun. That's the Hermann Lamm method. You should learn your criminal history, lads. Lamm used a lookalike wooden gun to bluff his escape out of Utah State Prison in 1917.'

Angel's mobile phone suddenly began to ring. He pushed down into his jacket pocket to find it.

It was Harker. He sounded impatient. 'I tried to reach you in your office. What are you messing about at?'

Angel stroked his chin. 'Phone's out of order, sir.'

'*Well get it fixed,*' Harker said. 'You should look after police equipment. There's DI Lord from Skiptonthorpe urgently trying to reach you. Whatever you're doing, drop it. Phone him back immediately. He said that he has some information that might assist you.'

'Right, sir.

Angel ended the call from Harker and immediately found Lord's mobile number from his phone's memory. He clicked on it.

Farleigh was still writhing on the floor, growling like a tiger, occasionally trying to rise to his feet. PC Ahaz was standing over him and watching him carefully. The other PC was still fastened to the radiator and wishing he wasn't.

'Ah, there you are, Angel,' Lord said. The tone of his voice indicated that he wasn't his usual buoyant self. 'I don't know how you are doing . . . but I've had a bit of a turn around here. I've had Muldoon's daughter all over me in tears. She's retracted her statement. It wasn't Stefan Muldoon's son-in-law who murdered him. When I last spoke to you, the evidence from her seemed to be cut and dried. She's gone back to her husband, his son-in-law. They've made it up. She says she only said what she did to get her husband to take more notice of her. Now I'm left without a clue and without a prisoner.'

Angel smiled. 'That's all right, Lord. I've got the guilty one here, and I've all the proof you'll need and a tin box full of motive.'

There was a pause. 'Really? That's great,' Lord said, sounding mortified. Then brightly he said, 'It's amazing what you can achieve when two forces work together as a team.'

Other titles published by
The House of Ulverscroft:

SHRINE TO MURDER

Roger Silverwood

In the Yorkshire town of Bromersley there's a serial killer on the loose. Detective Inspector Michael Angel and his team of regulars search for the killer. However, the available clues are as sparse as they are puzzling: witnesses observe that someone, wearing early Roman attire, is observed at each murder, and a laurel leaf is left beside every corpse. DNA evidence links a woman of oriental origin to the murders, but this profile doesn't fit any of the suspects. The investigations become more mystifying as Inspector Angel races against the clock to find the killer. Can he prevent further bloodshed?